# THE MISSING
# BRIDESMAID

BOOKS BY L.G. DAVIS

THE LIES WE TELL SERIES
*The New Nanny*
*The Nanny's Child*

BROKEN VOWS SERIES
*The Woman at My Wedding*

*Liar Liar*
*Perfect Parents*
*My Husband's Secret*
*The Missing Widow*

*The Stolen Breath*
*Don't Blink*
*The Midnight Wife*
*The Janitor's Wife*

# THE MISSING BRIDESMAID

## L.G. DAVIS

bookouture

Published by Bookouture in 2024

An imprint of Storyfire Ltd.
Carmelite House
50 Victoria Embankment
London EC4Y 0DZ

www.bookouture.com

ISBN: 978-1-83525-313-7
eBook ISBN: 978-1-83525-312-0

# PROLOGUE

The car's going really fast, and it's making my tummy feel funny. It's like when I go down the big slide at the park, but scarier.

I don't know where we're going. She said it's an adventure, but I don't like this adventure. I just want to go back home, back to Mommy.

I'm still wearing my bridesmaid dress and it's so pretty, like the ones in my storybooks. It has lots of puffy layers that make me feel like a princess, and it smells like Mommy's perfume because it was hanging inside her closet. But I lost my flower crown and my bright-white shoes when she took me away.

"Are we going back soon? To Mommy?" I whisper.

"Shh, you're supposed to be taking a nap." She looks at me through the mirror in front of her face. "Try to forget about Mommy, darling. You've got me now."

"But I'm scared." Tears start falling down my cheeks, and I try to open the car door, but it's locked. So, I hug my puffy dress and try to make myself very small, wishing I could disappear.

"You don't need to be, sweetie. Everything is going to be okay." Her voice is soft and kind, like it used to be when she was nice. But I don't know if I like her anymore, because I saw her do it.

I saw Mommy fall down with her eyes closed.

I need to go back and help Mommy, so she can marry Daddy. I don't want to leave her like that, lying on the floor...

But if I try to escape, what if this woman hurts me, like she hurt Mommy?

# ONE

## HANNAH

The front door clicks shut, and Nathan's even, heavy steps reverberate through the hallway.

"Hello, my love," he greets me with a warm smile, his intense blue eyes sparkling.

Now that we're together, I can hardly believe just how lucky I am to be in a relationship with my best friend. We've always had each other's backs, and I'd trust him with my life. He knows the worst parts of me, the dark secrets I have hidden in my past, and he loves me anyway. I can honestly say he's also the most handsome man I have ever laid eyes on, with his chiseled jawline and neatly combed dark hair.

Sometimes when he walks into the room, my heart still flutters, as if I'm a teenager with a crush. At forty-six, he barely looks a day over thirty, with hardly a frown line on his forehead, a tall, lean frame and impeccable style. But it's not just his looks that captivate me. It's the way he makes me feel like the most cherished woman in the world.

Nathan sheds his dark-gray suit jacket and hangs it on a hook by the door, smoothing out the sleeves. His movements are slow and considered; he has always been meticulous. I'm not the tidiest person by nature, so when we moved in together, it took a while for me to adjust to his organized way of living. But over time, I've come to appreciate the structure and stability he brings into our home.

"Welcome home, babe. How was your trip?" I reach up on my toes and press a gentle kiss to his lips.

Nathan opened his law firm here in Stoneview a few years ago, but many of his clients and trials require him to travel to other cities and towns in Florida. It's a constant juggling act for both of us, but we've managed to make it work somehow.

"Long." He runs a hand through his hair, disturbing the perfectly combed strands. "But you know how it is. The opposing counsel was relentless, but I managed to hold my ground, and we won in the end."

His shoulders carry the weight of stress, despite his success as one of the best criminal defense attorneys in Florida and beyond. He has always been dedicated to his work, following in the footsteps of his father, esteemed Florida judge Robert Howard.

The toll it takes on him is obvious, especially after his recent trial in Orlando, where he tirelessly worked on the case of a young mother who was accused of killing an elderly man in a hit-and-run incident, which she claimed was an accident. The trial was emotionally draining for Nathan, as he fought tooth and nail to prove the woman's innocence.

Some time ago, Nathan suffered a major blow when he lost a highly publicized murder case, his first ever loss. It was followed by two more losses, but his hard work and determination eventually changed his luck.

His name now commands international respect and he's greatly admired among his legal peers, but I know the memory of that first major defeat still haunts him.

I stroke his arm. "You smashed it, again. I'm so proud of you, baby."

"Well, thank you, love," Nathan replies, a glimmer of pride in his sea-blue eyes. "But let's not talk about work this evening. We have more important things to focus on: our long-awaited wedding!"

He's right: most couples who are as lucky as we are, with our adorable six-year-old daughter Lennie and our perfect beach-side house in a charming small town, would have got married ages ago.

But we're not like most couples, and we're not quite as lucky as we seem. Appearances can deceive, and there's a very good reason why it took us a long time to get to this point. A reason neither of us want to talk about.

"I can't believe we only have two months to go," I say, feeling a smile brighten my face and my heart. We are going to tie the knot on June twentieth, the first day of summer. After all, what better way to celebrate our love than on the longest day of the year?

He wraps his arms around my waist and pulls me close. "Me neither. Did you finally decide on the flowers you want us to have?"

I chuckle. I'm a florist, as passionate about my job as Nathan is about his. So this should have been an easy decision, but I've been indecisive for months. I create exquisite arrangements for other people's weddings all the time, and over the years my mind has been bursting with ideas for my own. Then when it came down to it, I found it really difficult to choose.

"Well," I begin, resting my head against Nathan's chest, "I think I've finally made up my mind. I want a combination of blush pink and ivory roses with accents of eucalyptus leaves, something in pale blue, and baby's breath. Simple, yet elegant. The colors remind me of Lennie; she loves pink so much and it's the same palette we have in her bedroom. What do you think?"

"I think I just want to marry you." Nathan's arms tighten around me. "I know how important flowers are to you, and your plan sounds perfect, but I'll only have eyes for you on our wedding day. They could be dandelions for all I care. What matters is that you're by my side."

"You're so right, my love." After everything we've been through, I'm just grateful we've made it to this point. For a long time I thought this would never happen, that I'd be the woman waiting to walk down the aisle to Nathan. My dreams really have come true.

"I'm always right." Nathan grins cheekily, then buries his hands into my chestnut curls and kisses me deeply. "I can't wait to marry you, Hannah. Now, where's our sweet little bridesmaid?"

As if on cue, someone walks into the hallway. But it's not our daughter Lennie, who is going to be the bridesmaid at our wedding. It's Josie, one of my assistants at my shop, Bliss & Twine.

Josie is twenty-five, and the epitome of youthful exuberance. She has fiery red hair—usually in a braid—to match her sparkling, larger-than-life personality. In jeans and a worn-out rock and roll band t-shirt, she may appear young and carefree, but she's a force to be reckoned with in the industry. She is so creative, able to turn ordinary blooms into breathtaking works of art. I call her the flower whisperer; it's as if she has a secret connection with each petal.

Josie and Lila, my other assistant, will be helping me with my wedding flowers, so they came over earlier to discuss the latest arrangements, but Lila left and Josie stayed behind to help me pick some stems from my garden for Bliss & Twine. I always enjoy her company; she's a breath of fresh air. She takes life with a confidence and transparency that I can't help but envy. If I hadn't faced so much pain as a child, and if I didn't have to carry the weight of my secrets, I think Josie and I would be very similar. But behind my enviable life and the bright smile I show to the world, there's a darkness I don't know if I can ever leave behind.

Josie is carrying a wicker basket filled to the brim with daisies and azaleas, and their sweet aroma fills the air as she sets it down on the hall table.

"Sorry for interrupting you two lovebirds," she says, a mischievous twinkle in her emerald eyes. "I just need to make my way back to Bliss & Twine with these beauties."

"Hi there, Josie," Nathan replies with a smile. He likes Josie a lot; more than Lila, who seems to get on his nerves a little. "Do you happen to know where our little bridesmaid is? You aren't smuggling her away under those flowers, are you?"

Josie laughs softly. "Oh, she's been practicing her flower-petal throwing in the garden, for the wedding. I told her to give you two a minute before she comes to say hello; I know how much you've missed each other."

Less than a minute later, Lennie comes running into the hallway, her pink dress twirling around her as she spins and her blonde locks catching the streams of sunlight pouring in through the window above the door. "Daddy!" She launches herself at Nathan and he catches her and spins her around, making her giggle with delight.

"Hey, my little princess. How's my favorite girl in all the world?"

While I say goodbye to Josie, Lennie grins at her beloved father, her wide brown eyes shining. "I missed you, Daddy. You went to work for so many days. Today, me and Mommy went to search for more shells on the beach for the wedding. I wanted you to come with us."

Lennie has always been drawn to the beach, and one of her favorite hobbies is collecting seashells. If we allowed her, she would spend the entire day searching for those little treasures. She uses them for all kinds of imaginative projects, from creating tiny homes for her dolls to making intricate artwork on the sand.

Nathan says she gets her creativity and love of nature from me, and even though I'm a big believer in nurture over nature, I like to think it's true that she has my positive traits. I worry about the other things she might have inherited from me too, though; the side of me I never want anyone to see again.

Nathan laughs and sets Lennie down gently on the floor. "It's only been two weeks, baby. But I'm sorry. I promise I'll make it up to you. Since it's still a while before you go to bed, how about we light a bonfire on the beach and roast some marshmallows?"

I fold my arms across my chest and raise an eyebrow at Nathan. He knows very well that tomorrow is a school day. Plus it's early spring, the nights are still chilly on the coast and Lennie recently had a cold.

He just grins at me mischievously. "What? We need some family time before the wedding madness kicks in at full force."

In spite of myself, I smile at the thought of a cozy bonfire on the beach, just the three of us. I can see that Nathan is exhausted, but he's really making an effort to spend quality time with us. Life is short, and Lennie's childhood won't last forever. I should grab hold of these opportunities whenever I can.

"Mommy, can we please?" Lennie clasps her hands together, jumping up and down with excitement.

"Okay sure, that does sound like a great idea," I say, laughing at her excitement. "We can make s'mores and watch for shooting stars. You can invite Whisper to join us if you like."

Whisper is Lennie's imaginary friend. She has been a constant presence in our lives for months now, and Lennie talks about her constantly.

It worried me to begin with and I wondered if Lennie was suffering as a result of Nathan's time away from home and the stress he was under during that recent trial. But Josie assured me it's perfectly normal—she had an imaginary friend herself, as a child.

Lennie's face falls a little. "Mommy, Whisper is sick. She can't come."

Nathan and I exchange a glance. Lennie's imagination is a powerful thing.

"Oh no, I'm sorry to hear that, sweetie." Nathan kneels to her level. "I'm sure she'll feel better soon, and maybe next time she can join us. Now come and help Daddy unpack."

As the April sun dips into the horizon, our small family gathers around the fire pit on the beach. Lennie's laughter rings through the air while Nathan chases her in circles, both their faces glowing with joy in the firelight.

I sit on a blanket, watching them play, feeling warmth and peace radiating through me as waves crash against the shore, the soft sound blending with the crackling of the flames.

"Gotcha!" Nathan shouts, scooping Lennie into his arms and spinning her around.

"All right, you two," I call out, spreading a picnic blanket onto the sand, "it's time for dinner."

Nathan sets Lennie down gently, and they race each other to the blanket, collapsing onto it in a tangle of limbs.

"Mommy, what did you make for dinner?" Lennie asks, her eyes wide with anticipation as I begin to unpack our meal.

"Some of your favorite things, sweet pea." I reveal a container of chicken salad sandwiches, fruit salad, and some chocolate chip cookies that I baked last night.

"Yay." Lennie claps her hands, while Nathan ruffles her golden hair affectionately. Above her head, he gives me a warm smile.

"Thank you," he mouths.

As we dig into our feast, the conversation flows easily, filled with laughter and lighthearted teasing. It's moments like these that help me forget the secrets that lurk just beneath the surface, the dark and turbulent history that Nathan and I share.

"Tell us a story, Mommy," Lennie begs, her mouth full of sandwich as she gazes at me.

"All right, let's see." I pause while I search my mind for something fun to tell her. "Once upon a time, in a land far, far away, there was a brave princess who fought against all odds to protect her kingdom..."

But as I tell the story, I'm pulled back into the past again and I can't help feeling that the joy and serenity we feel right now is as fragile as a castle built on sand.

When my mother was alive, she used to tell me that happiness is a fickle friend who comes and goes as he pleases, never a long-term visitor. At the time, I didn't understand what she meant, but now I do. I have a long habit of being superstitious. And after what I did—what we did—I sometimes feel that it's only a matter of time before karma catches up.

Even though I desperately want to forget it, our upcoming wedding is an inevitable reminder of the secrets Nathan and I keep.

"Mommy, what happens next?" Lennie's voice pulls me back to the present, her concerned expression mirroring Nathan's.

"Sorry, sweetheart." I force a smile. "I just got lost in my thoughts for a moment."

"Is everything okay, Hannah?" Nathan's sharp blue eyes search mine.

"Of course," I assure him, though my voice betrays me with a small tremor. "Just tired after a long day at the shop."

"Let's finish our meal, then we'll head inside for some rest," he suggests, reaching over to squeeze my hand.

"Sounds perfect."

I try to tell myself that no matter what fate has in store, we will face our demons together as a family, and we will emerge victorious. But the flames continue to crackle and pop, casting flickering shadows across our faces and making everything feel transient and dream-like. And as the firelight dances and wanes, I just hope that whatever is to come, one thing will remain constant: our love for each other.

I have everything to lose. But that's all the more reason to stay in the moment and cherish these perfect times while I still can.

Then in one magical moment before we pack up our things, Lennie spots a shooting star. It burns a trail across the night sky as I tell her to make a wish.

My wish is simple: that my past never catches up to me. That I get to keep the perfect life, the one I stole.

# TWO

## LENNIE

It's Saturday! My favorite day of the week. After eating lunch, I help Mommy make charts for where people will sit at the wedding. It's like a puzzle we get to solve together and it's so much fun.

Daddy likes everything clean and tidy, so we keep all the wedding stuff in the spare room downstairs, and me and Mommy call it the wedding room. It's my favorite room in the house because there are pretty decorations, fancy fabrics, and lots of colorful ribbons everywhere, and I don't have to worry about putting things away.

Mommy and I sit on the floor together and work on the seating charts.

"Lennie," she says, "why don't you add these sparkly stickers to the kids' seating chart? It will make it look even more special."

I nod and she hands me the cool stickers with stars, hearts, and flowers. They sparkle in the sunlight coming through the window as I carefully place them next to each kid's name. I can't wait for them to see it. And I can't wait for everyone to see my bridesmaid dress that Aunty Elena sewed for me.

Once we finish, Mommy gives me a big hug. "Let's do some yoga to unwind and have fun," she says, and I grin with excitement because I love doing yoga with Mommy. I can't do all the cool poses she can do yet, but I know I'll learn them one day. Sometimes we tell stories while we practice, and when I do the Warrior Two pose, I like to pretend I'm a princess on my way to rescue my imaginary friend Whisper from a fierce monster.

We go to the living room porch that faces the sea to do yoga together, and then when we're done, I ask Mommy if I can go play in my tree house.

"Okay, but not for too long, Lennie. Remember, we're going to the park soon," Mommy reminds me. "If you need me, I'll be in the garden."

"Okay. I'll come back soon." I run through the house and out of the kitchen door, heading straight to my tree house.

It was the best birthday surprise ever from Daddy when I turned five. It's like a real little house and it's on the side of the house where I'm able to see both the sea and the street, and where there is a big tree that Daddy said was perfect for a tree house. It has a balcony that's great for watching the sea or the garden and an awesome rope ladder to climb up and down.

Inside it I have my very own bed with super comfy pillows and blankets, and a special spot for reading my favorite books. It's like my own secret world where I can make anything happen with my imagination. No one, not even Mommy or Daddy, can come up without asking me first, because it's my secret place.

With each step on the ladder, I imagine myself climbing up the stairs of a tall castle in a flowy princess dress.

But when I reach the top and push open the door, I freeze.

There, sitting on the floor of my tree house with her legs crossed, is a woman I've never seen before. Or maybe I have, but I can't remember exactly. Her hair is very dark and it's in two braids that sit on top of her head like a Halloween costume wig, and her eyes are green like a dragon. She's wearing a long white dress, a bit like the one Mommy will soon wear at her wedding to Daddy.

"Who... who are you?" I stammer, taking a step back. Mommy and Daddy have always warned me about talking to strangers.

"Shh," she whispers softly, pressing a finger to her lips. "I'm your friend, Lennie. My name is Whisper."

"Whisper?" I blink a few times and my heart starts pounding hard in my chest. "But I can see you... You're right here!"

Whisper smiles and I see her beautiful teeth, white like Mommy's wedding dress. "I've decided to show myself to you, sweet girl. You see, I'm not just an ordinary imaginary friend. I'm your guardian angel. And I was sent to protect you from danger."

"Guardian angel?" I repeat. I never knew Whisper was an angel, and I wonder why she didn't tell me before. "What danger?"

"Come here, little one." Whisper stands up and comes to take my hand. "I'm here because your daddy is not a good man. He's dangerous, and I don't want him to hurt you."

"No." I frown and shake my head, step back, and clench my fists. "Daddy loves me. He won't hurt me."

"Sometimes, even the people we love can hurt us," Whisper replies, her eyes wide and bright. "You must trust me, Lennie. I'm here to keep you safe. Your daddy hit you once before, and I'm here to make sure it doesn't happen again."

"But... he's my daddy," I whisper, my voice trembling. "And he didn't hit me. I don't remember. He would never do that."

"You were too small to remember, Lennie, but he did. He doesn't really love you or your mommy, and if either of you make him angry, he might hurt you both again. I'm here to make sure that doesn't happen. You don't have to do anything. Just trust me and listen to what I say." Her voice is gentle and kind. "I will help you through this. Together, we will make sure you're okay. But today, let's just have fun together. What do you want us to play?"

I don't like what Whisper said about Daddy; it has made me feel sad and worried. But I think she must be wrong, and anyway I'm so happy I get to see her for real. She's my best friend in the whole world. "You can play with me, Whisper? You're really here?"

"Yes, Lennie," she says with a warm smile. "I can play with you, and I'm real." She touches my hand again. "You can feel me, can't you?"

"Yes. Thank you for hearing the wish I made when I saw the shooting star. I really wanted to see you."

"You're very welcome. Now, what shall we play?"

"I want to pretend we're pirates!" I squeal. I've played with Whisper so many times, but never like this; it was always in my mind. I almost think I'm dreaming, but I pinch myself to check, and I don't wake up.

Whisper's green eyes shimmer like emeralds. She's so beautiful, maybe even more beautiful than Mommy. "A fantastic choice, my dear Lennie! Let's set sail on the high seas in search of hidden treasures."

Together, we quickly turn the tree house into our pirate ship. We gather the blankets I have in the corner of my tree house and drape them around the walls to make sails.

"What do you have in that box over there? We might be able to find something we can use," Whisper suggests, pointing at an old wooden chest in the corner. It used to belong to Daddy, but when he built me the tree house, he said I could have it for my treasures.

"Let's look." I crawl to the box and open it. "There are only toys in here and this..." I pull out my sun hat and put it on my head. "Whisper, this can be my pirate hat."

Whisper giggles softly. "Oh, Lennie, you make the most perfect pirate captain! That hat suits you so well. Now, let's see what other treasures we can find in this magical chest."

We search through the wooden chest, discovering some binoculars, a shiny golden key, and one of my drawings.

"These will do just fine," Whisper says, adjusting the hat on my head. "We'll use the power of our imagination to turn these ordinary things into great treasures. Now, take the binoculars and look through them. What do you see, Captain Lennie?"

"I see Mommy; she's walking in the garden and looking at her flowers."

Whisper moves away from the window and puts a finger to her lips again. "We should be very quiet. No one can know I'm here."

"Why?" I whisper back.

"I'm your secret friend, Lennie. Only you are allowed to see and hear me. If anyone else finds out about me, I'll vanish and you'll never be able to see me again. And I don't want to leave you." She reaches out and squeezes my hand gently. "Do you understand why you can't show me to anyone? You mustn't even tell them what I look like."

I nod my head. "Yes, I understand. You're my special friend, my guardian angel, and I don't want you to leave. It's okay, Mommy is far away in her garden on the other side, near the street."

"Good. That's good. But we have to be very, very careful."

"Don't worry, Whisper. You can come here anytime, because you're my guardian angel and my best friend. But no one else is allowed to come into my tree house, only when they ask for permission."

Whisper smiles. "I like that, Captain Lennie. We'll keep this place hidden and safe, just for us and our treasures."

We continue playing in our tree house, pretending to be out at sea with pirates and mermaids. We imagine waves crashing against our ship and the air blowing through our hair. Whisper and I take turns being the brave captain. And the whole time we're playing, we keep our voices quiet so that no one else can hear us, only my toys.

But then, just as we spot an island in the distance where we're going to look for buried treasure, I hear Mommy's voice calling for me. "Lennie, it's time to go to the park." She doesn't sound very far away.

"I have to go. Me and Mommy are going to the park."

"Go, sweet Lennie. But remember, don't tell Mommy what I look like or that you're seeing me for real. If you do, I have to disappear forever."

"I promise, Whisper. When will you visit me again?"

"Very soon. But I can never tell you when. It's a surprise."

"Okay. Bye." I climb down the ladder and run to Mommy who is waiting by the kitchen door.

"You look happy, my love," Mommy says as she hugs me tightly. "Did you have a good time playing in the tree house?"

"Yes, Mommy," I reply with a big smile, my heart floating like a balloon in my chest. "Can we go to the park now?"

"Of course, sweetheart. Let's go to the park and have even more fun."

As we walk into the house, I look behind me at the tree house, wondering if Whisper is still in there or if she disappeared by magic.

Later, as we walk to the park, which is not far from our house, I ask Mommy an important question.

"Mommy, are guardian angels real?"

Mommy stops walking and turns to me. "Well, Lennie, some people believe in guardian angels. They believe that these angels watch over us and protect us from harm."

"I have a guardian angel too. It's my friend Whisper. She

wants to protect me from Daddy. She says he did something bad in the past, but I don't remember it. That's not true, is it Mommy?"

# THREE

## HANNAH

First thing on Sunday morning, I'm filling the washing machine with a pile of clothes that have been sitting in the laundry basket for days. As I reach for the detergent, my phone, which is on the counter, starts ringing loudly. I glance at the caller ID and see it's my friend Gloria, the owner of Honeywood, my favorite coffee shop.

Honeywood is only a few blocks away from Bliss & Twine. Ever since Gloria became the new owner a few years ago we've become quite close. I stop by almost every day for a chat and a chai, and to get some paperwork done in a different location, and it's always so good to see her. Sometimes my friend Elena joins us too, but it's been a while since all three of us have gotten together.

"Hey Hannah, I'm taking the day off," she says when I pick up the phone. "Want to do something fun and relaxing with me?"

"Wow, Gloria, you rarely take a rest day. Should I be worried?" I ask as I put the phone on speaker, so I can talk to her and continue doing my chores.

"No, it's all fine, I just need a break from the daily grind," she replies, sounding tired. "I know it's last minute, but how about we go to that spa that just opened downtown? I managed to get some complimentary passes for the grand opening today. We could ask Elena if she'd like to join us too and make it a girls' day out?"

The idea of a luxurious spa day sounds incredibly tempting, and I can already feel the tension in my shoulders start to ease at the thought. But Nathan and I were going to take Lennie for a picnic at the park. I hesitate for a moment, torn between the rare chance to relax with my friends and the promise I made to my family.

"That's such a lovely idea. A spa trip would be wonderful, and I'm really tempted, but I already made plans with Nathan and Lennie today."

"Not anymore." Nathan smiles mischievously as he walks into the room. "I can take Lennie to the park myself. You should go and enjoy some well-deserved pampering. You work so hard and deserve a break."

"Are you sure?" I ask, noticing the shadows under his eyes.

"Absolutely." He comes to kiss the tip of my nose. "Lennie and I will have a father–daughter day. We haven't done that in a while."

I feel a rush of gratitude for him and quickly agree to Gloria's invitation.

"Fantastic," Gloria says excitedly. "Let's meet at the spa in an hour."

When we hang up, I ring Elena to ask if she can join us, but she and her husband Darius are busy. I mentally make a note to plan a movie night with her and Gloria sometime, then quickly get ready, feeling a mix of anticipation and guilt for leaving Nathan and Lennie behind.

.   .   .

The Serenity Spa is an oasis of calm that evelopes me as soon as I step through the door. Soothing music plays in the background, and the air is infused with eucalyptus. Gloria is already there, sipping on a glass of cucumber water by the smoothie bar.

"Welcome, welcome!" She pulls me into a warm hug. "I'm so glad you could make it. We are going to have the most relaxing day."

Gloria is around the same age as me, but she looks so youthful, she could be a decade younger. Hair the color of rich mahogany tumbles down her back in loose waves, framing her heart-shaped face. Her hazel eyes are bright with excitement, and her smile is infectious.

She leads me to the changing rooms where we throw on our fluffy robes and slide into our slippers before heading to the relaxation area. Loungers line the room, each one offering a view of the indoor garden filled with greenery and trickling water features. We settle in, letting out contented sighs as we sink into the soft cushions.

After a few moments of peaceful silence, a spa attendant approaches us with a menu of services. Having made our choice, we are led to a private treatment room where two massage tables are waiting and candles are flickering softly.

As the massage therapist begins to work on my tense muscles, I feel the knots slowly unraveling under her skilled hands.

When I turn my head to one side, I catch a glimpse of Gloria, her eyes closed in bliss as she enjoys her own massage. But then she senses me staring and opens her eyes.

"Enjoying your massage, darling?" she asks dreamily.

"So much. I don't remember the last time I felt this relaxed." I let out a contented sigh. "Thank you so much for arranging this. It's exactly what I needed."

Gloria reaches out to squeeze my hand in response. "Of course. We all need a little self-care now and then."

She has such a tender heart and it hurts me to think that she has gone through some very painful times in her life. Times that she doesn't like to talk about much, just like me.

As we lie there, my thoughts drift to what Lennie said yesterday, about her imaginary friend wanting to protect her from her dad. I'm just about to mention it to Gloria, when she speaks first.

"You look worried and that's not allowed in this place. So, Miss Florist extraordinaire, how about we share stories about our funniest customers?"

I chuckle. "Oh, where do I even begin? Just recently there was the chili pepper bouquet, then a request for a wedding bouquet in a glass vase with live goldfish swimming in it for good luck. Can you believe it?" I shake my head. "I had to explain gently that it wouldn't be fair to the fish nor would it be practical."

Gloria laughs. "That's so odd. Did you manage to talk her out of it?"

"I tried, but she had a meltdown right there in the middle of my shop. I had to offer her a discount on a more traditional bouquet just to calm her down. What about you? Any memorable encounters with quirky customers at Honeywood?"

"Oh yes. We once had a customer who ordered an espresso, but insisted on making it himself because he did not trust anyone else to get it right. So, we let him use our espresso machine. He was so serious about his coffee-making skills that he brought his own special mug, a thermometer, and even a small digital scale to measure the exact amount of coffee grounds. It was quite a spectacle, and in the end, he refused to pay full price since he had made his own beverage."

"That's ridiculous." Laughter bubbles out of me, and I already feel lighter than I have in a long time.

The entire afternoon goes by in a blur as Gloria and I catch up on each other's lives.

As I drive home, I feel so happy and content, grateful for friends like Gloria who can turn what would have been an ordinary day into something so special.

Then a speeding car comes out of nowhere and almost crashes into me. I swerve to avoid the collision, my heart pounding. The other driver zooms off without a second glance, disappearing around a bend in the road.

Shaken but unharmed, I pull over to catch my breath.

But as I continue my drive home, a hard knot forms in my stomach. Was that deliberate? I try to push the paranoia aside, reminding myself that anxiety will only make things worse.

But it felt like a warning, telling me that I'm not allowed to be happy. That if I dare to let go and relax completely, something terrible will happen, because the universe knows I don't deserve to be free and at peace.

# FOUR

Bright and early on Monday morning, as the house settles into silence, I seize a few stolen moments for myself before plunging into the day's tasks. The sun pours through the living room window, casting a golden glow over the beach beyond.

The interior of our house has changed a lot from when I moved in, six years ago. I needed to make sure it doesn't remind me of the past, and the woman who lived here before me. She had decorated it in a minimalist fashion, all very modern and stylish, but to me it felt cold and sterile. I wanted to infuse everything with new life and warmth.

Now, colorful rugs and cozy couches invite relaxation, and I painted the walls in warm, earthy tones. A play space for Lennie has also been set up in one corner of the living room, complete with a tiny table and chairs, art supplies and shelves filled with books and toys. Even the screened-in living room porch has seen a complete transformation with the addition of potted plants that hang from the ceiling, their leaves draping down in a lush green curtain.

I'm sitting on the couch journaling my thoughts, but it's

impossible to resist the pull of my favorite spot—the yoga mat waiting patiently in the corner. So I get up and unroll the mat.

I'm blessed with good genes, but I've also worked very hard to feel good in my body and to take care of my mind and spirit. I love partying and drinking as much as anyone—it's all about balance—but I also practice yoga and meditate regularly. Honestly, I don't know what I'd be like without yoga; it helps me keep my demons at bay. And after what happened yesterday, when that car almost hit me, I desperately need the grounding and clarity that my yoga practice provides.

I inhale deeply, enjoying the calming scent of the essential oils I've diffused in the room. And as I release the stress in my body, I slowly flow from each pose into the next, relaxing into the familiar rhythm. This is like a ritual for me, my mat a sacred space where I can escape.

I love yoga so much that I've started doing some sessions with Lennie to instill in her at a young age the importance of connecting mind, spirit, and body, and finding inner peace. I hope that even if she has inherited some of my darker traits, yoga will help her to be her best self, just like it helps me. And at just six years old, she already shows an incredible eagerness to learn and embrace the practice, and I love watching her mimicking my poses. It's also a lovely way for us to bond.

Before Lennie was born, I went to a lot of yoga, Pilates, and kickboxing classes. But in early motherhood I no longer had the time, and I was also going through a period of intense emotion. I was so burdened with guilt that I didn't feel I deserved to do the things I loved. Therapy helped with that, though, and now as Lennie grows older, I am slowly finding time for self-care again. I really want to be the best version of myself for my little girl, and connecting with my body through movement helps me to feel more in control of my life, and of my mind.

Feeling energized after my flow, I make my way to the

kitchen to get a drink. Like the rest of the house, the kitchen has also been redesigned, transformed into a cozy, rustic space with framed photos of our little family on the walls. I replaced the countertops with warm, wooden ones and the cabinets now have a distressed, white farm-style finish. A large farmhouse sink sits below a window, allowing plenty of natural light to flood the room. I open the fridge to retrieve a handful of greens from my garden, and I whip up a blend of kale, spinach, banana, and a dash of almond milk for me, Nathan, and Lennie.

On my way up the stairs, my phone vibrates in my hand and I pause to glance at the screen, seeing a text from Gloria.

*Hey you, hope you slept well last night after all the pampering. I definitely slept like a baby! Thanks for coming with me. It was so much fun. Let's do it again soon, okay? See you later. Gloria*

I quickly type out a reply, thanking her for the wonderful afternoon.

Then I continue upstairs, heading for Lennie's room, where I gently push open the door, revealing a world of color and imagination. Part of the floor is littered with toys, ranging from stuffed animals to building blocks, evidence of her boundless creativity.

Nathan often finds himself torn between marveling at Lennie's artistic abandon and fighting the urge to tidy up, while I want her creative spirit to run wild. I think Lennie's room should be a place where she can unleash her imagination without any constraints.

But to stop from driving Nathan crazy, we keep the clutter on one side of the room on a multi-colored rug that we call her "fun zone." The rest of the room is meticulously organized with shelves filled with books, a small desk for drawing and writing, and a cozy reading nook tucked away in the corner. Her canopy bed has long, pink and silver, delicate fabric that cascades down in elegant drapes like a waterfall, creating a magical cocoon. But I usually keep it tied to the posts to prevent tangling.

The walls are painted white and blush pink, and they are covered with Lennie's artwork, paintings of imaginary landscapes, seashells, and magical creatures. Lennie loves to draw and her passion for art is evident in every stroke of the brush.

She's still a child and has so much to learn, but I'm honestly in awe of her raw talent. I catch a glimpse of her sketchpad and some crayons on the nightstand. She must have been drawing after I put her to bed last night, just like I did when I was little, although for me it was books. I'd sometimes wake up and read even though I wasn't allowed.

"Good morning, my little princess." I walk over to the bed where she's still sleeping peacefully. Her golden curls frame her face like a halo, and I can't resist running my fingers through them.

She stirs slightly, a smile tugging at one corner of her lips. Struck as I so often am by her beauty and innocence, I lean down to kiss her forehead.

"Morning, Mommy," she mumbles, rubbing her eyes with the back of her hand as she sits up.

"Morning, my loves," Nathan says, appearing in the doorway and greeting us with a bright smile even though I can see he's still tired.

"Morning, Daddy!" Lennie wriggles out of my arms to greet him, and Nathan swoops her up, tossing her into the air and catching her effortlessly, eliciting peals of laughter.

"All right, pumpkin, let's get you ready for the day." I pry Lennie from Nathan's arms and guide her toward her closet.

"Can we go to the beach after school, Mommy?" Lennie asks as we select her clothes.

"Of course, sweetheart." I ruffle her hair.

"Yay!" She claps her hands in excitement.

"Let's get you dressed first, though," Nathan interjects, helping Lennie into a pair of blue jeans, a maroon t-shirt, and a black sweater.

"While Daddy helps you get dressed, I'll go and make breakfast." I plant a kiss on Nathan's cheek before heading to the kitchen.

A while later, the scent of frying bacon fills the room. Nathan and Lennie settle at the table, their playful banter music to my ears.

"All right, Lennie, how many seashells did you collect with Mommy yesterday?" Nathan quizzes, sipping his coffee. He's not a breakfast person, he'll be perfectly satisfied with his smoothie and his hit of caffeine, but when he's home, he still makes sure he sits with me and Lennie.

"Fifteen shells." Lennie takes a gulp of her smoothie. "Mommy counted them. One of them had a tiny crab inside."

"Wow, that's a lot." Nathan feigns amazement, as he smiles at her fondly.

"Breakfast is ready." I set down plates of scrambled eggs, crispy bacon, and toast. I like to make something special on Mondays, to start the week right.

Once we are done, I hand Lennie her backpack, a pink bag covered in her favorite fairy cartoon characters. Nathan helps her adjust the straps, ensuring they're secure and comfortable on her shoulders.

"Let's not forget your lunchbox," he adds, placing it gently into her backpack.

Lennie beams up at him. "Thanks, Daddy."

"You're very welcome. Come on, time for school." Nathan takes her hand, and we head for the door. She skips all the way down the garden path, and Nathan and I grin at each other. It never gets old, seeing our little girl so happy. After he helps her into her car seat, his blue eyes meet mine. "I'll drop off the little munchkin, then I'll go straight to work. Have a good day, darling."

"You too. Busy day ahead?"

"I have a client to visit at the jail, and a lot of catching up to do at the office. Then I have some case files to review. So yes, quite a lot to do. But I'll be back in time for dinner."

I place my hands on his clean-shaven cheeks and kiss him. "Okay, see you later."

As he drives off with Lennie, I stand at the end of the garden, watching my family disappear down the street.

As they turn the corner, I'm left alone with my thoughts, and the shadows that have been following me around lately, ever since we fixed the day of our wedding. Ghosts from a past I'm trying to ignore.


After school in the afternoon, Lennie and I gather the seashells we've collected on the beach and pack up our belongings, making our way down the private path leading to our house. We go round the side first, under her tree house, and head to the garden, so I can check on my sunflowers.

Even though they have been struggling a little, I'm relieved to see that they're holding on. Still, I make a mental note to cut off any withered blooms and tend to the soil tomorrow. Lennie meanders around, her small hands grazing the petals and leaves. Smiling, I inhale the sweet scent of flowers and the earthy undertone beneath it.

As a florist, I've seen many gardens in my lifetime, but this one holds a special place in my heart. It's my sanctuary, and I'm so proud of what I've done with it. It's filled with stunning colors, from the deep purple of the lavender bushes to the pale pink of the roses, and there are neatly trimmed hedges around the border. I chose flowers that would attract bees and butterflies, which are already starting to increase in number this spring, and in one corner a small fountain bubbles, surrounded by a bed of blooming water lilies.

Before I moved into his home, Nathan had a lovely garden, but it was nothing compared to what it is now. I've spent countless hours tending to each plant and planting new ones, nurturing them all with care and love, coaxing them to reach their full potential. Every bloom, every petal, is a testament to the time and effort I've invested in this place. I wanted it to really feel like my own, to be infused with my spirit, not that of the woman who lived here first.

Some of the wedding flowers will be sourced from this very garden. It's a way for me to carry a piece of home to the Glass Parlor, our gorgeous wedding venue. At first, I didn't want to have the reception there, as it was the exact same place where Nathan had been due to marry his ex, when they were engaged all those years ago. But my friend Elena talked me into it, and she's right. It's a beautiful place, with stained glass and painted floors.

I'm convinced the flowers from our garden will dispel any bad vibes that linger in the air. Some might think it silly of me, but I believe that the love and positive energy I planted here will create an atmosphere of joy and happiness. Lennie is especially excited that the flower crown she will be wearing at the wedding will also be made from the flowers of our garden. I recently shared a drawing of my design for the crown with her, and her eyes lit up with genuine delight. It will be an elegant yet simple headpiece, delicately woven with some of the same flowers that will make up my bouquet.

"Sweetheart, should we pick some flowers for the dining table tonight? Daddy will be eating with us, so let's make it special," I call out to Lennie, who has now settled down by the fountain and is busy plucking petals off a daisy.

"Yes, Mommy! Let's pick the prettiest ones!"

Kneeling beside her, I watch as she chooses each flower, her small hands nimble and delicate. She carefully places each one into the white wicker basket I keep on a bench near the fountain.

"I think these should be enough for a beautiful centerpiece. We'll use some of your shells to make it even more pretty." I stand up and help pull her to her feet. "Let's go and prepare dinner."

Soon after we go into the kitchen, I see Nathan's Mercedes pulling into the driveway. I know he said he'd be here for dinner, but he's back much earlier than usual. Normally, he wouldn't be home before half past six.

"Mommy, Daddy's home." Lennie's face lights up and she runs to the corridor to meet him, with me following behind.

"Hey there," Nathan says as we open the door to him.

Something's not right.

I'm not sure what it is, but he's definitely not his usual self. His voice sounds strained, and instead of scooping Lennie into his arms and swinging her around as he normally does, he simply smiles weakly at her and kisses her forehead.

"Babe. You're home early," I say, trying to keep my tone upbeat as I kiss him. "Everything okay? You look—"

"Um, can we talk away from the little one?" He rubs the back of his neck, avoiding eye contact, and I nod, my throat tightening. As usual, I'm fearing the worst.

Even though I always try to be, I'm not naturally the most positive person. I get anxious, obsessive even, tending to let my mind wander into the darkest corners, anticipating the worst possible scenarios. That's why I practice yoga: nobody needs it more than me.

I settle Lennie at the kitchen table with a book and a snack of yoghurt and fruit, then join Nathan in the living room. "What's going on?" I ask softly, searching his face.

Then he takes a deep breath, his eyes clouded with pain. "I

got a call from one of my uncles. It's my father... he passed away."

My hand flies to my mouth. "Oh my God, Nathan. I'm so sorry." I reach for him, but he steps back, his eyes glistening.

"Are you okay?" I ask tentatively, wanting to offer comfort but unsure how to do so.

Nathan's mother left him and his father when he was a child, and he has always looked up to his father, following in his footsteps and drawing inspiration from his strength and determination. But their relationship became strained in recent years, as Nathan realized with the clarity of adulthood that his father didn't deserve to be idolized so much. He doesn't like to talk about it, even though there's nobody who would understand more than me, but I know his father sometimes took out his stress on his son, with bursts of temper that were frightening and harmful. Nathan must be feeling an overwhelming mix of emotions, from sadness to guilt to confusion.

"Yeah, Hannah," he says, his voice cracking. "I'm okay. I just... I need some time alone. To process."

I nod. "Of course. Take all the time you need," I murmur, but my heart is aching as I watch him leave the house, his broad shoulders sagging. It's devastating to watch him crumbling.

He heads to the beach, his hands buried in his hair, and I can't take my eyes off him as he finally stands at the water's edge, staring out at the waves crashing against the shore, before dropping to his knees, his head bowed. I know he wants space right now, but I feel such a powerful urge to go to him, to comfort him in his time of need. But this is not about me. I have to respect what he needs to do, as he grieves.

So instead, I go to the kitchen, where Lennie and I get started on dinner. She babbles away happily as she stands on a chair and mixes a pan of sauce for me on the stove. I envy her innocence in this moment, her lack of awareness of the pain that life can bring in the blink of an eye.

The memories of my own mother's death flood my mind, taking me back to that terrible day when I found her lying in her bed with her long brown hair spread out around her head like a halo. I recall the numbness that took over my body then. The way my world froze, a moment drawing out into infinity.

It changed me forever. What will Nathan's grief do to him?

# FIVE

## LENNIE

I open my eyes to find the sun smiling at me through my curtains. Mommy said it's the weekend, so I don't have to go to school. I'm allowed to play all day. My stuffed animals are happy that I'll be able to play with them too. Mr. Buttons, the teddy bear Aunty Elena bought me when I was born, who wears a brown suit with lots of buttons on it, is still sleepy. But I give him a morning hug.

"Good morning, Mr. Buttons," I whisper. It's nice to say hi, even if he doesn't say it back.

I slide out from my warm blanket, and my feet touch the cool, wooden floor.

I can't wait for all the fun things waiting for me today. Maybe Whisper will visit me again. I haven't seen her since last weekend, but in my head, she keeps telling me that she will come back to see me soon. Sometimes I wish I had a sister, so we could play together. But it's just me, Whisper, and my stuffed animals. And that's okay.

In the bathroom, I stretch on my tippy-toes to reach my toothbrush. I see a girl with freckles and curly hair like sunshine in the mirror, and I talk to that girl, pretending someone else is there, spending time with me like a sister.

After I've brushed my teeth with my strawberry-flavored toothpaste, I go to my closet and pick out a blue dress with teeny white stars all over it.

"All right, Mr. Buttons," I say, holding him close when I'm finished getting dressed, "it's time for my breakfast. I'll see you later." I kiss him and leave the room with Whisper next to me.

"Whisper, do you think Mommy's making pancakes today?" I ask as we walk hand in hand down the hallway toward the stairs. I still haven't told anyone that Whisper isn't always invisible, or that I know what she looks like now. I don't want her to vanish because she's my best friend in the world.

"I certainly hope so, Lennie," comes the soft voice that only I can hear. "Your mommy knows how much you love pancakes."

Whisper loves to whisper in my ear, and that's why I gave her that name. I tell Mommy and Daddy about her sometimes, and Mommy just smiles and says it's okay to have an imaginary friend. She also said sometimes the things in our heads are just as real as the things outside of them.

Daddy doesn't believe in Whisper, but he pretends to. When we had a bonfire on the beach last week and saw a shooting star, I made a wish that one day Whisper would show herself to me so I could see her, and that Mommy and Daddy would finally see her too. Now my wish has come true, but I can't tell Mommy and Daddy until Whisper says it's okay.

I want Daddy to be happy, and I miss him so much when he goes away, even though all this week he has been sad and grumpy. I even heard him snap at Mommy sometimes when she tried to talk to him. Yesterday Daddy was so unhappy that he didn't even read me a bedtime story, which is my most favorite thing ever. He does the voices really well, and he's so good at pretending to be different people.

Maybe Whisper could make Daddy happy, if only he could

talk to her. And then maybe she would change what she thinks about him too. She says he's a bad man, but to me, he's the best dad ever. He's been sad these days, but he will get better soon, and I'm going to do everything I can to make him smile again.

As me and Whisper reach the staircase, I suddenly feel a little bit scared, like someone is watching me. I look around, but there's no one there. It's just me and Whisper.

"Did you feel that?" I ask her.

"Feel what, Lennie?"

I shrug. "Nothing. Let's go see what Mommy's cooking for breakfast." I rush down the stairs, my blue starry dress swirling around my legs.

"Careful, Lennie," Whisper warns, but I struggle to hear her over all the yummy kitchen smells and the sounds of pots and pans clattering as I skip into the kitchen.

The room is warm and filled with the delicious smell of fresh pancakes. I watch as Mommy flips them in the air like a real chef. I hope I can have mine with blueberries, yoghurt, and maple syrup. That's my favorite way to eat them.

"Good morning, Mommy," I say, smiling at her.

She's so beautiful, in her dark-blue dungarees and her white apron. I hope when I grow up, I'm as pretty as her. My hair is lighter than hers, but everyone says I have her dimples and her nose.

"Morning, sweetheart," she replies, her eyes crinkling at the corners as she smiles back at me, but I think she also looks a little sad, like Daddy was yesterday. "I thought we could have a special weekend breakfast today. Sit down, and I'll get you a plate."

"Yay, thank you, Mommy." I sit down at the kitchen table, swinging my feet as they dangle toward the floor. As I wait for my food, I say to Whisper, "I knew she made pancakes. Aren't we lucky?"

"Very, very lucky," she whispers back.

"Here you go, Lennie," Mommy says, placing a plate of steaming, fluffy pancakes in front of me. My stomach rumbles and I clasp my hands together.

"Thank you, Mommy," I say again. "These look so yummy. Whisper thinks so too. She's here too, Mommy. She loves your pancakes."

"Is that so? Well, I'm glad Whisper could join us today. Did you have any nice dreams last night?"

"I dreamt of a magical world where the sand was made of sugar and the waves were like cotton candy." I spoon some yoghurt and blueberries onto my plate and watch as the little blue balls tumble around.

"Wow, that sounds wonderful. Tell me more about it, sweetheart." She pours a little syrup over my pancakes and then sits down at the table.

"Whisper came with me," I continue, taking big forkfuls of pancakes and looking at the empty chair next to us, where Daddy usually sits. "We rode giant seahorses around the ocean, and we found a treasure chest full of stones in the colors of the rainbow."

"Sounds like quite the adventure." Mommy strokes my hair gently. "I'm glad you had Whisper there with you. Speaking of adventures, why don't you go get your sketchpad and crayons after breakfast? We can head down to the beach soon. You can draw the waves."

"Really? Can we go now?"

"Finish your breakfast first, sweetie. Then we'll go."

"Okay. Will Daddy come with us?"

The smile on Mommy's face disappears as she looks down. When she looks up again, her eyes look a bit shiny. "Sweetie, Daddy is packing. He'll be going away tomorrow for a few—"

"To the funall?"

"It's funeral, but yes." Mommy frowns. "Where did you hear that word?"

"I heard you and Daddy talking in the night. He was very sad."

"Yes, sweetheart. Daddy is feeling sad right now, but we'll be here for him."

I nod. "What's a funall?"

Mommy takes a deep breath. "It's an event people have when someone dies and goes up to heaven. It's a way to say goodbye and honor their memory. Remember when your yellow bird Charlie died, and we buried her in the garden?"

I nod, my heart sad because I miss Charlie. "Yes, I remember."

"It's like that, but bigger," she explains. "The funeral is for grown-ups, though, so you don't have to worry about it. Just focus on having fun today, okay?"

"Okay, but who went to heaven?"

"Someone very important to Daddy, but like I said, you don't have to worry about it. Daddy will be back soon, and we'll all be together again." She turns to the window. "Look at those clouds. Can you see the shapes they make? They look like fluffy, white sheep, don't they?"

I nod. When Mommy doesn't want to tell me something or wants to cheer me up, she always makes me think about something else.

After breakfast, we go to the beach and I want to ask more questions, but I don't want to make Mommy sad again. Sometimes Mommy says she's happy even when I know she's sad. That's a lie.

After we come back from the beach, we find Daddy in the living room, sitting on the couch with his head in his hands. He looks up when we come in, and I see the sadness in his eyes. Mommy goes to him and wraps her arms around him, and they hug for a long time.

I stand there watching until Daddy stands up and kisses me on top of my head. Then he goes and makes a hot tea for him and Mommy before he goes back upstairs. He doesn't say he's going to play with me like he usually does when he's home.

Mommy sits me down on the couch with a mug of hot chocolate and turns me to look at her. "You know what, Lennie? I don't think it's a good idea for us to let Daddy go to the funeral alone. What do you think?"

"So, we can go with him?"

"No, my love." She puts both her hands on my cheeks. "I'm afraid a funeral is a grown-up thing. I should go with Daddy."

I feel tears jumping into my eyes. "You're leaving me alone?"

"No, of course not, darling. I thought it might be a good idea for you to stay with Aunty Elena and Uncle Darius? You'll have a great time together, and we'll be back before you know it. Maybe she'll make you some of her delicious lemonade and cookies."

I nod, feeling a bit sad but not wanting to show it.

At least Whisper will be at Aunty Elena's with me.


In the morning, on Sunday, Mommy and Daddy drive me to Aunty Elena's wedding shop. I love it there; it's a magical place with sparkly dresses and colorful ribbons. It makes me think of fairy tales and princesses.

We find her standing by the door, wearing a flowy colorful dress and a long necklace made of wood pieces. Aunty Elena is very pretty. I like her black hair, especially when she puts head-bands and flowers in it. Right now, she has it up in a little pony-tail with a pencil through it.

She smiles at me and holds out her hands, "Hey there, Lennie. Ready for some fun?"

I nod slowly, still a bit unsure about being without Mommy and Daddy. I like Aunty Elena, but I'd rather be with them. I wish they'd let me go to the funall too.

"We love you, Lennie," Mommy says as they hug me good-bye. "Be good for Aunty Elena, okay?" Then the door closes, and I'm left standing there, holding Aunty Elena's hand.

"Aunty Elena," I whisper, "why is Daddy so sad?"

Aunty Elena sighs, her eyes looking sad too. "Sweetheart, your daddy's heart is hurting because someone very special to him is no longer with us. Going to a funeral helps people say goodbye and remember all the good times they had together, when someone leaves and goes up to heaven to be with the angels."

"But why can't I go to the funall too?"

She shakes her head gently. "I'm afraid it's just for grown-ups, darling. But don't worry, we'll have our own special day together, just you and me. I'm so excited you're sleeping over tonight. How about we start by making something beautiful?"

"Like what?"

"Like a wedding dress." She winks. "Wouldn't that be so much fun?"

I nod, thinking about the shiny beads and colorful threads she always has in her shop.

As Aunty Elena leads me away from the door, I look through the window and see Mommy and Daddy driving away in our car, and I wave to them, but they don't see me.

"Aunty Elena," I ask again, pulling at her dress, "will Daddy still be sad when he comes back?"

Aunty Elena bends down, her eyes serious now. "Some-times, sweetheart, the sadness stays with us for a while. But we'll do our best to make him smile again, won't we? Now, let me show you the magical world of sewing. We'll make some-thing so pretty that everyone will be amazed. How about we make a wedding dress for the doll you left at my house last time you came to visit? I have her with me."

"Mirabella?" I say, my eyes widening.

"Yes, Mirabella. We'll make her the most beautiful wedding dress anyone has ever seen."

I follow her inside, still thinking about Daddy and hoping that I can make him happy again soon.

But in my head, I hear Whisper reminding me that just like Aunty Elena said, sometimes sadness doesn't go away.

What if Daddy always stays like this?

And what if it's like Whisper said last time? What if now that he's so sad, my daddy doesn't love me anymore?

# SIX

## HANNAH

At 1 p.m. on Monday, I step out of the car in Clearwater. The ground beneath my feet is muddy from the earlier rain, and the heady scent of wet earth lingers in the air.

In the distance, I can see a field of flowers, the bright colors of azaleas, purple coneflowers, and tickseed flowers dulled by the gray clouds. As we gather around Nathan's father's grave, the sky opens again and raindrops thud on his casket. My heart feels heavy as I watch him being laid to rest in the cold ground.

To be perfectly blunt, my sadness isn't for Nathan's father. I didn't really know him and I feel furious with him for how he treated Nathan. He was hardly what anyone would call affectionate, and he was always the perfectionist, pushing his son to succeed at everything. Failure was never an option.

But I feel a tremendous sense of sadness for Nathan. He's lost his father, a person who should have always been there for him, and I know only too well that no amount of anger or resentment can change how much that hurts. No matter how terrible he was to him, he was still his father, and that bond simply cannot be broken. And at least his dad stayed with him when he was a child, while his mother just left him, something I'll never understand.

I stand by Nathan, our fingers interlaced. The breeze tousles my hair, and I shiver—not just from the cold, but from the eerie stillness of this small cemetery.

The gravestones seem to lean in, whispering secrets about those who rest beneath them. Cemeteries have always made me feel deeply uncomfortable. I'm ashamed to say that I haven't even visited my mother's grave since her death. I tried several times, going as far as the cemetery gates, but I just could never bring myself to go any farther. The weight of her absence felt too heavy, and the thought of her lying there under the ground, with me unable to touch her or hear her voice, was unbearable. And as soon as visions of her lying on that bed flooded my mind, I turned my car around and left.

Nathan stands rigid, his gaze fixed on the casket, lost in memories that I can only guess at. He told me once that his father never once read him a book, or sang him a nursery song. I think that's why whenever he has the time at home, he's so devoted to Lennie, determined to give her as much of his attention as he can, even when he's exhausted from work.

I wonder what he's reminiscing about now, if there are any crumbs of affection from his father that he can retrieve from deep within his memories. I squeeze his hand, trying to offer some silent reassurance, but he doesn't respond at all. Wherever he is, I can't reach him.

The cemetery is small and old, its gravestones weathered and cracked with fading letters etched in them. I look around, attempting to find a familiar face, but I'm met with a sea of strangers.

Nathan's relatives blend into the backdrop of his past. He's so distant from his family that he didn't feel the need to introduce me to any of them over the years. He obviously doesn't trust them, or like them at all.

When I asked him to introduce me to some of his relatives at the church earlier, he shook his head. "This isn't the time," he whispered. "Anyway, I don't want them near you. They're not worth knowing."

Last night at the hotel, he mentioned that after his mother left when he was a kid, very few of them reached out to check up on him. Not many of them are invited to our wedding. I guess, being an only child like me, he has grown accustomed to solitude and self-reliance.

I let the topic go, even though I wish I could be involved in every part of his life, even the most painful parts of the past.

After his father is in the ground and the soil has covered up his casket, I watch Nathan navigate through the mourners, exchanging nods more than words. An older man draws a momentary connection from him, perhaps a distant uncle; I think I remember something about him. But the rest of the guests remain faceless figures from Nathan's history.

As my gaze sweeps over the crowd, I notice a woman in the distance, dressed traditionally like everyone else here, in black with only a hint of her face visible beneath her large hat. She stands alone, detached from the rest of the mourners. Even from afar, there's something about her presence that intrigues me. My curiosity piqued, I consider making my way over, but she walks away swiftly. Who was she, and why didn't she join everyone else?

Then I'm distracted by a man with a bristly white beard who asks Nathan if he will join them at his house for a small gathering. Nathan hesitates, glancing at me for a moment before turning back to the man. "Thank you, but I'm afraid we can't," he says wearily. "We're driving back home now."

"I need to get out of here," he murmurs as soon as the man walks away, and I nod. The desire to escape this place weighs on me as heavily as the grief that radiates off my husband. I'm definitely ready to leave and get back to my daughter.

It's hard not to think about my own mortality after a funeral. I want to die old and gray with lots of grandchildren around me, and I want Lennie to know with every fiber of her being how much I loved her. I want her to feel my love with her always, even when I'm no longer there.

Back in the car, Nathan sinks into silence, and as I drive through the rain-soaked streets, I steal glances at him, wanting to comfort him but feeling unable to do so. He seemed grateful when I offered to come with him, but I still have the feeling that he wants his space, and I need to respect that.

His broad shoulders, which are usually squared with confidence, are now hunched down, making him seem smaller. His hands fidget with the edge of his seatbelt, his strong fingers tracing the same path over and over as if searching for comfort in the repetitive motion.

When he meets my eyes briefly, I notice the lines on his forehead, which are more pronounced than I've seen them before. They tell a story of sleepless nights and restless thoughts. Last night he was tossing and turning for hours.

I extend my hand, gently placing it on his in a gesture of comfort and support. The warmth I offer is met with a slight twitch but his eyes remain fixed on the passing scenery.

"Babe, there was a woman at the funeral wearing all black and—"

"Most people wore black."

"Yes, but she had a large black hat that covered most of her face too. She was standing on her own, close to the gate of the cemetery. I couldn't see her clearly, but there was something a bit strange about her."

Nathan is quiet for a moment, then he lets out a breath. "It was probably just some random mourner paying her respects," he says heavily. "Funerals tend to attract all sorts of people."

"But why didn't she join everyone?"

He turns to me. "Look, Hannah, please don't waste your time thinking about those people. They don't matter. They're not my family; you and Lennie are. You'll never have to see them again."

When I remove my hand to put it back on the wheel, Nathan runs his through his disheveled hair. I know it would probably help if he just allowed himself to cry, but he can't seem to bring himself to do it. Maybe he's worried that if he lets go, the pain will consume him entirely.

As we approach Stoneview a little while later, Nathan's body language remains unchanged. I have a heavy weight in my stomach, but I still enjoy the drive through the small, quiet town.

It's such a beautiful place, I know I'll never take it for granted. The narrow cobblestone streets wind their way through, and front porches brim with color from pots of flowers. It seems to me sometimes that Stoneview is frozen in time, with its weathered store signs and old cottages. Every corner holds a piece of history; it's impossible not to feel a sense of nostalgia.

Elena, who loves history and has a whimsical nature, is always wondering what it was like to walk these streets in centuries gone by. She likes to picture how people dressed, what they dreamed of, what stories were lost with them, fading into the mists of time.

Stoneview is the perfect place to raise a family and create lasting memories. It's a warm, safe community where I know my daughter is surrounded by people who will look out for her and treat her with kindness.

But as I look at Nathan, his face etched with sadness, I wish the magic of the town we grew up in could provide him with the healing he needs, the same magic it had when we were kids running around on these very streets.

It might just be the impact of the graveyard and the funeral leaving me fragile and anxious. But I can't help the feeling that his father's death has marked a change in the atmosphere: a shift toward darkness. Not just sadness, but danger.

I can sense it in my gut; I just hope I'm wrong.

And I hope the darkness isn't coming from inside of me, again.

# SEVEN

Elena and Darius's house is a pretty little cottage near the town center, with a white picket fence surrounding the front yard. The fence is lined with roses of various colors, their delicate petals gently swaying in the breeze, and it wraps around a well-maintained lawn.

Gardening is not Darius's or Elena's thing, so I come over every now and again to help out, but she and Darius do try to keep the yard looking beautiful, and they have the coziest porch on the street. It boasts rich colors and ornate decorations, with the wicker furniture scattered with cushions in jewel tones of red, purple, and gold. There's a vintage Turkish rug on the wooden floor, and antique oil lamps lining the railings. When the sun starts to set and the lamps are lit, their soft glow is utterly enchanting.

As we walk up toward the house, I can see the living room through the large window facing the driveway. It's packed with old photographs, antique furniture, and wooden shelves lined with classic novels, all illuminated by the warm light of a table lamp.

Elena has lived here since she was a child, and even though

it looks very different now, her home often makes me feel nostalgic. When we were in school, every time I visited, Elena's mother would give us the best homemade lemonade, sharp and sweet, and warm chocolate chip or peanut butter cookies. The smell of freshly baked treats and Elena's mother's kindness made me feel comforted and cared for. Since my own home environment was so different, I cherished every moment I spent there.

Sadly, Elena's mother died, and her father, who suffered from Alzheimer's, gradually forgot even the memories of his beloved wife. He passed away a few years ago, with only fragments of her in his mind.

Elena lived with him in this house until he died, and she has never wanted to move away from the place that held so many precious memories. Darius, who I liked from the moment we met, moved in here with her after they got married.

Before we have the chance to knock, the front door flies open and Lennie bounds out, her eyes sparkling with excitement. Elena is just behind her, smiling warmly at us. I crouch down to Lennie's level, pulling her into my arms and holding her tight, suddenly overcome with emotion.

Sometimes it really hits me hard in the chest: I love every bone in my daughter's body. She is everything to me and nothing matters as much as her. She is immeasurably precious and, without a doubt, having her is the best thing that has happened in my life. It's like she gave me a second chance; a sign from the universe that even someone like me can be granted true happiness. Even after everything I did, I was gifted the pure joy and love of motherhood.

"Did you have fun with Aunty Elena?" I ask, breathing in the scent of coconut oil, which we use to moisturize the sensitive skin on her scalp and neck.

"Yes! We made a wedding dress for my doll, Mirabella. It looks just like yours, Mommy."

I brush her rosy cheek with the tip of my finger. "Wow, that sounds lovely, sweetheart. I'm sure Mirabella looks stunning in her new dress."

Elena reaches out to hug Nathan. "I'm so sorry again for your loss, Nathan." He returns the embrace, but I can see his body is tense.

"Daddy!" Lennie wriggles away to go to him, throwing herself into his chest as he crouches down and wraps his arms around her, but his eyes are far away.

Elena comes over to hug me as well, then she puts her hands on my shoulders. "Are you sure you don't want Lennie to spend a few more nights with me and Darius, just to give you both a little time to process the loss? It was fun having her around; you know it's no trouble for us."

Before meeting and marrying Darius, Elena never showed any desire to have children. But recently she has had a change of heart. At forty-six, she worries that she may no longer be able to get pregnant, and while they have discussed the option of adoption, I can sense that she still harbors a deep longing for a biological child of her own. For now, she finds every excuse to spend as much time as she can with Lennie, her goddaughter.

"Thank you so much, Elena. You're so kind, but I think it's best if we go back home for tonight. Lennie needs her own bed and routine."

Elena nods understandingly. "Of course, that makes sense. Just know that I'm here for you both whenever you need anything."

"I know." I squeeze her shoulder, feeling a surge of gratitude for her unwavering support during all the difficult times we've been through.

Then Darius steps out of the house. He's a little older than Elena and has a charming salt-and-pepper beard that gives him an air of refined maturity. They are a lovely couple, complementing each other in ways that only true soulmates do. Elena has really found her match with him; they both share a fascination with the past and have a passion for vintage style. Today Darius is wearing a tailored three-piece suit that looks like it comes right out of the 1920s. In contrast, Elena has on a loose top decorated with delicate floral designs, paired with billowy wide-legged pants.

"Nathan," Darius says, his deep voice laced with sympathy, "I'm truly sorry about your father."

"Thank you, Darius." Nathan's voice is cracked as if he's not spoken in years. "I appreciate your support so much."

Darius is a psychiatrist, and I'm grateful when he offers a therapy session for Nathan, but Nathan politely declines.

"That's very kind, but I think right now I just need some time to process everything on my own."

Darius nods. "Of course. Just know that I'm here, and please don't hesitate to reach out."

"Thanks, man." Nathan sighs. "We better get going, Hannah."

"Silly me! I forgot Lennie's things. I'll be right back." Elena runs back into the house and returns a few moments later with a small bag filled with Lennie's belongings. I take it from her and help settle my daughter in her car seat.

But before I get into the car, Elena puts a hand on my shoulder and whispers, "Let me know if I can help with Lennie at all, hon, so you can just focus on being there for Nathan right now. He looks like he could use all the support he can get. I've never seen him looking so broken. Not even after everything that happened before."

Elena knows so much about me, including some of the trauma Nathan and I went through in the past, but there are things I have kept hidden from her for years. She's a kind and generous spirit, but I don't think even she would forgive me, not if she knew what Nathan and I did before we had Lennie.

· · ·

On the way home, Lennie chatters excitedly from the back seat despite the heavy atmosphere in the car. But her babbling only serves to make Nathan's silence all the more deafening.

When we arrive home, Nathan goes straight upstairs, his footsteps slow and heavy.

To give him space, Lennie and I spend the evening baking his favorite coconut cookies in the warm, inviting kitchen. Lennie's small hands eagerly mix the ingredients while I guide her, trying to distract both of us.

And as I tuck her into bed, I wonder when light and laughter will come back to our home, with Nathan doting on her once again and cherishing the time he has with us.

She looks up at me with those wide innocent eyes, searching for reassurance. "Why is Daddy still sad, Mommy? Didn't the funall make him better?"

I pause for a moment and force a smile. "He's just tired, baby. He needs some rest. Everything will be okay, I promise."

She gives a little nod, her hand reaching out to grip mine. "Will you read me a story?"

"Of course, my love." I choose a book from her shelf, but my mind is elsewhere and I know I'm not doing justice to the story.

Once Lennie finally drifts off, I tiptoe out and head to our bedroom. It's dimly lit, shadows dancing on the walls. Nathan is lying on the bed, still fully clothed and utterly lost in his thoughts. I approach cautiously, sitting on the edge of the bed.

"Nathan," I whisper, and my voice feels uncertain and unwelcome in the silence. He doesn't respond, his gaze locked on some distant point beyond the ceiling. I reach out and gently take his hand in mine, and his hand remains limp seconds before he withdraws it.

Needing something to lift my spirits, I leave the room and make my way to the kitchen, where I return Gloria's call from earlier today.

"Honey, I just wanted to check up on you," she says. "Are you and Nathan okay?"

I lean against the kitchen counter. "We're trying to be, but it's tough. Nathan is not himself. It's like a part of him has shut down."

"I know, sweetie. Grief can do that. Is there anything I can do to help? Whatever you need, I'm here for you."

"I know you are, and that's more than enough. Thanks, Gloria."

When I hang up the phone, my eyes land on the wedding binder on the counter, a joint engagement present from Gloria and Elena. It has a white cover, with sparkling gold lettering spelling out our names and the date of our approaching nuptials.

My fingers tremble as I flip through the pages, stopping at our engagement photo. We have two months until the big day, but my mind is consumed with anxiety instead of excitement. Will Nathan have healed enough to enjoy celebrating our love? Or is his father's death the first nail in the coffin of what should be our perfect day?

Could this be another warning, a reminder that because of what we've done, our happiness and freedom will never last; that it will soon be taken away?

As I sit there staring at the engagement photo of us on our private beach, my mind drifts to the woman with the large, black hat again. I can't shake the feeling that she was more than a mere stranger in mourning. Something seemed familiar about her, even though I didn't know anyone there. And the way she moved away just as I was walking toward her, it was like she didn't want me to see her face. But I push these uncomfortable thoughts aside.

"Don't be silly," I tell myself out loud, as I close the binder.

When I return to our bedroom, Nathan is no longer there, so I go in search and find him sitting at his desk in his home office playing chess with himself. It's something that always helps him relax. I have yoga, Nathan has chess. He taught me the rules a while ago, but he prefers to play alone, using the game as a way to quiet his mind. I watch silently from the doorway, my heart aching. I wish I could do something to ease his pain.

The office is fit for a successful lawyer, with its mahogany desk, shelves lined with law books, and framed diplomas adorning the walls. As usual, everything is neat, in its place and carefully organized. He moves the chess pieces slowly and with purpose, his brow furrowed.

I inhale the familiar scent of aged leather and cedarwood and try to keep my voice as calm and gentle as possible. "Nathan, are you okay?"

He slowly looks up, his eyes bloodshot and weary. "Honestly, I don't know," he finally murmurs. "I just need some time alone. You should go to bed." Absentmindedly, he picks up the gavel his father gifted him when he graduated from law school, a polished, heavy wooden hammer that he keeps in a prominent place on the desk. Its handle is smooth and worn from years of use, and its head is a dark, deep brown with intricate carvings. On one side, there is a small engraving of Nathan's father's initials: R.J.H., which stand for Robert Julius Howard. I've noticed that he often touches it when deep in thought or worried about something. Now he taps it gently against the desk, next to one of the antique fountain pens that he loves to collect and uses only for important legal documents.

Before stepping out the door, my gaze drifts to the many photos around the room of Lennie, Nathan, and me, smiling on vacations and outings, reminding me of happier times. And as I close the door, I wonder again how long it will take for Nathan to adjust to life after this loss. When will he go back to being the same man I know and love, the amazing father he is to Lennie?

# EIGHT
## LENNIE

I wake up super early and see Whisper next to me on the bed. She's holding Mr. Buttons in her arms. I rub my eyes and yawn. Then I give her a big smile because I love it when she stops being invisible. She has done it three times already since Mommy and Daddy came back from the funall.

"Here, Lennie, this little guy fell from your bed when you were sleeping."

I take Mr. Buttons from her and hug him. "Thank you."

"You're welcome. You know what? One of these days, I'll leave a special present for you in the tree house because you've been such a good girl and didn't tell anyone that you really see me sometimes."

"I'm good at keeping secrets." I hug Mr. Buttons tighter and kiss the top of his head.

I almost told Mommy twice, but then I remembered and zipped my lips tight.

When I look back at Whisper, I notice that her face is different, and her eyes look a little sad.

"Why are you sad, Whisper?" I reach out to touch her hand.

She sighs, her green eyes shining with tears. "Lennie, my darling, I'm upset to see your father not loving you anymore."

"But he does, Whisper. I know he does."

"Sweetie, he doesn't spend time with you anymore, and he's capable of doing very bad things, especially when he's upset. It makes me sad that you don't believe me."

"But it's not true. Daddy loves me. Mommy said his heart is hurting and that he just needs some time to get better. She said he's not angry at me, he's just sad."

Whisper's cold hand pets my cheek. "I know it's hard for you to understand. But when people feel sad, they can do bad things. I've known your parents for a long time. And I know your daddy's sadness will turn into anger and he will change, and then he will hurt you and your mommy."

I squeeze Mr. Buttons so hard, I almost burst him. My heart is all mixed up. I don't want to believe Whisper, but I don't think guardian angels lie.

I close my eyes and take a big breath. What if she's right? What if Daddy gets so sad that he turns into a bad man and hurts me and Mommy?

"It's okay, Lennie." Whisper puts a hand on my shoulder. "I'll be here to protect you; I'll do everything in my power to keep you safe. But I have to go now, before your mommy comes to wake you. Remember, don't tell her that I'm not invisible anymore, or what I look like. It has to be our little secret."


At breakfast, my pink and sparkly plate is on the table and Mommy made the fluffiest pancakes ever, this time with choco-late chips as a treat. She has a secret ingredient in her pancakes that she shared just with me: it's called nutmeg and sometimes she lets me add it myself. I'm good at adding secret ingredients.

I love it when we have a special breakfast, and Mommy says it's the most important meal of the day. But I don't feel happy because Daddy is not here to drink his coffee while we eat. He has not joined us for breakfast for seven days. I counted them all on the calendar I got for Christmas.

I think maybe Whisper was right: maybe Daddy doesn't want to be around me anymore.

"Mommy, does Daddy not love me like before?" I ask.

Mommy's smile disappears and a line appears between her eyes. "Oh honey, Daddy loves you more than you can imagine." She taps the tip of my nose with her finger. "You are his favorite person in the whole world."

"You're my favorites in the whole world too: you and Daddy and Whisper."

Mommy is smiling again now, but she dabs her eyes with a napkin.

"Are you crying because I made you sad?" I ask.

"No, baby, these are tears of happiness that you are in this world." Mommy's voice sounds a bit shaky. "Sometimes we cry when we feel happy as well as when we're sad. And when we're sad, crying is a good thing, because it makes us feel much better."

"Maybe Daddy should cry like you, so he can feel better."

Mommy takes a deep breath. "Sweetheart, Daddy is going through a really tough time right now. He is just trying to find his own way of dealing with how he feels." She shrugs. "He might decide to cry eventually. But remember, it's very important to be patient and understanding with him. He still loves us lots and lots, even if he's sad."

I nod and take a bite of pancake, but it doesn't taste as good as it usually does.

I miss Daddy's silly jokes and the way he spins me around.

"Lennie," Mommy says, "how about we go to Aunty Elena's shop after school so you can try on your bridesmaid dress again, now that she's taken up the hem a bit? Then afterwards, you can come and help me make some bouquets at Bliss & Twine."

I nod, feeling excited because I love trying my dress on and helping Mommy, Lila, and Josie at the flower shop. But then Mommy wants me to eat more breakfast even though I'm not hungry. I only eat a little bit and tell her I'm done, but she still makes me take one more bite before we leave for school.

"I'm not hungry, Mommy. Can I please stop?"

"Okay, sweetie. Just have a bit of milk, and then it's time for school."

"I miss Daddy driving me to school," I say. Whenever he was not traveling, Daddy always used to be the one who took me to school, before he got sad. I liked it when he told me funny stories about the people we saw on the way. And sometimes I asked him to include Whisper in the stories too, and he did.

"Daddy will take you to school again soon, my darling. I promise. But it's fun driving with Mommy too, isn't it?"

"Yes, Mommy," I say with a small smile. "Driving with you is nice too. But I miss Daddy."

"I know, sweetie. Me too."

# NINE

After the school bell rings, I meet Mommy outside and she keeps her promise. She drives me to Aunty Elena's shop to try on my dress. As soon as we arrive, Aunty Elena gives me a glass of lemonade like she said her mommy used to make when she was a child.

Mommy and I sit on the soft couch, and Aunty Elena disappears for a moment. Then she returns holding a beautiful, sparkly dress hanging from her arm. It's my bridesmaid dress, and it's the color of snow, with tiny pink and blue flowers and a skirt that poofs out like a cloud.

"Here it is, Lennie, fit for a princess," she says, her eyes glowing.

I put down my lemonade on the small table, careful to use one of Aunty Elena's coasters so I don't make it sticky, and jump up. "It's so pretty. I can't believe I have a real princess dress."

Aunty Elena nods, her large feather earrings waving. "Of course, sweetheart. You're my princess and you always will be. Now, let's try it on again and see how it looks. Come with me to the changing room."

Mommy follows us and watches Aunty Elena helping me

put on the dress and the little white shoes with pale blue bows that match it. They are a bit tight, but they look so pretty.

"Oh, Lennie, you look absolutely beautiful!" Aunty Elena says when she's done.

I look in the tall mirror and smile at myself. "I like it a lot." I turn around. "Look, it twirls with me."

Mommy laughs, and her eyes are happy again.

Aunty Elena hands me a matching purse and a flower crown with fake flowers just for practicing. "You'll be the loveliest bridesmaid."

I can't stop smiling. "Do you think Daddy will like it? Will it make him happy?"

Mommy kneels down and smoothes a strand of hair away from my face. "I'm sure it will, honey. Daddy is going to be so happy on our wedding day, and you're going to be the perfect bridesmaid."

Aunty Elena claps her hands. "Now, let's make sure everything fits perfectly. Stand still, Lennie, and let me adjust the straps."

"It's perfect," Aunty Elena says finally, stepping back to look at me. "You're a vision, Lennie. And guess what? You get to take the dress home with you today."

"Yay!" I twirl around one more time and then I have to take it off before Mommy and I leave to go and make some bouquets.

On our way out of Aunty Elena's shop, I hold Mommy's hand, swinging it backward and forward. "Mommy, can we get ice-cream too?"

She chuckles, ruffling my hair. "Of course, sweetie. But let's go to Bliss & Twine first, and then we'll treat ourselves."


Mommy's shop is like a big, secret garden. When we open the door, a soft bell jingles, and the smell of flowers surrounds us like a hug.

It's my favorite place in the whole world, except maybe my tree house. There are flowers everywhere, standing in buckets and smiling at me. Red ones, yellow ones, pink ones—so many that I can't even count them all. The colors are so bright, like a rainbow has spilled all over the room.

Right in the middle of the shop, there's a small fountain, and the water dances happily, making gentle splashing sounds. I run over to it, giggling as I dip my fingers in the cool water. Mommy says it's a wishing fountain, so I close my eyes tight and make a wish. I wish for Daddy to come home early today and for my family to be happy again.

Next to the fountain, Lila and Josie are arranging flowers. They always help Mommy in the shop. I like to call them flower fairies.

Lila is shorter than Mommy, and she wears hats or scarves that cover her hair, with big glasses and red lipstick. And Josie is tall with long red hair like a fairy that she twists into a braid. It's Josie who talks to me most, but they are both very nice and sometimes when I come to the shop, they give me chocolates. Lila always admires my drawings, and she once gave me a box of sparkly pens that are perfect for drawing flowers.

Mommy talks to them for a bit and thanks Lila for the cup of coffee she gives her, before she takes my hand again. "Come with me, sweetie." She leads me to the back of the shop where a little table is waiting and she hands me a bunch of flowers and a pair of scissors. "Let's create a bouquet together for the shop. We'll make it like a fairy's secret garden."

We tie the ends of the flowers together with a red ribbon. Mommy's hands guide mine as we carefully arrange each stem, and I stroke the soft petals and bright-green leaves. At the end, Mommy gets some sparkly glitter from a drawer and sprinkles it over the bouquet.

"There," she says finally. "Our fairy garden bouquet is

complete. I'm sure it will make someone very happy. Now, we better go and have that ice-cream I promised you."

I shout goodbye to the flower fairies and then Mommy and I walk out hand in hand. Mommy's hand is a little bit cold and shaky; it's been like that a lot lately and I'm not sure why, because the sun is shining and warm.

After walking along the street for a while, I notice a woman wearing white clothes, sitting in a dark car on the other side of the road, in front of the donut shop. She's wearing a cap that hides most of her face, but I think she's looking at us.

"Mommy, do you see that lady?" I ask, tugging on Mommy's hand.

Mommy looks around. "Which lady, sweetie?"

"The one with the cap... in the car." I twist around to point at the car. Mommy stops to glance in the direction I'm pointing, but now the woman is nowhere to be seen.

"I saw her, Mommy. I did. Now she's gone."

"Maybe you imagined it, Lennie?"

I hold Mommy's hand a little tighter as we continue walking. "I don't think I imagined it, Mommy. There was a woman, and she was watching us."

"Oh, sweetie, why do you think that she was watching us?"

"I don't know. I just felt it, like a tingling on my skin."

Mommy squeezes my hand. "Don't worry, Lennie. Sometimes our minds play tricks on us. We can't always trust everything we think we see, or everything our minds tell us."

I look around again to see if the woman got out of the car and is walking behind us, but she's not there anymore.


After we eat ice-cream, we go back home, but Daddy is still at work. So, I go to my tree house to play for a bit. I climb up the rope ladder, and I feel so happy. The tree branches are swaying and whispering, and I can hear seagulls. When I get up to the top, I take a big breath and smell the salty ocean air. But then I see something new on my bed.

A cuddly panda bear! I already know it's from Whisper. This must be my special present for keeping our secret.

"I will call you Snowy," I say, hugging the bear.

I play with Snowy for a while until Mommy calls me in for dinner. But before I go down the steps, I see someone standing far away, past the garden and the driveway, and on the street. It looks like they're standing still, watching me. My tummy starts doing flips and my whole body feels shivery. I remember what Mommy told me before, that sometimes our minds play tricks on us. My legs feel so wobbly, but I take a deep breath and climb down the ladder of the tree house.

Later, before I go to bed, Mommy makes me a glass of warm cinnamon milk, and I'm drinking it when Daddy walks into the kitchen. He just arrived home from the office and he's loosening his tie. He kisses Mommy and then me, but his lips are cold.

I want to hug him, but he goes to the fridge and gets a bottle of water. Then he opens the cabinet to remove a glass, but he closes it a little too hard. I jump, and some of the milk splashes out of my glass. Daddy turns around, his eyebrows raising when he sees the spilled milk on the floor.

"Be more careful, Lennie," he snaps, his voice loud and different. "You're a big girl now, you should know how to drink properly."

"I'm sorry, Daddy," I mumble. I'm not used to Daddy being angry with me. "I didn't mean to. It was just an accident."

Daddy's sadness is turning into anger, just like Whisper said.

"Nathan," Mommy says, and her voice is also a little loud, "I know you're stressed, but she's just a child. She's going to spill things."

"She's six years old. She should know how to hold a cup properly by now."

Feeling very sad with tears coming into my eyes, I put my milk on the table as carefully as I can while Mommy wipes the table.

As they continue to argue about me, I run out of the kitchen and upstairs to my room.

"I think Whisper is right, Daddy doesn't love me anymore," I say to Mr. Buttons as more tears heat up my eyes. Mr. Buttons doesn't say anything, but I think he believes it too.

# TEN

## HANNAH

In the first week of May, a few weeks after the funeral, I stand before the mirror in my walk-in closet after putting Lennie to bed.

I look tired, my face is pale and I'm wearing my dressing gown with no makeup on, but I still picture myself walking down the aisle. Anticipation bubbles up within me like champagne, but there's also an underlying current of anxiety, one I increasingly can't ignore.

Taking a deep breath, I try to center myself and I remember the word I learned in my months of trauma therapy. The one that's supposed to bring me back to my safe place: grounded. *Grounded.* My safe space is my garden, right here in our home, and as I murmur the word out loud, I'm transported there. Sitting on the grass, my fingertips brushing the ground, breathing in the delicate scents and hearing the gentle hum of bees.

Since Nathan's father's funeral, he has barely said a word to me or Lennie. It's as if he isn't the same man anymore. He's retreating into himself, turning to his solo games of chess for comfort instead of letting me in. If it were just about me, I could handle it, I would find it easier to be patient with this grief, but I am really worried about Lennie. Watching her try to get her father's attention to no avail is so painful. I've tried to talk to him about it, to see if I can encourage him to spend some quality time with her, but he just brushes me off with a nod or a grunt. The invisible barrier between us seems so strong and impenetrable that it's almost physical, growing wider every day.

When I leave the closet, I sit on the bed next to Nathan, who came here to lie down after dinner, saying he had a headache. After a few minutes, he finally lifts his head to look at me. His eyes are tired, and the now all-too familiar sadness in them still causes a deep ache in my heart.

"Hey, babe," I say softly, reaching out to touch his arm. "I love you. Are you okay? Do you want to talk?"

He doesn't answer me right away, instead taking a few deep breaths before turning his body to face me fully. "I don't know," he admits, his voice rough with emotion. "I'm sorry I've been so distant from you, my love. I just feel so lost right now. This hit me harder than I expected."

It's the most he's said to me in two weeks, and I snuggle into him, resting my head on his shoulder as he wraps his arms around me. We sit in silence, his sadness saturating the air between us. I don't know what to say so I just hold him back, afraid to move in case he breaks away.

Finally, he pulls back slightly. "I just don't know why I feel like this. It's not like he was much of a father." Anger briefly flashes in his eyes before being replaced by sadness once again. "He might have stuck around after Mom left, but he barely showed me any love or kindness at all, not once." His voice is filled with a mix of bitterness and sorrow. "But I can't help feeling this unbearable emptiness inside me, now I know he's really, truly gone."

I kiss his lips softly and stroke his arm. "I know, baby, but even though he hurt you so much, he was still your father. It's okay to feel lost and confused about everything that's happened. But you're not alone in this, I'm here for you... and so is Lennie." I pause for a moment. "She misses you."

Then I feel him let me go before he actually does. He stands up from the bed and walks over to the window, where he looks out over the balcony toward the ocean.

"I need to... I have work to do," he finally mutters.

"You never told me about your new case. What's it about?" Nathan knows I'm his greatest supporter and he usually enjoys telling me about what he's working on. If his work is the thing that will get him talking to me, then I think it's best to focus on that instead of pushing him to open up about his grief before he's ready.

"Nothing major, just a small case that came up unexpectedly," he replies, avoiding my gaze as he continues to pace. "It's just a matter of tying up loose ends. Nothing for you to worry about. Get some sleep."

He comes to kiss my cheek then walks out the room, pulling his navy dressing gown over his blue and white striped pajamas. Not long after, I hear the door to the office slam shut.

I swallow the lump in my throat and try to brush aside the hurt that's threatening to consume me. I know Nathan isn't pushing me away intentionally, but it still stings.

I can't get myself to sleep, and after a while I head to the office to check on him, bringing him a cup of coffee. I find him hunched over a stack of documents, and he accepts the cup with a brief thank you, barely glancing up at me.

"Hey, I know you've got a lot going on, but can we talk for a moment?" I say, a little nervously.

He pushes a hand through his hair. "I wish I could, but I'm kind of busy right now," he replies without looking up, his tone dismissive.

"Please, Nathan." My voice trembles. "I feel like we're

losing you, me and Lennie. It's really hard seeing you distance yourself from us like this."

He finally looks up at me, his expression guarded. "That's not my intention. This is just how I handle stress. I lost my father, Hannah. Try to understand."

I try to keep my voice steady. "I do understand Nathan, I really do. I know how painful it is to lose a parent, and I'm so sorry for what you are going through. I wish I could do something to help ease your pain, but you keep shutting me out. This should be a time for us to come together, not grow apart. We're a team. We need to face these challenges together." I fight back the tears, but it's a losing battle. "Lennie's worried about you too. She needs her dad. Look, we really need to talk about what happened last night... the milk. You've never snapped at her like that before. She was really upset."

"Enough, Hannah!" He slams his hand down on the desk, and his sudden outburst sends a jolt through me. "I can't talk right now, okay? Can't you respect that?"

"Yeah, fine," I whisper, defeated. Then I turn to leave, but not before catching a glimpse of the anger burning in his eyes, an unfamiliar expression that terrifies me to my core.

I've seen that anger before. But never toward me. Never toward Lennie.

Before walking out of the room, I meet his eyes. "I know you're going through a lot, but our daughter needs you. I need you. Please don't shut us out, or take this out on us." He doesn't respond and his gaze drops back to the papers in front of him.

Heading to Lennie's room, I find her still fast asleep with Mr. Buttons in her arms, her innocent face so sweet and peaceful.

I brush a curly strand of blonde hair away from her face, guilt washing over me. Guilt that I'm failing at fixing us. She was so excited about the wedding and now, with Nathan pulling away, it's like the light has gone out of her world.

Before I leave, I notice a panda bear with a cream ribbon around its neck that I haven't seen before. I didn't notice it when I put her to bed earlier. It looks new, and it's lying on the vintage rocking chair Elena gifted me when Lennie was born.

I pick it up, and for a moment, warmth spreads through my chest. Nathan must have got it for her. He may be going through hell, and he's not himself, but he's reaching out to her in his own way. He's doing the best he can. I return the panda to the armchair and lean in to kiss Lennie's forehead.

Back in our bedroom, I do some yoga to try to relax, and by the time I finish my final stretch, Nathan still hasn't come to bed. Needing someone to talk to, I pick up my phone and dial Elena's number. I know that if she's asleep already, she'll have her phone on silent, but she's a night owl and we often have chats this late.

She picks up on the second ring, and I'm immediately calmed by her voice.

"Hey, Elena. Do you have a minute?"

"Sure. What's wrong? You sound terrible."

I let out a bitter chuckle. Elena is always so honest; I appreciate that about her. "Unfortunately, that's exactly how I feel... terrible." I take a deep breath. "Nathan and I are not in a good place. He's been so distant since the funeral, and I don't know how to fix it. He's getting angry, even losing his temper at Lennie. It's not like him at all... I'm scared, Elena, that he might not recover from this. I guess this whole thing has brought back trauma from his childhood, from his relationship with his father, and it's hitting him really hard."

There's a pause before Elena speaks again, her tone gentle and balanced. "That must be so difficult. I'm sorry. Have you tried talking to him, telling him how worried you are?"

"Yeah, I have. But he just tells me he needs space, and that's not exactly ideal right now especially given that we're getting married soon."

"Well, losing a parent is really painful, you know that. And like you said, it has probably brought up a lot of unresolved issues for him. He hasn't had the easiest life."

"I know, but it's honestly like he's changing into a completely different person. I'm not even sure he wants to get married anymore. And the way he's been with Lennie... You know how much he normally dotes on her, he's always been such a wonderful dad. But yesterday he shouted at her, really yelled, for spilling her milk. I could see she was scared and it was awful."

Elena's silence is deafening. I know that she is trying to come up with something to say to me, something that will make me feel better. But there's nothing she can say, nothing anyone can say.

Finally, she speaks. "Hannah, listen to me. Nathan loves you and Lennie; he's just struggling to cope with his grief. You need to be patient with him, give him the space he needs, and try to support him as best you can. He'll come around. I promise."

I thank Elena for her words of comfort, and we move on to talking about a bride whose wedding she had been planning for months only for her to elope with the best man at the last minute. Elena is a wedding planner as well as owning her own shop, and she always has the best stories. Soon I do feel a little better. But when we end our call, anxiety settles back on me.

The truth is, I've seen what Nathan is capable of when he's broken and angry; I saw it years ago. I just never thought it would be directed toward me, or Lennie.

Nathan hasn't done the work I've done to deal with my trauma, my pain, my guilt. He just buried it deep inside him and refused to go to therapy. Until now I thought he'd found so much happiness in our little family that he'd never go back to those dark days. Never again have a reason to unleash the darkness buried within him.

But I'm starting to think I was wrong.

# ELEVEN

The next day, I'm sitting in my office at Bliss & Twine as I try to refocus. I have been so occupied with my personal life lately and I have let many of my work responsibilities slip through the cracks.

Lila and Josie have been picking up the slack as best they can, but it's not fair to burden them. Today, I'm determined to get everything back on track and regain control of my business.

With a sudden burst of energy, I stand up and gather my scattered papers. "I'm heading to Honeywood," I say to Josie and Lila as I walk out. "I'll work there for a bit. If you need anything, you know how to reach me."

"I'll give you a call if necessary," Josie tells me, smiling. "But don't worry, we can handle things here."

I step out into the bright sunlight and pause for a moment to draw in a deep breath. The air is warm and carries the scents of fresh bread from a nearby bakery, and the faint hint of salt drifting in from the sea.

Main Street is bustling with activity, and I smile at familiar faces, exchanging brief greetings with some of the people I've known since I was a child, until I turn onto Maple Avenue.

Since Gloria took over, Honeywood has undergone a makeover that has made it even more welcoming than before. It has a Scandinavian design; simple and earthy with plant pots scattered throughout brimming with deep-green leaves. Fairy lights twinkle over rustic wooden tables, and the rich, inviting smells of fresh coffee and cinnamon buns fill the air.

When I step inside, I immediately feel relaxed, greeted by cool air conditioning and the happy hum of conversation.

As I approach the counter, a familiar face smiles back at me. It's Judy, a waitress who has been working at Honeywood since before Gloria arrived.

Judy greets me with a flash of her white teeth, "Hey, Hannah. The usual today?"

"Yes, please."

I make my way to the table by the window that has become my regular spot. From here, I can watch the passersby.

Sometimes I wonder how many people in Stoneview are hiding secrets, like couples who might look loved up and content but are struggling behind closed doors. But as I gaze outside, I remind myself why I'm here—to work. So, I spread my papers across the table and pull out my calculator.

Soon enough, Judy brings me my chai and I take a sip, the blend of spices dancing on my tongue.

"Perfect," I say with a contented sigh.

"You really love your chai, don't you?" She smiles.

"There's no one who loves it more than me," I say, grinning. "How is your baby boy doing?"

"Sam is doing great, thank you. He's still learning and growing every day. He's such a happy little boy." Her face lights up as she thinks about her child, like any proud mother.

"I'm so glad to hear that. He's a cutie."

I've seen Judy with Sam a few times around town and watching them made me wonder if Nathan and I might have more kids. Judy is struggling to conceive now, but she desperately wants Sam to have a sister or brother, and I think maybe Lennie would benefit from the company of a sibling as well. Even though the newborn stage was tough with all the sleepless nights, I miss it now that she is getting older.

"Gloria said to let you know that she'll be with you soon."

"Tell her to take her time. I'll be here a while, I have some work to do, and I'm starting to think this place has become my second office."

Judy chuckles softly and nods. "Well, it's always a pleasure having you here. You bring a warm energy to the place."

"What a lovely thing to say, thank you so much, Judy." I feel my cheeks flush.

"Nothing but the truth," Judy says. "Anyway, I'll let you get on. Let me know if I can bring you anything else."

I watch as she walks away and know that I should start working, but instead, my hand reaches for my phone and I call Nathan's number. My heart sinks when he doesn't answer. Before his father died, he used to call me multiple times a day, but now it seems like I'm always the one calling him, trying to stay connected.

Just as I'm about to dive into my work, Gloria appears from the back and joins me at my table. She greets me with a kiss on my cheek before sitting down. Her dark hair is neatly pulled back in a topknot and she's dressed in the usual smart black trousers and white shirt she wears when working.

"Are you okay?" she asks, her hands clasped on the table. "You seem a little off."

"Yeah, I'm okay." I force a smile, but I know my eyes will be betraying me.

Gloria notices my pain immediately and moves to sit next to me, wrapping her arm around my shoulders. "Hey," she whispers, "what's going on? I know Nathan is grieving and it must be so hard."

"I feel like a terrible person," I admit. "Nathan has just lost his father, I should be giving him all the time and space he needs. But I can't shake this feeling that I'm losing him. He's becoming more and more distant from Lennie and me every day."

As Gloria pulls away, I see her blinking rapidly and I know she's thinking about her own experience. "Grief takes time," she says softly.

"I know." I reach for her hand and give it a squeeze. "You are one of the strongest people I know. I can't even imagine what you went through. If I were in your shoes... I don't know if I could handle it... losing a child."

"Oh, I'm not strong at all. Don't let appearances fool you." She laughs. That's how she copes, using humor to cover up her grief. "Anyway, Nathan will get there eventually. At least to a place where it gets a little easier to wake up in the morning."

"Yeah. I just wish there was something I could do to help. Lennie is really struggling with this too."

Gloria nods. "Some people need to grieve alone. Just be there for Lennie."

I never bring Lennie to Honeywood as I'm too afraid of stirring up painful memories for Gloria, of the daughter she lost before she moved here.

She opened up to me about that pretty quickly after I first met her. It was all clearly still so raw back then. But she never told me the full story, and I don't push her, knowing it's her choice when, how, and if to share.

We are close, but there's still quite a lot I don't know about her. She was born and raised in Sarasota, and her twin sister died shortly after birth. She loves Chinese cuisine and acoustic guitar music, enjoys late-night walks, and has a passion for painting and collecting artwork from different places around the globe.

But I have a feeling there's more about her past that she

doesn't want to share with me yet, and I understand completely. We all have our secrets, me more than most.

"I have some paperwork to do as well. I'll join you," says Gloria.

She walks away and returns with her laptop and another cup of chai for me, and a green tea for herself. Despite being the owner of a coffee shop, she doesn't enjoy drinking coffee anymore. It used to be her go-to for caffeine, especially during her years as a waitress. But one day, she suddenly couldn't stomach the taste. It was as if her taste buds had turned against the very thing that had kept her going through long shifts and early mornings. Now she opts for herbal and green teas instead. But despite losing her taste for coffee, she still finds comfort in its aroma.

"On the house," she says, taking a seat.

"Sometimes I wonder how you make any money, Gloria," I say with a smile, as I reach for the chai. "You give away too many freebies."

"No need to worry. They're not really free. Wait until the end of the year; if it turns out I didn't make much profit, I might just charge you retrospectively."

We both laugh before getting to work, taking occasional breaks to chat, and the bustling café fades into background noise.

I treat myself to a fresh bran muffin, reminding myself to take care of my energy levels. I think I am either coming down with something or feeling the impact of the worry about Nathan. I keep getting headaches and dizzy spells.

An hour later, feeling rejuvenated, I stand up to leave.

"Same time tomorrow?" Gloria asks.

"You got it."

. . .

A few hours later, I'm in the kitchen cooking dinner with Lennie, feeling much more positive after my heart-to-heart with Gloria and a productive day at work. Lennie is such a bright little spark today too. She even brought me herbs from the garden, saying she picked them with Whisper.

I've made lasagna, one of Nathan's favorite dishes, with a rich tomato sauce and a smooth bechamel. I honestly think it's one of my best, and I hope it makes him happy. But just as I'm setting the table, a wave of dizziness hits me. I pause and lean against the nearest wall for support, taking deep breaths to calm myself.

These sudden episodes of lightheadedness seem to be getting more and more severe. Should I brush them off as fatigue and stress? Or should I go and see someone?

After a few moments, slowly I continue to lay out the cutlery and plates. I really hope I'm not getting sick. I need to be strong for Lennie and Nathan, to be their rock, now more than ever.

# TWELVE

As I tuck Lennie in for the night, I press my lips to her forehead, breathing in the scent left from her rose bubble bath. I always want to linger over these precious moments, but tonight I'm taking my time even more than usual.

Being here with Lennie allows me to delay the inevitable, I guess. Because inside the master bedroom, there are conversations that need to be had: difficult conversations.

I tried so hard to give us a lovely family meal, with jazz playing in the background, Nathan's favorite food, and Lennie on her best behavior. But Nathan was irritable throughout, and he spent a lot of time on his phone, something we've always tried to avoid at mealtimes.

Elena and Gloria told me to be patient, to give Nathan some time to get back to himself, and I understand where they're coming from. But we have a wedding coming up in six weeks and we need to make a decision about it. I really hate the thought of postponing, but I'd rather marry him later on than have him remember our wedding day as a time when he was grief-stricken and depressed.

The thing is, though, I'm genuinely scared. I have a feeling that if we don't get married on the date we agreed, something else will come in the way and we will never do it at all. After all, we've been together for seven years and we still haven't tied the knot. A nagging voice in my head taunts me, telling me that we will never be allowed to have our dream wedding and a happy marriage. Not after what we did.

Finally, I stand up from Lennie's bed, and her eyes are still just a little bit open in the semidarkness.

"Are you sure you don't want me to call Daddy so he can say good night?" I ask her.

Instead of responding, she turns her head away from me and her body follows so she's facing the wall instead. My breath catches in my throat as I watch my daughter distance herself from her father, just like he's been doing to her.

Since his father's death, Lennie did everything she could think of to get close to Nathan, but lately she's been pushing him away. I guess that's the only way she can protect herself from continually being rejected.

I place a hand on her shoulder, squeezing. "Sweetheart, you know your daddy loves you, right?"

"No. He doesn't love me anymore." Her voice is so low I almost don't catch the words.

"Why do you keep saying that?" I gently turn her to face me.

She holds tight onto the duvet cover, pulling it up to her nose so all I can see are her eyes, and says nothing.

I sit back down on her bed and take a slow breath. "Lennie, he does love you, very much. He's just going through a difficult time."

I'm tempted to tell her the truth, that it was Nathan's own father, her grandfather, who died. Maybe then she would understand why he's so sad. But Nathan made me promise not to. He doesn't want Lennie to ask questions that would make him talk about the man who hurt him so much, and the childhood he'd rather forget. His father never even met Lennie; Nathan wanted to keep them apart.

"Daddy doesn't love me," Lennie says, blinking away the tears in her eyes. "He's sad because of me."

I pull her onto my lap, holding her tight. Then I brush the hair from her face and give her a kiss on the cheek.

"I'm sorry you feel that way, and I'm sorry things have been hard lately. But that's not true, Lennie. Your daddy really, really loves you," I repeat. "Once he gets better, you'll be able to do all the things you used to do together. We'll have another bonfire on the beach."

"I don't want a bonfire." She buries her face into my neck. "I don't want to play with Daddy."

I turn her to look at me again. "Baby, where's all this coming from?"

"Daddy hit me, Mommy," she says, her bottom lip trembling. "Whisper told me. I don't remember, but she saw it."

My heart plummets. "Whisper told you that? What exactly did she say?"

"Whisper said Daddy hit me, and that he might hurt me again, and you too."

I hold her tight, reeling from her words. What on earth could have put that idea in her head? My poor, darling girl. She must be feeling so confused, and so hurt. "Well, sweetheart, I promise you that Whisper is not telling the truth. Your daddy would never ever hit you or do anything to hurt you. Yes, he's been unhappy recently and I know it has upset you a lot, but I promise he isn't doing anything to hurt you on purpose."

I want to stay there, hold her in my arms forever, but I'm close to breaking down in tears and I need to protect her from that. I keep my voice steady. "Now, you should get some sleep and we can talk about this tomorrow, okay?"

"I don't want to say good night to him," she repeats fiercely.

"Okay, that's fine. You don't have to. It's okay, Lennie. I'm here. You're safe."

I'm finding it very hard to breathe right now.

My hands shaking, I cover her up again and give her another kiss, and then I leave the room.

Standing outside her door, I lean against it, my hands clasped in front of me as I take several deep breaths. I know I can't tell Nathan what Lennie said right now; it would crush him. But we do need to talk. Something has to change.

When I've gathered myself together, I go into our room and find Nathan sitting up in bed, leafing through one of his thick law books. But I know he's not reading because he's flipping through way too fast.

I close the door softly.

"Hey, sweetheart." I take a few steps toward the bed and sit down. "I've been thinking... Do you think... Should we postpone the wedding?"

"No." His voice is sharp and quick, and finally his eyes flick up to look at me. "Don't be ridiculous. The wedding will go on as planned. I'm not letting my father ruin that for us."

"But Nathan, it's just around the corner and you are clearly not ready to walk down the aisle right now."

He puts down his book and lifts the duvet, his eyes fixed on mine. "Come here, darling."

For the first time in weeks, I detect some warmth in his voice, and I go over to him.

"I'm sorry I've been so distant." He kisses the side of my face. "It's just been hard, you know? I would never have expected grief to affect me like this."

"I know, so maybe the best thing to do is just to call things off for now. It doesn't mean we won't get married eventually." Even as I say the words, my heart aches.

"But we did so much to prepare already, and Lennie is excited. We can't let everyone down. Not after—"

Even though he doesn't complete the sentence, I know what he was about to say.

Nathan's last wedding ended in a nightmare, so I can understand why he doesn't want anything bad to happen to this one. I've been working so hard to distance myself from that day, so I'm frustrated that he's bringing it up now. But maybe I have no choice but to accept it's something that will forever remain with us.

"Nathan. This is not the same. It's a totally different situation."

"Yeah, I know." He loosens his grip on me for a moment and runs a hand down his face. "But..." His voice drifts off and he shakes his head. "The wedding will happen, my love. Everything is going to be okay, I promise."

I want to freeze this moment, to hold on to it before it melts away. Before the pain swallows us whole and he becomes unreachable yet again.

"How's Lennie?" he whispers, and my breath solidifies in my throat. "Is she already asleep, or can I go and say good night to her?"

I'm silent for a while, wondering what the best thing to do is, for Lennie. I'm finding it hard to think clearly, my thoughts are blurred at the edges, my head pounding. Finally, I wonder if maybe it would be good for him to reach out to her, to reaffirm his love.

"That's a good idea."

With that, he gets out of bed and walks over to Lennie's room and I follow behind, hoping to see a moment of tenderness between them. But he's barely through the doorway before Lennie shouts at him to leave her alone.

He turns back, and his face is drawn, his eyes full of pain. "I'm going out for a drive," he says and leaves me standing outside her room, pressing a hand to my chest and feeling my heart thumping rapidly.

After calming Lennie and waiting until she falls asleep, I decide that the only thing that would soothe me now is my garden. Grabbing my worn-out gloves and trowel, I make my way out the door.

The garden is lit up by a gentle glow as the moon spills its pale light over the rows of flowers and shrubs. I also have several strands of fairy lights intertwined amongst the foliage, leftover from last Christmas. Lennie loved them so much that I decided not to take them down.

I kneel down in the dirt, and with steady hands, I pull out the weeds that have grown in between my rose bushes. The sound of the roots detaching themselves from the soil brings a cathartic release. But the feeling only lasts for a fleeting moment before the tears that had been threatening to spill all evening finally escape, mingling with the soil as I continue my task, becoming more and more aggressive with each yank of the weeds.

Pulling off the gloves and throwing them aside, I let my fingers dig deep into the rich earth. The pain in my chest still refuses to subside, and I find myself venting my frustration on the weeds. When I eventually stop and sit back, panting, I notice that I have not only destroyed the weeds, but also damaged some of my beloved plants in the process.

The sight of broken stems and crushed petals fills me with guilt, and I gently cradle the wounded plants in my hands, tears mixing with the dirt on my fingertips. I curse myself for allowing my emotions to get the better of me, for taking out my frustrations on these innocent plants that normally bring me so much joy.

Closing my eyes, I take a deep breath and try to gather my thoughts. Then, suddenly, I feel a driving urge to open my eyes.

There's a strange energy in the air, something that makes the hairs on the back of my neck stand on end.

Slowly, I open my eyes, and look around the garden, but there's nothing out of the ordinary. It's only when I pull myself to my feet and head back to the house that I lift my gaze to the windows of the house and see Lennie looking out, watching me.

To my utter horror, it looks like someone else is there, right next to her.

Running through the garden, my heart pounds in my chest as I reach the kitchen door. I burst into the house as if it's on fire and Lennie is upstairs. Who is in my home? Is my daughter safe?

My footsteps echo through the empty hallway as I leap up the stairs, leaving a trail of soil behind me.

My hand is trembling as it hovers over the doorknob and I push open Lennie's door.

To my relief, my daughter is still fast asleep in her bed.

There's no one else in the room.

I must have imagined it, I think to myself, as a wave of relief and embarrassment washes over me.

But I could have sworn that I saw someone standing behind my daughter.

# THIRTEEN

I'm parked outside Lennie's school, drinking my smoothie as I watch my little girl walking with her head bowed toward the front doors. Her backpack is slung over one shoulder, the weight causing her slight frame to lean slightly to the side.

Lowering the flask into the cup holder, I grip the wheel tight, biting back tears, trying not to break apart. I have a full day ahead and can't afford to let my emotions consume me. As soon as I get to the flower shop, I have a flood of emails to respond to, orders to box for Josie and Lila to deliver, and a stack of invoices that need to be sorted and filed. The demands of running a small business never seem to end, but today, they're a welcome distraction.

If Nathan picks Lennie up from school today, I'll put in some extra hours at the shop. It's been a while since I've stayed late, and the thought of having some quiet time to myself feels comforting. Having me out of the picture will also give Nathan and Lennie a chance to reconnect, especially after what happened this morning.

Nathan wanted to drive Lennie to school like he used to, but Lennie threw a tantrum and refused to get in the car, demanding that I take her instead. She only mellowed down when I agreed to drop her off. On the way, I tried my best to make her understand how much her dad wanted to make things better, that he missed doing the things they used to do before. It took a while, but then to my surprise, she suggested that he should pick her up today.

Before I drive off, I call Nathan to let him know.

"Honey, I'm really sorry about earlier. I don't know what's going on with Lennie."

"I do." His voice crackles slightly through the line. "She's trying to punish me for not being present. But I've really been trying, Hannah. I've been trying to climb out of this hellhole."

"I know. I know how hard it has been for you. It will get easier with time, it really will." I pause. "By the way, Lennie said you can pick her up from school instead."

"She did?" His voice lifts with a mix of surprise and hope.

"She did. And maybe you can take her out for some ice-cream? Or you could take her to the park. Spend some quality time together, just the two of you. I think that would mean a lot to her," I suggest.

"You really think that would help?"

"I do. Lennie just needs to know that you're there, that you still love her. She's hurting right now, but I know she'll come around." I pause. "Nathan, you haven't noticed anything strange around the house lately, have you?"

"No, why do you ask?"

"I just... last night I was in the garden after you went out for a drive. I looked up to Lennie's bedroom window, and I honestly thought I saw a woman in there with her. So I ran to her room, but there was nobody there. I realize I must have been seeing things, but she seemed so real. Nothing like that has happened to me before."

There's a brief silence on the other end of the line before Nathan finally says, "That's not quite true, though, is it,

Hannah? You know as well as I do that you haven't always had control over your mind. I think maybe you just need to get a bit more rest, but you have to tell me if something like this happens again, or anything that feels like your mind is spiraling."

I sigh, and promise that I will. I don't tell him about the dizziness, headaches, and sense of confusion I've been feeling lately though. I don't want him to blow this out of proportion, and he has enough on his plate right now.

I now wish I hadn't mentioned the woman in Lennie's room, but since last night, I haven't been able to get her out of my head. This morning before I went into her room, I heard Lennie talking to someone. And when I went in, again there was nobody there. She said she was talking to Whisper and that they have a secret.

I didn't push her for details and I'm always careful not to challenge what she says about Whisper. Josie said it's important for children's imaginations to have the freedom to flourish, no matter how vivid they are. But I don't like the idea that this imaginary so-called friend is convincing my child to keep secrets from her parents.

I'd never say this to Nathan, but the really superstitious part of me even wonders if Lennie is talking to a ghost. Maybe that's who "Whisper" really is... and maybe that's who I saw in her bedroom window.

I do believe in life after death, although I'm not sure what format it takes. I'm open to the idea that spirits might linger if they have unfinished business to attend to. But I can't think who would want to cause harm to us or Lennie.

Nobody who is dead, that is.

"Anyway, you could use a bit of self-care," says Nathan. "Go and get your nails done later or something, and I'll pick Lennie up from school. I'll plan something nice for us to do together, something special."

"Great. And if all else fails, take her to collect shells on the beach."

He chuckles. "Yeah, our little mermaid sure loves her shells."

After I hang up the phone, I call Elena and she suggests that before I head to work, we should meet up for a quick breakfast at Honeywood.

Despite the amount of work waiting for me, I can't resist. "Sure, I'd love that."

Fifteen minutes later, I am sitting across from Elena at a table for three because we both know that it's only a matter of time before Gloria joins us for a chat.

Elena is wearing a black and gold kaftan and her short hair is pushed back by a wire headband with tiny pearls that glimmer in the soft morning light. Her sense of style always makes her look younger than she is; it's like time has frozen for her.

"I'm so glad we could do this," she says, reaching for the menu. "Since you have a wedding coming up, breakfast is on me. So, what would you like? Don't hold back."

"Oh, that's very kind of you." I pick up my own menu, a heavy leather-bound book with gold lettering. "I think I'll have the avocado toast with poached eggs," I say, scanning the page. "And I'll also have a side of crispy bacon."

Judy approaches our table, tying her burgundy apron behind her. Her green eyes sparkle as she grins at us, "Morning, ladies! Are you ready to order?"

"We are," Elena replies, returning the smile. "I'll have the buttermilk pancakes with a side of fresh berries, please."

I give her my order too, and Judy nods. When she walks away from our table, Elena clasps her hands in front of her.

"How are things at home? Is Nathan opening up a little more?"

"Sometimes. But one minute everything is fine and the next it's not. Last night I actually suggested we postpone the wedding."

Elena's eyebrows shoot up. "You didn't!"

"I just thought maybe it would give him some breathing room, and honestly it's hard to think of marrying him when he's in such a bad place mentally. He's not himself right now. So I don't know if it's the best time, even though I've been wanting this day to come for so long. The thought of postponing is breaking my heart, but I don't know what else to do."

"You really love him, don't you?" she asks like she doesn't already know.

"Yes, and I'm so afraid. What if I lose him?" I cover my face with both hands, unable to hold back tears. "I feel... I feel so helpless."

Elena places a comforting hand on my arm. "Listen to me," she says, her voice filled with compassion. "You and Nathan have been through so much together, and I am certain your bond is strong enough to help you make it through anything. It's okay to have doubts and fears, but don't let them consume you. Trust in the love you share with Nathan, and trust in yourself." She squeezes my hand. "Nathan is going through a lot right now, but so are you. Why don't you speak to someone, a professional?"

"I don't know, Elena. I'm not the one who just lost a father. And therapy is really tough. It was good for me but it was such a lot to go through emotionally. I'm not sure I can face that right now."

"Okay, but how about you just speak to someone who's a friend?"

"You're not suggesting I speak to Darius, are you? Wouldn't that be awkward?"

She doesn't respond immediately because our food arrives, and we take a moment to thank Judy before turning our attention back to each other. Elena's eyes search mine, her concern palpable.

"It doesn't have to be Darius. I just want you to take care of yourself, and he'd offer you sessions for free, and he really is brilliant at what he does. You know that therapy can provide a safe space for you to explore your fears and anxieties without judgment. I still don't get why you stopped seeing your therapist, after all the trauma you experienced in your life."

"Because I'm fine now. I can handle things on my own."

The idea of seeing a therapist makes me shrivel up inside. Even though it did help, it was one of the hardest things I've ever been through. And right now, especially with the wedding coming up, the thought of bringing up memories that I've worked hard to leave behind terrifies me.

It's years ago now, but I'm ashamed to say that there was a time in my life when I lost control of my mind. I did things I would never have thought I'm capable of, things that make me feel deeply ashamed now, even though I've tried to work on myself really hard since then, trying to cultivate a spirit of gratitude and forgiveness toward others.

Seeing a therapist was a necessary step, but the wounds have healed. I don't want to be reminded of that fragile version of myself, the one who spiraled so far into darkness.

One of the most painful memories therapy dug up was the day I lost my mother, walking into her room and finding her dead on the bed surrounded by the divorce papers my father had served her.

No, sitting on a therapist's couch is definitely not something I want to do again. I'd rather turn to yoga and my garden for solace. There's something about the dirt between my fingers, the smell of the earth, and scent of flowers that never fails to bring me respite and perspective. Alongside yoga, gardening has become my sanctuary, my own personal form of therapy.

"You don't have to worry about me, you know?" I wipe away a few tears, pick up my fork and force a smile. "I'll be fine... we'll be fine."

After all, I've been to hell and back, and I'm still here, still standing.

"Well"—Elena cuts into a pancake—"I'll be your therapist then. You know I'm here for you anytime you need to speak about... anything."

"I know that." I give her a smile. "And I appreciate you more than anything, both me and Nathan do."

"And I'm grateful for you both too."

The way Elena is with both of us, it's hard to believe that she once dated and even got engaged to Nathan. But Elena realized that they were not right for each other long before he and I got together, and she always wanted him to find someone who would truly make him happy. And I really hope he is, or at least he soon will be again.

"Well, since you're my self-appointed therapist, something happened last night, and I need to talk to somebody about it."

"Sounds serious." Elena leans forward, her eyes wide with concern. "Tell me."

"I don't know what to think of it. Last night Lennie refused to say good night to Nathan. She keeps saying he doesn't love her anymore. She even said her imaginary friend told her he hit her."

"Hit her? Are you serious? That can't be true, surely?"

"Of course not. It's just because he's been hurting her feelings by pushing her away so much lately. I know he would never hit her. I'd never stay with him if I even thought he was capable of that."

"Yeah, Nathan would never hurt his daughter. It's just not in his nature. He loves Lennie more than his own life."

"I know, but she's really got this thing about him not loving her stuck in her head. She's changed; she isn't the same around him. This morning, he wanted to take her to school, and she just started screaming and crying, as if he's some sort of monster. It was awful, it hurt his feelings so much."

"It definitely sounds like she's just confused, like you said, and she's expressing her pain in this very dramatic way. Kids can have wild imaginations, you know? And Lennie more than most."

"Exactly. And she did say it was her imaginary friend Whisper who told her that her dad hit her."

I feel a little better already, having got this off my chest. But the way Lennie reacted around Nathan this morning looked like fear, genuine fear, and this thing with Whisper is getting out of control. Dismissing the at best whimsical, at worst ludicrous idea that Whisper could be a ghost, I know it's normal for children to have imaginary friends. But is it normal when those friends tell them horrible lies about their parents?

Maybe I should look into Lennie getting some therapy, if this thing doesn't resolve itself soon.

"Look, hon, I hate to dash off," Elena says as she finishes her plate, "but I have a wedding fair to go to this afternoon, and I need to prepare. Can we continue this conversation later?"

"Of course," I reply. "Enjoy the fair, hon, and thanks for listening."

Elena gives me a quick hug before grabbing her coat and heading toward the door. As soon as she's gone, the weight of my worries settles back onto my shoulders, and I'm unable to pull myself together until Gloria finally takes a break from work and sits with me.

"Why do you look like someone with a one-way ticket to hell?"

I let out a bitter chuckle, feeling a knot forming in my stomach. "Honestly, it seems like I've already arrived at the gates."

# FOURTEEN

When I finish filling Gloria in on everything that has been going on with Lennie, she's quiet for a while. Then she calls another one of her waitresses over and tells her to bring us two chais.

As soon as our drinks arrive, she takes a sip of hers, with her sharp, stunning eyes fixed on me. I've come to notice that she's quite a thinker, not the kind of person who just reacts impulsively. Instead, she always takes time to gather her thoughts, analyzing the situation from all angles before forming an opinion.

As she gazes at me intently, I can almost see the gears turning in her mind. Finally, she sets her cup down gently and leans in closer. "Hannah, I know you think this is just a child's imagination, but I think you need to dig deeper into this." Her voice is low and serious. "Lennie's behavior and her words about Nathan cannot be ignored. There has to be something behind it."

"But I know what's behind it. She's hurt because he's not been spending time with her lately, and he's been temperamental, snappy with her, and she's not used to that." My voice wavers, and I pick up my cup and inhale the comforting blend of cinnamon, nutmeg, and cloves.

"She has such a vivid imagination, Gloria," I continue. "Her invisible friend, all the games she invents... I really think this is just another example of her creating stories in her mind."

Gloria sighs. "I understand that, and maybe you're right." She leans back in her chair and pauses. "I've known Nathan for as long as I've known you, and I really don't want to suspect him of anything sinister, but—" She stops herself and looks away.

"But what?" I press. The chai suddenly tastes bitter.

Gloria slowly meets my gaze again. "If I'm honest, I've seen things that have worried me, Hannah. I've seen him get angry before. Do you remember that big flower festival you invited me to here in Stoneview years ago, when Lennie was really little, soon after I moved here?"

My mind flickers back to that day. Nathan had been unusually tense, snapping at me over the smallest things. I had brushed it off as stress from work.

"Yeah." Gloria picks at her nail, her voice hesitant. "I saw him lose his temper, with Lennie. It was just a brief moment, but it concerned me a little. I didn't say anything then because I thought it was a one-time thing, but now that you're telling me this, I think you should know."

"I don't remember him getting angry with her at all." I pick up a napkin and absentmindedly tear it into shreds.

"You weren't there; you were busy setting up your stand. It happened so quickly. I got chatting with Nathan and Elena while one of your assistants from Bliss & Twine was showing them around the vendor booths. Lennie was toddling every which way and she accidentally knocked over a display of delicate glass ornaments. And Nathan just snapped. His face turned red with anger, and he yelled at her so loudly that people around us stared. When he grabbed her arm and pulled her away from the stand, she made a sound like he was hurting her."

The image of Nathan's face turning red with anger flashes through my mind, an image that seems almost foreign in the context of the gentle father I've known him to be for so long.

Before his father's death, I'd never heard him raise his voice at Lennie, not even when she played with the precious gavel his father gave him. That day, he simply took her tiny hand in his and helped her search until they found it tucked away in the toy box.

When Lennie apologized, he picked her up, wiped her tears, and told her gently to be more careful next time. The same day, he bought her her very own gavel, a cute miniature version with a pink handle, to make her feel important and included.

And now it's as if a curtain has been pulled back, revealing a side of him that I never knew existed.

Is he a different man when I'm not watching?

Gloria's words hang heavy in the air, and there's a gnawing feeling deep within me.

When I don't say anything, she blows out a breath. "All I'm saying is that you should be careful. I like Nathan, but nobody is perfect, and he's obviously going through something right now too. It's important to pay attention to the signs, no matter how subtle they may be. People can change, and sometimes we only see the side of them that they want us to see."

"I know you mean well, but you're wrong, Gloria. Nathan is a great dad. That incident at the festival was just a moment of frustration, and it was years ago. We all have our breaking points, don't we? That doesn't make him a bad parent."

Gloria smiles almost sadly. "You're very right. We all do have our breaking points. But can you really trust Nathan not to lose his temper badly with either of you, not ever? Particularly now that he's grieving and struggling so much?"

I stare at her, her words like drops of freezing water dripping down my spine. The image of Lennie's tear-streaked face flashes in my mind. What Gloria said happened at the festival must have been a one-off, surely? Just a rare occurrence fueled by frustration and exhaustion. I remember Lennie was having a tough toddler day; she kept fussing in the sweltering heat.

"Look, I really appreciate your concern," I finally say, my voice trembling slightly. "But I know you're wrong about this. Nathan has been through a lot lately with losing his father. It's understandable that he is on edge right now, but don't worry. Lennie is safe. She just misses him, and she's confused, that's all."

Gloria's concerned expression softens. "I hope you're right, sweetie. I truly do. But promise me one thing, okay? Promise me that if you ever feel even the slightest hint of danger or discomfort, you'll reach out for help. Promise me that you won't brush off your intuition just because you want to believe the best in Nathan."

I give her a small nod, my throat tight. "I promise," I whisper.

Gloria glances behind her at a group of customers walking into the café. "I'm so sorry, love, but the place is getting busy. The morning rush is upon us and I need to get back to work. Just remember what I said, okay? Take care of yourself and your precious little girl."

I walk out of the café feeling lightheaded. The world around me seems muted, as if I've stepped into an alternate reality where everything is slightly off-kilter.

A short while later, I finally settle in for the day at Bliss & Twine. It's just Lila and me today as Josie is out running a flower crown workshop.

Lila has a habit of chatting a million miles a minute, and while normally I enjoy her cheerful company, today I find her constant questions about Lennie and Nathan and the upcoming wedding intrusive and exhausting, so I leave work early.

I take Nathan's advice and go to a salon for a manicure, where I try to distract myself by skimming through photos of floral arrangements and inspirational quotes on Pinterest.

While I'm at the salon, Nathan calls to let me know that Lennie *did* allow him to pick her up but refused to do anything else with him.

Finally, I reach my own limit and shed a few tears, trying to hide them from the chatty woman who is painting my nails in a soft pink color that I chose for Lennie's sake.

That night, when a migraine hits me hard, Nathan pushes his grief aside and brings me endless cups of tea and meds, treating me with so much kindness that I almost forget about the conversation I had with Gloria earlier. But her words keep floating to the surface of my mind.

*People can change, and sometimes we only see the side of them that they want us to see.*

# FIFTEEN

I'm standing inside the bridal suite at the Westerwood Hotel, and soft sunlight is filtering through the lace curtains.

"Wow, Hannah, this is the most beautiful bouquet I have ever seen," Gianna, my client, says as she takes it from me. "You've outdone yourself." She examines the arrangement and then her dark-brown eyes meet mine.

Despite Gianna's youthful appearance, there's a certain depth in her eyes that gives off an air of maturity far beyond her years.

I've been designing floral arrangements for years, but the genuine gratitude in her face makes it feel like the first time.

"I'm so glad you like it, Gianna. It was a fun project."

To be honest, it wasn't exactly fun. She is one of the most demanding brides I have ever worked with. I spent countless hours researching and gathering the perfect combination to bring her vision to life, only for her to keep changing her mind every time I thought I had nailed it.

Josie usually delivers the bouquets to brides, but after putting so much work into this one, I just had to witness Gianna's reaction firsthand. Now, I breathe a sigh of relief, glad that it all worked out in the end. I felt quite frazzled when I arrived, as I got lost on the drive over even though Nathan and I have been to this place many times for special occasions, including our own engagement party. It's not like me to lose my way in the town I grew up in, but my mind has been so foggy and distracted lately.

Suddenly Gianna puts down the bouquet and throws herself into my arms. I'm a little taken aback, but I allow myself a smile as I hug her back. Being a florist is stressful at times, but it's also incredibly rewarding when you see the joy on your clients' faces.

"Hannah, I can't thank you enough for putting so much effort into making my dream wedding come true," she says as we pull apart.

"This is just a small part of it, Gianna."

"I know, but flowers play a big role in creating the atmosphere, and I couldn't have asked for anyone better than you." She looks down at her beautiful bouquet. "The wedding planning was really stressful, so it's amazing to see things come together so perfectly."

I glance at my watch. "Well, you'll be walking down the aisle in just about an hour."

"Yes, it's finally happening," she says, her voice filled with excitement and a hint of nervousness. "I'm so happy we decided to have the wedding during the week, so not many people would be able to attend. It makes it much more intimate, don't you think? And less scary. Honestly, the thought of hundreds of eyes on me would have been a nightmare."

I smile at her. "I'm sure it's all going to be exactly as you dreamed it. I'll leave you now so you can finish getting ready."

"You're right. I better get moving," Gianna says, urgency creeping into her voice. "Thanks again, Hannah."

"You're so welcome," I reply with a warm smile. "It's been an honor to be a part of your special day."

Back in my car, I'm just about to start the engine when I feel a sharp pain in my head. It intensifies, a relentless throbbing, and I reach for the bottle of aspirin in the glove compartment, hoping that the familiar relief will wash over me soon.

I went to see a doctor two days ago, but she didn't seem too concerned about the awful headaches I've been getting, dismissing it as stress or lack of sleep. But this pain feels different, more severe than before.

I take a deep breath, trying to push away the discomfort, but it persists, wrapping around my temples. I can't ignore it any longer, it's overwhelming, and fear grips me as I realize that something could be terribly wrong.

Finally the pain subsides enough for me to think clearly. But I certainly can't drive, not in this state. I could call Nathan to pick me up, but I know he's in court right now. So I grab my phone and dial Elena's number.

"Hey, gorgeous bride-to-be," Elena answers cheerfully. "What's up?"

"Elena, I need your help," I say urgently, my voice trembling. "I've got this terrible headache, and I don't really want to be alone right now. It's quite severe and I'm dizzy. I don't think I should drive. I'm parked in front of the Westerwood."

"What are you doing all the way out there?"

The Westerwood is a little on the outskirts and it would take her a while to reach me. Maybe I shouldn't have called her. It's not fair of me to ask her to drop everything and run to my rescue. Like me, she has a business to run.

"I had a delivery to do." I hesitate, considering if I should just tough it out and drive home myself. But as another wave begins to surge through my head, I know I can't risk it. "You know what? Don't worry about it. I'll take a taxi."

"Nonsense," Elena responds firmly. "Just sit tight and try to relax, okay? I'll be there soon, and I'll take a taxi, so I can drive your car back."

"Only if you'll let me pay for the taxi."

"Deal. I'll be there as soon as I can."

Hanging up the phone, I lean back in my seat and close my eyes, trying to find some respite. In the brief spaces between the waves of pain, my mind keeps going back to Nathan and the arguments we've been having lately about the littlest things.

This morning, I somehow forgot that he doesn't take sugar in his coffee and he snapped at me. I was furious at myself for not remembering such a simple detail. And there have been so many other things like this. The arguments have been getting worse and more frequent too, and I can feel the strain on our relationship increasing with each passing day.

No wonder I'm getting headaches. The stress is eating away at me.

The wait for Elena is so long that I find myself dosing off, my head lolled back against the headrest. In my dreamlike state, I'm transported to a place and time where the arguments with Nathan don't exist, and my little girl is her happy self again. All is well in our family bubble, and the three of us are enjoying one of our bonfire nights on the beach.

A knock on the window startles me awake, and I blink rapidly, trying to shake off the remnants of my dreams.

It's Elena, her face etched with concern as she gestures for me to roll down the window.

As soon as I do, she asks, "You okay in there?"

I nod and rub my temples. "Just fighting this killer headache. Thanks for coming, hon. I'm so grateful for the support."

"No problem." Her eyes continue to scan my face. "You look exhausted. Have you been getting enough rest?"

I sigh. "Not really." I step out of the car and go round to the other side, so Elena can take the wheel.

Once settled in, she turns to face me, a frown between her brows. "Should I drive you to the hospital?"

"No, that's not necessary," I reply, forcing a weak smile. "I've been under a lot of stress lately, but I'll be fine. I already feel a bit better. I'm thinking I could actually go back to work."

"Not too fast, woman. We don't want you pushing yourself too hard. Your health is more important than anything else right now. How about you come with me to the shop instead? It's a slow day and I could use some company. That way, I can watch over you for a while just in case you start to feel worse."

I'm reminded once again of what a great friend Elena is. But I can't ignore the sinking feeling I often get when I'm with her. The knowledge that if she finds out who I really am and what I'm capable of, this friendship I cherish so much would crumble into ruins.

"I don't know, Elena. I've already taken up so much of your time. I think—"

"Let me sweeten the deal a little. I have a bottle of fresh lemonade waiting for you in the fridge and it has your name on it."

"Well, in that case," I say, capitulating, "how can I resist?"

Elena recently came across a recipe book that had belonged to her mother, and one of the recipes she fell in love with is the signature lemonade from her childhood. She's been experimenting with it ever since, adding little twists of her own, like rosemary or lavender. It has become her specialty, and she takes great pride in it.

When we get to the studio and I sit down with a full glass, she joins me, a serious expression on her face.

"I know you don't want to discuss this, but I think these headaches have a lot to do with everything you're bottling up inside you. I really think you should at least have one session with Darius. Just one, to unload some of the weight that's been burdening you. It might help alleviate some of the stress."

As much as I hate to admit it, Elena might be right. But at the thought of talking to Darius, fear curls around my heart.

He's not just any therapist; he's her husband. I've been so out of sorts lately and if I'm honest, a little confused. I'm afraid I might say the wrong thing to Darius, something that might make it back to Elena and bring my secret to light. I can't allow that to happen.

I take another sip of the lemonade, before I meet Elena's gaze. "I promise to think about it," I lie.

I don't like it about myself, but I'm good at lying to Elena.

# SIXTEEN

I have a strange dream that night. I'm inside Lennie's tree house and I'm a child again, playing with her toys. The walls are covered in drawings and scribbles, my scribbles. Many of them are of the ocean, sea shells, and flowers, but I know I'm the one who drew them.

I'm not only in Lennie's tree house, I feel like I'm actually her, on the outside at least. I'm wearing one of her favorite dresses, a purple velvet one with white lace trim.

As I twirl in the dress, a doll with a missing arm catches my eye, and I reach out to pick it up. As my hand touches its face, a flood of sadness rushes over me. Dropping it onto the small bed, I hug my legs and rock back and forth, tears streaming down my cheeks.

After finally pulling myself together, I reach into the box of toys that I had pulled from under the bed and rummage inside it for another doll, this one with a pristine appearance. With trembling hands, I carefully cradle the new toy in my arms, feeling a strange sense of comfort.

Suddenly, a voice echoes through the tree house, a voice

that sounds hauntingly familiar. It's soft and gentle, like a whisper on the breeze. I know immediately that it's Elena.

I move to the small window and see her on the ground, looking up, watching me.

Unlike me, she's an adult, dressed in a long kaftan with intricate patterns. It billows in the wind, and she raises her hand to shield her eyes from the sun.

She doesn't look happy, and as I hold my doll to my body, and gaze down at her, my heart fills with a sudden mix of guilt and fear.

She's clearly angry with me, but I don't understand why. Did I do something wrong?

I try to call out to her, but my voice is lost in the wind, so I scramble to my feet and open the tree house door, racing down the steps to reach her. But even when my feet touch the ground, no matter how fast I run, the distance between us only seems to grow.

It's as if an invisible force is pulling her away from me, and I'm left with a deep sense of longing, aching to bridge the gap between us. The soles of my feet pound against the earth and my breath comes in ragged gasps, but it feels as though I'm running in place.

Panic grips me as I realize that I'm unable to get to her, no matter how hard I try.

I frantically wave my arms and scream her name, hoping she will hear, but she doesn't reach out for me, doesn't help me close the distance between us. She just stands there watching me. Her eyes, usually warm and welcoming, now hold a hint of sadness. It's as if she knows something I don't, something that prevents her from coming any closer.

I come to a halt, my breath heaving in my chest, and I stand there, locked in a moment of despair, my small hands holding the doll tightly. Why won't Elena come to me? She's my best friend, like a sister to me. What's keeping us apart?

Tears well up in my eyes as I watch her turn to walk away in the direction of the beach, her kaftan trailing behind her.

I stand there, rooted in place, unable to understand why she's leaving me behind. My heart breaking, I watch her silhouette grow smaller and smaller against the vastness of the shoreline.

Feeling defeated and alone, I head back to the tree house and climb up. The door slams shut behind me, enclosing me in my little corner of solitude, but the space feels strange and cold. I collapse onto a beanbag chair, cradling the doll in my arms, seeking comfort in its familiar presence as I inhale the scent of aged wood and sea air.

I wake up with a start, my heart pounding in my chest and sweat dripping down my forehead. Even as the dream fades away, the image of Elena's disapproving gaze lingers in my mind. It takes a few moments for reality to properly settle back in, but when it does, fear grips me.

Could this be a sign? What if Elena knows my secret?

"Nathan," I whisper, nudging him gently, then flicking on the nightlight.

He stirs in his sleep, blinking groggily. "What? What's going on?" He picks up his phone from his side table, squinting at the screen. "It's one in the morning, Hannah."

I pull my knees to my chest the way I did in the tree house in my dream. "I think Elena knows."

He yawns. "Knows what?"

"Our past. What happened that night. I don't want to say it."

Nathan sits up now, fully awake, his eyes searching mine. "But why would she find out now? It's been years."

I take a deep breath, trying to steady myself. "I don't know. I just... I have this feeling, this gut instinct that she might know."

"What brought this on? Have you said something to her? I told you to be careful—"

"No, I haven't said anything," I assure him, desperation seeping into my voice. "It's this dream I just had. It felt so real. She was in it, and I could see it in her eyes, the pain, the anger."

"You dreamed about her?"

I nod, beginning to cry. "She looked at me like she knows."

Nathan takes me by the shoulders gently, his eyes searching mine. "Elena has no idea. Please, Hannah, you need to calm down. You're getting yourself worked up; it's not good for you."

"But I'm so scared. I keep thinking about it, what we did. You know I sense things sometimes, and this feeling, it's overwhelming."

Nathan's grip tightens. "Hannah, please stop this. We've come too far to let paranoia get the best of us. We can't let it ruin everything." He lets go of my shoulders and buries his hands in his hair. "I need you to keep your wits about you, stop yourself spiraling."

I nod, wiping away a stray tear. "But Lennie... if it comes out—"

"It won't!" His voice is harder now, sharper. "We have taken every precaution to make sure no one finds out. Now will you please stop dwelling on this?"

"But we need to think about what to do if something happens, Nathan. We can't just bury our heads in the sand. We have to be prepared."

Nathan gets to his feet and strides to the window, yanking the curtains open even though there's no sunshine outside. "Look, I understand that you're scared, but dwelling on the what-ifs will only fuel your stress levels and you know that could be dangerous for you, for all of us." His voice is tinged with frustration as he turns to face me. "I can't talk about this anymore, not now. I'm too tired."

I want to let go, but my gut instinct tells me that I can't

ignore this feeling. My dream felt too vivid, too real to simply dismiss as paranoia. Nathan may be convinced that we have taken every precaution, but I'm not so sure.

I take a deep breath and gather the courage to speak up once more, walking us into a full-blown argument that lasts late into the night. Voices rise and fall, accusations hurled like flaming arrows. The tension in the room becomes palpable, suffocating us as we stand on opposite sides of the battlefield. In a brief ceasefire, Nathan goes to fetch us both a glass of water, and he tuts at me when I ask him to add in a splash of whisky.

"If you're so determined to bring up the past, Hannah, why don't you just do it, then?" He grabs his phone and shoves it into my hand. "Go on and call the cops. You might as well end this charade now."

I just stare at him in shock, breathing heavily. I know he's right. The more I think about my fears, the more I will attract destruction and pain into our lives. I believe what you focus on will expand and manifest. I need to keep it together, to keep thinking positively. For Lennie, for Nathan. My precious family.

As I slowly and deliberately calm my nervous system while Nathan glares out across the ocean from our bedroom balcony, I look down at the phone he gave me, and I notice something strange.

There's a text from Lila.

*How is little Lennie? I hope you're taking care of my girl.*

I had no idea Nathan and Lila were in touch. I didn't think they liked each other very much, frankly. And why would she text him about Lennie instead of me? Why would she, my assistant, be inquiring after Lennie at all? I know she likes her, but isn't it a bit much to call her "my girl"?

But when Nathan comes back in and we continue with our

stress-fueled, meandering argument, thoughts of Lila fall away from my mind, and I don't ask him about it.

She's always been a bit of an oddball, a little nosy perhaps and certainly not the most respectful of people's boundaries. But she's harmless, she means well. And right now, she's the least of my worries.

# SEVENTEEN

## LENNIE

I sit on my bed, hugging my favorite teddy bears as I hear Mommy and Daddy arguing through the walls.

I think they don't love each other anymore.

I squeeze my eyes tighter, wishing I could squeeze out their voices too. But they're still there making my ears hurt.

"Look, let's just... Let's get some sleep. We'll talk in the morning," Daddy finally says.

"Sure. Like sleep solves everything," Mommy replies, but her voice is quieter now.

After they stop yelling, I talk to Whisper in my head for a while to try to calm myself down, but then I hear something: Mommy's voice.

"Sweetheart?" Mommy's whisper fills the silence, and the door creaks open. "Lennie, are you still awake?"

I nod, my head feeling heavy. She comes in and sits on my bed, and when she sees my tears, she wipes them away with a soft touch. "Oh, honey, I'm really sorry we were loud." She hugs me for a long time. "Can I get you a warm glass of milk with honey? Will that help you sleep?"

"Okay," I whisper, and she disappears for a moment and

when she comes back, she's holding my favorite unicorn cup that I won at a fair.

"Mommy?" I hold the cup with both hands and take a sip. "When you and Daddy shout it makes my ears hurt." I look into my milk and a tear falls inside, but I don't care.

Mommy brushes a strand of hair away from my face and tucks it behind my ear. "I know, sweetheart. I'm so sorry you had to hear that. Sometimes grown-ups get upset and they don't know how to express it in the right way. But I promise you, we still love each other and we love you."

"*You* love me, but Daddy doesn't love me anymore."

"Of course he loves you, sweetie," Mommy says quickly. "He loves you to the moon and back, Lennie. Always remember that."

I don't believe her, but I don't say anything. I just drink my milk until it's finished.

"Try to sleep now, okay?" Mommy says when I'm done. "Everything will be better in the morning." She kisses my cheek, her lips making my skin warm.

"Okay, Mommy," I murmur, even though I still feel sad. "Can you sleep in my room tonight?"

Mommy sighs. "No, baby, I can't sleep in your room. I'm not feeling very well. But I promise you, you won't be alone." She holds up my new panda bear Snowy, the one from Whisper. "You have so many friends to keep you company. They'll watch over you while you sleep."

"Okay." I hold Snowy close, feeling his soft fur against my cheek. Mommy is right, I have lots of friends to keep me safe. I smile at Snowy and give him a little squeeze before placing him next to me on the pillow.

Mommy stands up and goes to turn off the main light, leaving the nightlight because I'm scared of the dark.

"Good night, Lennie," she says before closing the door.

"Night night." I close my eyes, trying to imagine that tomorrow will be a happy day.

Sometime during the night, a soft sound wakes me up again. I rub my sleepy eyes and squint, seeing a person sitting in the rocking chair by my bed. It's Whisper! Again, she's wearing white clothes just like a real angel.

I want to call out to her, but she puts a finger to her lips and shakes her head. "Shh, Lennie," she says in a low voice, "your mommy and daddy mustn't come in and see me, so we don't want to wake them. It's our little secret, remember?"

I nod.

"Good girl." She opens her arms wide for a hug, and I jump out of bed to go to her.

"Whisper, are you... are you really my guardian angel?"

"Of course I am. Who else would look after you in the middle of the night? I came because I know you're sad, and I want to make you feel better." She strokes my cheek with her warm finger. "You feel sad, don't you?"

I nod. "Mommy and Daddy were shouting. How did you know?"

"I'm your guardian angel, remember? I know everything that happens around you." Whisper looks serious. "Do you want to know what they were fighting about?"

I bob my head and Whisper scoots closer. "So, you have that big school play coming up next Friday, right?"

I nod again, surprised by how much Whisper knows about me. "Yes, I'm playing Cinderella."

"Well," she continues, "your parents were fighting because your daddy told your mommy that he won't be able to make it to the show. He said he has to work late that night."

I feel a big lump in my throat as I hear Whisper's words. "But Daddy always comes to my shows. He promised he'd be there," I say softly, trying not to cry but my voice shakes a little.

Whisper takes my hand. "I know, Lennie, but like I said, your daddy doesn't love you anymore. There are many things he used to do that he won't do anymore."

"But my mommy said Daddy loves me to the moon and back."

"Sometimes grown-ups lie, Lennie. They lie because they think it will protect you, but it only hurts more later."

"Did Daddy really hit me when I was little?" I ask, climbing back into my bed and under the covers. "I don't remember it."

Whisper leans forward and taps my nose. "Memories are tricky things, little one. They can hide in the shadows, waiting for the right time to come out. But you can trust me, and right now you have to do everything to stay away from him. Your daddy has a temper, and you must try not to make him angry."

More tears start to fill my eyes, but Whisper strokes my hair.

"Hush, now. Don't cry, my brave little one. Remember, I'm here to protect you, always." She places a hand on my shoulder. "Now let me tell you a bedtime story."

When I say nothing, she begins to tell me a story of a little girl who lived by the sea, and whose drawings became real every night when everyone was sleeping.

"Everything the little girl wished for, she drew, and it became real. She would draw magnificent castles with towering spires, and the next morning, they would be standing tall on the shore."

After Whisper has been talking for a while, I start to feel sleepy, and my eyes begin to flutter closed.

"Good night, Lennie," Whisper says finally, tucking me in. "And remember, our secret stays safe between us. Don't tell your mommy and daddy that you've seen me for real, or what I look like. I'm for your eyes only."

"Secret," I mumble, already half-asleep. "I promise."

# EIGHTEEN

## HANNAH

It's the day after I had that strange dream about Elena, and I'm walking back to the shop after a quick breakfast at Honeywood. It's a busy day in town today, with throngs of people, mostly tourists. I'm making my way through them when I see a familiar figure.

A woman is standing with her back turned next to a street vendor's cart, examining the trinkets and souvenirs on display. A chill runs down my spine. It's her. The woman I saw at Nathan's father's funeral.

She's tall and stands gracefully, her shoulders pushed back to show off an elegant posture. Her hair is tucked away under a sleek black hat. The way she carries herself, she reminds me of a ballet dancer. I watch as she delicately picks up a small wooden figurine and studies it, her slender fingers tracing the carvings.

The weird thing is, she's wearing exactly the same outfit she wore at the funeral. Coming to a stop in front of a souvenir shop, I watch her from a distance. She seems oblivious to the world around her, fixated on the trinkets.

There's just something about her that makes me feel uncomfortable; I wish I knew who she is and what she's doing here. It's a silly thought, of course, because loads of people come to Stoneview, it's one of the most popular small towns in Florida, but nonetheless something about her just seems off.

I decide to trust my gut and approach her cautiously, trying not to draw too much attention to myself. Maybe I can talk to her, find out how she's connected to Nathan and why she stood at a distance at the funeral.

But as I walk toward her, she turns abruptly away from the vendor's cart and starts heading down a narrow alley tucked between two buildings.

I weave my way through the bustling square, my heart pounding. The alley is dimly lit, with sunlight peeking through the buildings and shadows looming in the corners.

I'm wearing heels today, so I quickly slip them off, feeling the cool cobblestones beneath my feet as I make my way down the alley. The sound of my footsteps echoes softly. As I round a corner, I catch a glimpse of the woman disappearing through a red, narrow door. But when I get to it, it's locked and there is no sign on the door.

I hesitate for a moment, contemplating whether I should knock.

This is stupid, I scold myself silently. What am I doing, following a stranger down a deserted alleyway?

Turning my head, I see a small, wiry elderly man peering at me from the entrance of an adjacent alley. His eyes dart back and forth between the locked door and me, and without a word, he steps forward and approaches me. He appears to be in his late seventies and he's wearing a worn-out tweed jacket. His shoulders are so hunched that they almost touch his ears, and his thinning hair is a mess of unruly gray strands.

"Lost, are you?" he rasps.

"I... I was following a woman," I stammer. "She went through this door, but it's locked. Did you see her?"

His gaze intensifies, his eyes narrowing even further, and he scratches his unkempt beard.

"Ma'am, I didn't see her," he finally responds. "But that door... it's been locked for years. No one uses it."

"Are you sure? I saw her go in," I insist, my voice trembling.

The man shakes his head. "I live near here. I know this neighborhood like the back of my hand, and I'm telling you, nobody uses that door. You must be mistaken, my dear."

I feel a shiver run through me. How could that woman vanish through a locked door that hasn't been opened in years?

"I... I don't understand," I mutter, my voice barely audible. "She can't have just disappeared."

"Are you sure you saw her at all?" the wiry man asks drily.

I feel a little unsteady at his words, and lean against the door. Was the woman a product of my own frayed mind? She seemed so real, so tangible.

"I... Thank you. I should probably go," I stammer, my voice shaky.

With a forced smile, I turn away and begin to walk back toward the crowded street, the woman still lingering on the edges of my thoughts.

Then suddenly, I think I see her again, in front of me, pushing through the crowd. And this time she's walking directly toward me, and I can see her face.

It's a woman I knew years ago, who once lived in my house, engaged to the man I'm now preparing to marry.

A woman who thought I was her friend.

I'm frozen, people jostling around me, as the woman comes toward me. And then her face changes, right before my eyes, its features adjusting themselves grotesquely as her whole body grows taller.

It's not her at all.

It's Nathan. And that look in his eyes, it's one I've never seen directed at me before. One I hoped I'd never see again.

My whole body is trembling, and as I squeeze my eyes shut, I repeat the mantra I learned in therapy. *Grounded. Grounded.* Gradually I come back to myself.

When I open my eyes again, nobody is walking toward me. I'm surrounded by a sea of people and Nathan is nowhere to be seen.

What the hell is happening to me? I wonder, as I slowly make my way toward a bench in the town square and collapse onto it before dropping my head into my hands.

After regaining my composure, I'm about to get back to my feet when my phone rings, jolting me out of my thoughts, and I fumble to answer it.

"Where are you?" Elena asks as soon as I pick up. "I'm at your shop and you're not here. We had some things to go over for the wedding, remember? Josie told me you went to Honeywood, but I called Gloria and she said you left a while ago."

A while ago? I glance at my watch. In my mind, I didn't leave the café more than fifteen minutes ago, but my watch says otherwise. It's almost forty minutes since I left, yet it feels like mere moments have passed with me wandering through town, chasing shadows.

Is it happening again? Am I losing the careful hold I've kept over my mind all these years?

I take a deep breath. "Elena, you were right. I need to talk to someone."

# NINETEEN

The moment I step into Darius's office, a wave of unease washes over me. I shouldn't be here, sharing my troubles with him.

It's a risk I didn't want to take, but what happened yesterday scared the hell out of me. It's also obvious that Nathan thinks I'm losing my mind again, and he doesn't even know the half of it. So maybe he's right, and if so, I need to get on top of this now.

I considered seeing another therapist who's not connected to Elena, but I feel safe with Darius and he was willing to fit me in last minute. It was so easy; one call and it was settled that I would come to his office first thing in the morning.

As long as I'm careful what I say, I should be fine. I can do this.

"Take a seat, Hannah." He gestures toward the leather armchair opposite his desk.

The moment I sink into the seat, my anxiety dissipates a little. The air smells faintly of aged paper and leather, and as I look around, I find myself drawn to the polished mahogany bookshelves lining one wall. I run my fingers along the fringes of an embroidered throw pillow next to me.

"Comfortable?" Darius's voice cuts through my thoughts, gentle yet somehow probing.

I nod, swallowing hard. "It's nice here," I murmur, my gaze lingering on an ornate clock perched on the mantel, its pendulum swinging with a soothing reliability.

Darius leans back in his worn leather chair, his hands steepled and fingers entwined. As always, the salt-and-pepper beard lining his jaw grants him a distinguished look.

"Tell me what's been troubling you, Hannah." His tone is soft, inviting.

Is this a mistake? How can I bare my soul to him when I'm keeping a secret that could destroy the friendship I cherish with his wife? Not only that, it would ruin my whole life if it came to light. My family would come crashing down in an instant.

Nathan doesn't even know I'm here.

*Safe topics*, I tell myself. Stick to safe topics.

My fingers curl into the couch as I exhale shakily. "I've been so scattered lately," I admit, the words tumbling out in a rush. "Forgetting things... misplacing them."

"Can you give me an example?" Darius's voice is steady and non-judgmental.

"Yesterday," I start, my eyes fixating on a small scratch in the mahogany desk, "I spent hours looking for my keys and tore the house apart. They were in the freezer, next to the peas and carrots." A humorless laugh escapes me. "Who puts their keys there?"

"Stress can often make us confused and forgetful," he suggests, leaning forward, the silver flecks in his hair catching the light. "Weddings, especially, can be quite stressful."

"Yes. Especially when Nathan..." My voice trails off, and I force myself to meet Darius's steady gaze. "He's been so distant since his father passed. It's like he's there, but not really with me."

"Loss can create barriers," he says softly. "Grief has its own timeline. For some, it's longer than others."

"I just want to help him," I murmur, "to bring him back from wherever he is."

"Being patient is part of helping. Perhaps allowing him space to feel his loss without pressure could be beneficial. Have you considered inviting Nathan to join you in a session? I know he told me that he wanted to handle things on his own."

"He still wants to do that," I say quickly, too quickly. "He... he has his own way of dealing with things."

Silence drifts between us. Then Darius leans back into his chair, the leather creaking.

"Of course," he says finally, giving me a small, understanding smile. "Just know that the offer stands if ever he feels ready. We can talk about anything."

"Thank you. I'll—I'll let him know."

"Is there anything else you would like to discuss, something that has nothing to do with Nathan? Remember, Hannah, taking care of yourself is just as important in times like these. Perhaps we could talk about something that goes back a little deeper than your recent stress and forgetfulness?"

Another wave of silence stretches between us.

I should get up, leave, put distance between myself and this well-intentioned man who doesn't know the shadows lurking in my heart. But instead, I remain seated, a prisoner to my own indecision.

I shift uncomfortably in my chair, then clearing my throat, I lean forward. "The day before yesterday, I had a strange dream."

There's no reason I can't talk about it. I can tell him about the dream and leave Elena out.

"Is that so? Tell me about it."

I swallow hard, trying to steady my nerves. "I was... I was a child again." I pause to look at a vintage globe on a nearby shelf. "I was in Lennie's tree house. It felt so real, like I was her."

Darius dips his head to the side. "Was it a comforting place for you?"

"Comforting? Yes, but..." I hesitate, biting back the image of Elena's angry expression. "But there was sadness too, and confusion."

"That's not surprising. Sadness can often manifest in dreams when we're facing change. You're getting married soon, and even though that comes with joy, there could be some fears that you might lose yourself in this new chapter of your life. It could also be that there's a part of you that longs for the simplicity and innocence of childhood, a part that feels over-whelmed by the responsibilities of adulthood."

That all makes sense. Planning the wedding, running my business, and taking care of both Nathan and Lennie... it feels like a constant juggling act. Perhaps, deep down, I yearn for a time when life was more carefree and uncomplicated. Only, my childhood was never like that.

"There's more. I've been seeing things as well. Things that are not there."

Darius studies me. "Seeing things? Can you elaborate on that?"

I take a deep breath before telling him about the woman I thought I saw in Lennie's bedroom window. He just watches me silently, and I don't know what he's thinking.

"I think the first time something like that happened was at Nathan's father's funeral," I continue. "I thought I saw a woman there. She was standing away from the other mourners and I found it strange. I walked toward her and she turned around, as if she didn't want me to see her, then she walked away. Nathan said he didn't see anyone like that there." I clear my throat and drop my gaze to my hands. "Then yesterday, I was in the square and I thought I saw her again, wearing the exact same clothes."

"Did you get to talk to this woman?"

I shake my head, my stomach clenching. "No, I tried to run after her, but she vanished through a door. Someone nearby told me that that door had not been opened in years. And he didn't see the woman."

"I see. Can you describe her?"

"Like I said, she wore the same clothes she had on at the funeral. All black, and a large, black hat. And then a few minutes later I thought I saw her again, and this time she was walking toward me. I could see then that she was someone from years ago, a former friend, nobody important. But her face turned into Nathan's, so I knew I must have been imagining the whole thing. But, Darius, in the moment I really thought she was real."

Darius nods. "It's not uncommon to experience hallucinations or delusions in times of heightened stress or emotional turmoil," he says, his voice soothing. "The mind can play tricks on us."

"Right." I chew on my lower lip.

The stress again. It all comes back to that. I'm not sure if that should make me feel better or worse.

"Tell me," he continues, "have you been experiencing any physical symptoms lately?"

"Actually, yes. I've been having intense headaches and periods of dizziness. The headaches come out of nowhere and they're so strong that sometimes I can't function. I'm also finding it hard to sleep."

"That doesn't surprise me in the slightest. Headaches and sleep disturbances can often accompany high levels of stress. Your mind and body are clearly struggling to cope with the emotional burden you're carrying." He pauses. "I'll prescribe you some medication to help manage the headaches and improve your sleep. That should provide you with some relief while we work on addressing the underlying issues."

I nod. "Thank you, Darius. I appreciate your help."

"Of course." After handing me the prescription, he stands up to walk me to the door. "How about we schedule another session? Same time next week?"

"Maybe. I'll call you," I say.

"That's perfectly fine. Just don't wait too long. It's important to maintain momentum."

Momentum. Yes, that's what this feels like—a descent I can't slow down, a fall with no end. "Thank you, Darius," I say and quickly leave.

Hot air hits my face as I step outside their house, the mid-May sun unusually strong and beating down on me. I squint, trying to adjust my eyes to the brightness.

People bustle around me, their movements a blur. I glance back once, half-expecting to see Darius watching from the window.

What if I've said too much?

What if he has somehow read my mind, seen secrets I can't even admit to myself?

# TWENTY

## LENNIE

It's lunchtime on Sunday and me and Mommy are sitting alone at the kitchen table. Daddy is at the office even though it's the weekend. But even if he was home, he wouldn't eat with us.

"Sweetie, can you... can you pass me the water?" Mommy's voice is very low, and her eyes are squeezed shut.

"Here, Mommy." She opens her eyes and I hold out the glass with both hands. "Is your head hurting again?"

"Yes." As she takes the glass, her fingers touch mine. They feel cold and I feel a squirming worry in my belly. Mommy's hands are always warm.

"Thank you, darling. You're my good girl." She tries to smile, but her head hurts her again and she closes her eyes tight. Her forehead is all crinkled up, like the drawings I make when I press too hard with my crayons. I wish I could rub the lines away like I do on paper with an eraser.

Mommy opens her eyes again and takes a long drink of water before putting the glass down slowly. "How about some dessert?"

I watch as she reaches for the bowl of fruit on the counter—oranges, grapes, apples, bananas. And then it happens. Her hands get weak, and the bowl falls from her fingers, tumbling down in slow motion. It crashes to the table and fruits are everywhere. The grapes roll to the floor.

"Damn it!" Mommy curses and presses a hand to her forehead. I'm not used to hearing her say bad words.

"It's okay, Mommy. Don't worry, I'll clean it up."

"No, don't worry, baby." Her hand goes to her temple, pressing hard. "Why don't you go out to play? I'll clean up here and call you when I'm done, so we can eat ice-cream." But her voice sounds strange.

"No, Mommy, I don't want to leave you alone. I want to stay here with you."

Mommy touches my cheek and smiles. "It's okay, my sweet girl. You don't have to worry about me. Go on to your tree house."

I was there before lunch and Whisper was with me. She said she would wait for me to come back. Maybe she can help me make some more secret potions to help Mommy feel better.

"I'll be back soon, Mommy." I get to my feet and give her one last hug before walking out the door.

"Whisper?" My voice trembles as much as my fingers holding the last step. "Mommy's head is hurting again. The medicine we made last time didn't work."

"Ah, sweet Lennie," she says, stepping closer and hugging me. "You're such a good daughter to worry about your mother."

"She dropped our fruit bowl. It fell on the table and the fruits rolled out." My bottom lip quivers.

"Your mother needs more help, doesn't she?" Whisper's tone is thoughtful and kind.

"She does. Can you make her better?" I beg. "Please?"

"Of course, Lennie. We will make a stronger magic potion for her, one that will chase away her pain for good."

"Really?" I clasp my hands together. "Thank you, Whisper! What do we need to make the potion?"

"I already have everything we need. While you were having lunch, I went to the garden and got some herbs." She reaches under the bed and pulls out small bundles of fresh herbs. "This time, we'll make a potion with chamomile, lavender, rosemary, and a little special ingredient."

"What's the ingredient?" I ask.

"This." She opens her hand and in her palm is some powder that looks like sugar. "This is a magic powder with special healing powers."

"Can it make Mommy happy too? She's very sad."

"Yes, this special ingredient has the power to heal not just the body, but also the heart and soul."

"Okay," I murmur. "Let's do it, let's make the magic medicine for Mommy."

"I have to warn you, Lennie. Like last time, you can't tell your mom about the potion. Just find a way to add it to her food at dinner without her noticing. If she sees you, it will not work." Then she gives me some of the herbs and tells me what to do.

I crush them on one of my plastic toy bowls. "Make Mommy better," I tell the ingredients.

"Good, Lennie," Whisper says. "Focus on that. Your love is the most powerful magic of all."

"Will it work fast?" I ask.

"Patience, child." She ruffles my hair. "Some spells need time in order to work."

As the final ingredient is mixed in, I feel proud of myself.

"Now it's perfect and ready to work its magic," Whisper says, her voice filled with hope. She takes a small bottle and puts the potion into it, closing it with a black cap.

.  .  .

"Do you want some salad, Lennie?" Asks Mommy later, pushing the bowl toward me.

"No thank you. My tummy is full."

"Is everything all right, sweetheart? You seem quiet." Mommy frowns.

"Yes, Mommy. Everything is fine." I fake a smile, looking at the empty seat where Daddy used to sit. "I just miss playing with you on the beach."

Her smile disappears, her eyes blinking a few times before she takes a bite of lettuce. "I know, baby. I miss it too. I'm sorry I've been so sick lately."

"It's okay. You'll get better soon." I breathe in deeply. "Mommy, can you get me some water? I'm feeling a little thirsty."

"Of course, sweetheart." She gets up from the table and heads to the kitchen. As soon as she disappears, I take out the bottle from my pocket and sprinkle a few drops of the magic potion onto her plate.

# TWENTY-ONE

## HANNAH

The salty scent of the sea mingles with the clatter of dishes and muted conversations as I push through the glass doors of the Mariner's Catch, a seafood restaurant I have loved for years.

A giant lobster pot hangs over the entrance, and the wooden floors creak beneath my steps like the deck of an old ship. Elena and Gloria are already seated at a table near the large windows overlooking the bobbing boats and noisy seagulls at the harbor.

"Sorry I'm so late," I murmur, sliding into the booth across from them. I had completely lost track of time, which is a regular occurrence these days.

"Don't worry about it, Hannah, it's just us," Elena says as she pours herself a glass of water.

"Exactly. It's not an interview." Gloria smiles warmly, her eyes crinkling at the corners.

"You must both be hungry, so let's go ahead and order." I reach for one of the three menus and glance through it.

"Great idea. How about we order the Seafood Tower?" Elena suggests. "It has a bit of everything."

"Sounds perfect," Gloria agrees. "I'm terrible at making decisions anyway. Are you in, Hannah?"

"Sure," I say.

It's been a long day. Although my headaches are a little better, I'm still battling dizziness and forgetting things, and it's really starting to get to me. And the latest fight with Nathan this morning didn't help.

When the Seafood Tower arrives, it's a mouth-watering display: tiers of fresh oysters, jumbo shrimp, crab legs cracked just enough to reveal the tender flesh, and scallops seared golden-brown, nestled beside lemon wedges and cocktail sauce.

We dig in, the clinking of our forks against the chilled metal platter blending with the noise of the restaurant. I love seafood, but I find myself mechanically chewing, my thoughts else-where. I don't even hear the conversation between Elena and Gloria. I try to force myself to engage, but my mind is full of turbulent anxieties and thoughts.

"Everything all right?" asks Marlene, our waitress, as she walks by, balancing plates on her hands and arms.

She's in her fifties with a gap-toothed smile and an air of genuine warmth. I know her quite well as I did the flowers for her daughter's wedding last year, and we spent endless hours discussing floral arrangements and color schemes.

"Delicious, thank you," I reply with a smile. "How's Jenna?"

A shadow flits across Marlene's features. "Oh, Hannah," she sighs. "It's kind of you to ask. Unfortunately, Jenna and Michael decided to go their separate ways."

There's an uncomfortable silence.

"I'm so sorry to hear that," I say finally.

Marlene's professional mask slips back into place. "Thank you. It's been tough, but Jenna's strong. We both are. Enjoy your meals."

She walks away and we continue chatting for a while.

Then Elena leans forward. "Hannah," she says softly, peering at me with those eyes that miss nothing, "how have you been feeling lately? And when will you book your next session with Darius?"

"I'm fine." The lie tastes sour on my tongue. "Just tired."

"You know we're here for you, right?" Gloria adds. "If there's ever anything—"

"Thank you, guys," I interrupt before she can finish. "I appreciate it, truly. But everything is well."

I glance at Elena, knowing she won't be satisfied with such a vague answer. "I'll call Darius soon to set something up."

"Good," Elena says, nodding. "He's worried about you, Hannah. He didn't tell me the details, of course, but he did mention you were in a really bad place. Promise you'll really call him?" she presses, her tone gentle yet firm.

"I promise," I assure her, locking away the dread that surfaces at the thought of another session with Darius. Another opportunity for him to dig up the past.

"Good." She smiles.

Then another paranoid thought hits me in a rush. What if Elena suspects that I'm hiding something, and is using Darius as a means to uncover the truth?

Panic threatens to spill over. I can't let Elena suspect anything. I must maintain control.

"Let's just enjoy tonight." I muster a smile as warm as the freshly baked bread that arrives at our table.

Gloria nods, relief softening her features, while Elena's gaze lingers on me, searching, questioning. But she lets it go with a nod and turns her attention to the steaming mussels that are set before us.

"Well," she says, lightly, "I'm enjoying making the few changes on your wedding dress, and it's coming along beautifully. I love the vintage-inspired lace detailing on the sleeves."

"Can't wait to see it," Gloria chimes in, sipping her wine.

"Thank you, Elena. I know it'll be perfect," I manage to say.

"Of course," she replies, but there's something in her tone, a knowing edge.

A perfect wedding, a perfect life, a perfect lie. How long can one maintain the illusion before it all crumbles?

Gloria raises her glass. "Cheers to Hannah and Nathan, and to a future brimming with love and happiness."

"Cheers," I whisper, and as soon as I've emptied my glass, I pour another and drink it just as quickly.

The dessert arrives twenty minutes later, rich chocolate cake with raspberries and a dollop of whipped cream on the side.

"Have you ever heard of hypnotherapy, Hannah?" Elena says as I take my first bite.

"Only vaguely," I reply, savoring the dark chocolate.

She leans in, her eyes bright. "Darius has just completed hypnotherapy training and he thinks it might help me unlock some of my hidden memories."

The cake turns to ash in my mouth.

"Hidden memories?" I say, my voice strained.

"Yes, about the accident that left me concussed all those years ago. I have these huge gaps in my memory. If I could fill them in, it might help me process the trauma." Her fingers toy with the edge of her napkin, folding and unfolding the fabric.

The room immediately tilts and the walls draw in closer. Sweat beads at my temples despite the chill from the harbor breeze wafting in through the open windows.

Elena continues. "He's hoping to try it out on me before offering it to clients. Wouldn't it be great if it works? It would be such a breakthrough."

Why is she talking like that? Like she already knows which memories are waiting to be uncovered?

My throat constricts. I cough, once, then again, louder.

"Are you okay?" Gloria pats my back.

"Fine," I gasp as I reach for my glass of water. "Just went

down the wrong pipe." I take a drink. "Hypnotherapy, wow," I manage to say, steadying my voice. "Sounds intriguing."

"Doesn't it?" Elena smiles. "I know I've kind of come to terms with losing my memories of that day, and I know it could be painful to have them back, but there's a part of me that's curious. I'm sure I can handle it, right?"

"True," I whisper, forcing a smile. "But are you sure it's safe? I imagine there are risks involved?"

Elena's brow furrows. "Risks? Like what?"

"False memories, for one." The words tumble out. "Sometimes people can have thoughts planted in their minds that never actually occurred. It could be damaging."

"Darius wouldn't let that happen," Elena counters.

"Of course not intentionally," I agree, "but you never know how these things can go. The mind is a fragile thing."

"You're right. Still, if there's a chance it could help, I'd like to try it." Her voice holds a note of determination.

Soon our conversation drifts back to more everyday things, and after a little while I push back my chair. "Excuse me. Nathan is working late, I should get going and relieve the babysitter." I kiss both of them on the cheek and tell them I'll transfer the money for the bill later.

I drive home mechanically until I find myself at the beach. The ocean sprawls before me—a dark space under the moon's pale glow. I stumble onto the sand, my high heels sinking with every step, and the salty breeze lashes against my face.

Then I collapse and curl up tight, pressing my forehead to my knees.

"Please, Elena, don't remember. I don't want to lose another friend," I whisper.

I'm not sure how long I've been there for, curled up on the sand, before I finally make my way inside, but Lila seems a little annoyed at me when I get in. It's later than we'd agreed when she offered to babysit earlier, saying she could use the extra money as she's saving up for interior design school. I'm chatting to her about Lennie in the kitchen when Nathan pulls in the driveway, and Lila swiftly excuses herself, saying she'll make her way home along the beach.

As she slips out through the living room windows, I wonder what put a bee in her bonnet. She seemed anxious about something, not her usual chirpy self, and her annoyed reaction to me being late home was quite uncharacteristic.

At one point in my life I'd have shown more concern, tried to find out what was going on with her. I've always tried to be a good employer, treating Josie and Lila with empathy and respect. But I just don't have the emotional bandwidth to inquire into Lila's personal life. I need to look after my own family, first and foremost.

Then I remember that text from Lila, the one I saw on Nathan's phone. It had completely dropped out of my mind. What on earth is going on with me?

Did I even see that text at all?

# TWENTY-TWO
## LENNIE

The heavy curtain is soft against my cheek as I peek out onto the big stage. The lights are so bright that they make the people look blurry. But I know they're all waiting for me, Cinderella, to come out again.

I hold on to my dress really tight; it's a pretty blue princess dress with sparkles that catch the light and make me shiny. Just like I'll be at the wedding.

"Remember, Lennie," whispers Mrs. Patterson, whose breath smells like mint, "big smile when you go back out there."

"Like this?" I try to show her my best smile but it feels shaky, like my lips don't know what to do.

"Perfect," she says. "Just like that."

The stage smells dusty. It tickles my nose and I have to squeeze it so I don't sneeze.

Finally, Mrs. Patterson claps her hands together and says, "Okay, everyone, get ready!" Then we all move around, laughing and making noise as we get ready to come out of our hiding place behind the curtain.

My heart beats really loud, louder than the sounds all around me.

"Remember your cues, sweetie pie." Mrs. Patterson squeezes my shoulder softly, and then she goes to talk to another teacher.

I peek through the curtain again, but I don't see Daddy.

Mommy said he would come, but he's not here. Only Mommy and Aunty Elena are sitting in the second row. Mommy keeps looking back like she's waiting for him to come in, but he doesn't. Whisper was right.

"Sweetheart, it's time," Mrs. Patterson says. "Your audience is waiting for Cinderella to go to the ball."

The music comes on and I go on the big stage.

I dance with my magic shoes, just like I practiced. But as I twirl, I keep looking for Daddy in the audience. He's not there and Mommy looks sad.

When everyone claps at the end, I look one more time and see Daddy sneaking in at the back of the room. But it's too late, he missed everything.

As we ride back home, Mommy and Daddy are whispering, and Daddy keeps apologizing to me.

"Sorry, pumpkin," he repeats, but I don't want to look at him. So, I turn away and stay silent.

"How could you be late?" Mommy's voice is getting louder. "You promised our daughter, Nathan."

"I told you it would be difficult for me to come. I had a meeting with a client." His voice sounds tired and sad. "I tried to end it early but then I couldn't find my keys. They weren't in my jacket pocket, where I usually keep them. You know I always, always have them in the same place. I still don't know where they are, and it's all of them, house, car, office. At least I have a spare set I can use until they turn up."

"You've never lost your keys before, so that's convenient. *But you need to know that this mattered,* Nathan. It was important to Lennie, it should have been important to you too," Mommy says and then they don't speak anymore.

. . .

Back at home, I hear Daddy stomping up the stairs, followed by the loud slam of the bedroom door.

Mommy takes some pills in the kitchen, her hands shaking a little bit. Her headaches are getting worse, and my secret potion is still not working. I put it in her food every day, like Whisper told me to, but when is it going to start working?

"Time for bed," Mommy says softly, leading me to my room. She tucks me in and smiles, but her eyes look far away, like she can't see me.

"Good night, sweetie," she whispers before closing my door with a soft click.

I wait until the house is quiet, then I whisper into the dark, "Whisper? Are you there? Please come help me. I need you to take the sadness in my family away."

# TWENTY-THREE

## HANNAH

"Ah, Hannah, right on time," Elena greets me when I walk through the door of the Bridal Bliss. "Let's see if any adjustments are needed, shall we?"

I nod and slip behind the faded velvet curtain, changing into the wedding dress that hangs off my frame more than it did at the last fitting.

"Darling, you've lost more weight," Elena says as I step out. She clucks her tongue, her fingers brushing against the fabric at my waist, then gently lifting my chin to study my face. "I'm getting worried about you."

"Really, I'm fine," I lie smoothly, dodging her probing eyes. "I just don't have much of an appetite lately."

"Stress can do that to you," she chuckles, though her brow remains furrowed as she pins and tucks the dress around my diminished figure. "But you must take care of yourself."

"Of course," I reply lightly. "I'll try to eat more. Promise."

"Good." She steps back, examining her work. But her eyes still hold that flicker of worry.

When she's done pinning and tucking, we sit down to drink

some of her homemade lemonade and I begin to feel calmer, Elena's chatter distracting me from my worries.

"Oh, I have a bit of an update," she says after a while. "I started hypnotherapy with Darius."

"Really?" I swallow hard and set down my glass. "And how's that going?"

She takes a breath, her fingers tracing her glass. "I think it's working. I know you were worried that it could be dangerous, but so far, I haven't experienced anything negative. I find it weirdly relaxing, actually."

"Working?" I feel my right temple start to throb. "Have you remembered anything specific?"

Her face shifts slightly, her eyes narrowing as if trying to focus on a blurry memory. "Just fragments," she replies. "Flashes of light, sounds, nothing concrete."

"Nothing concrete," I repeat, relief washing over me. "That's good. I mean, it must be hard not seeing the full picture."

"It is," she agrees. "I'm sure it's only a matter of time before everything comes back to me. I just feel that there's something important, something significant that I'm missing." She pauses to take a sip. "Darius said the mind has a way of protecting us from what we're not ready to face."

"Maybe," I nod. "Anyway, let me know how it goes. And thank you for the dress fitting. You're a miracle worker, as always." I put down the glass and stand, eager to escape the room that suddenly feels too small.

"Of course, honey. Take care of yourself, okay? I was telling Gloria the other day that one of these days we need to go to the cinema together. It's been a while."

"Sure, that sounds like a plan," I reply with a forced smile.

When I leave, I think I see that strange woman again on the street across from me, but I blink several times and she's gone.

. . .

That night, the house is so quiet. It's the kind of suffocating stillness that feels heavy and oppressive. After putting Lennie to bed, I walk softly down the hallway, the soles of my slippers whispering on the hardwood floor.

I make my way to the living room, sinking onto the couch with a sigh, and a few minutes later, Nathan comes to join me.

"Everything okay?" he asks and goes to stand next to the mantel.

"Yeah, just tired."

He doesn't move, doesn't sit beside me. Instead, he stands there, an unreadable expression etched into his handsome face. "You're not just tired. You've been off since you came home today."

My heart hammers against my ribcage. I haven't told him that Elena is undergoing hypnotherapy; I've been dreading the conversation. But he needs to know.

"It's Elena, she's undergoing hypnotherapy with Darius. To help her remember that night." The words tumble out in a hurried rush.

The air between us crackles with tension, and I watch as Nathan's posture stiffens, his jaw clenching hard. "Hypnotherapy? Since when? Why didn't you tell me?"

"Because I didn't want to worry you." My voice rises, defensive and brittle.

"Worry me?" He barks a sharp laugh. "She could remember everything, Hannah. Everything!"

"She might not. She only had a few sessions and she said she's only getting fragments. Maybe nothing more will come to her."

Nathan begins to pace and I can see the tension rising in him, reaching a fever pitch. Then he stops suddenly, his eyes locking onto the vase on the mantel, a simple ceramic piece holding an arrangement of wild flowers that Lennie gathered a few days ago.

"You should have told me. If she remembers what we did to my ex, and to *her*, we would go to jail. We would lose Lennie. Damn it, Hannah!" His voice rises into a shout.

And then he moves in a blur, his hand wraps around the neck of the vase, and before I take the next breath, it explodes against the wall, shards and petals raining down. The sound reverberates through the room, through my bones, and my stomach leaps into my chest.

As I watch the veins popping out on his forehead, I can't breathe. Can't think.

All I can do is stare at the destruction he caused, at the fragile blooms now crushed and lifeless on the floor. Nathan's grief, his pain—it's become a living thing, wild and untamed. And it's only now, in the wake of his fury, that I realize the depth of the gaping hole that has opened up between us.

"I'm sorry," he mutters, swearing under his breath, but I barely hear him over the roaring in my ears.

"How could you? What the hell, Nathan?" I manage, the words scratching my throat like sandpaper.

"I'm really sorry," he chokes out again. "I didn't mean—" Then he collapses to the floor next to the shattered remains of the vase. He grabs his head in his hands, the weight of his actions finally crashing down on him.

The anger that had consumed him so fiercely just moments ago has vanished so quickly, replaced with clear remorse. The sight of this powerful man reduced to tears should stir sympathy within me. It doesn't.

"Stop," I whisper, my voice steady despite the trembling that threatens to take over my body. My heart beats frantically in my chest.

The intense emotion I'm feeling right now isn't about the vase or even about the hypnotherapy. It's about every moment I tried to convince myself things would be okay, to deny how bad they were getting, to ignore the signs right in front of me. I can see it all so clearly now.

"That wasn't okay, Nathan," I say with tears in my eyes. "I know you've been grieving for your father. But this... this is something else." As I stand, my resolve hardens like steel. "Lennie and I need to leave."

He looks up at me, and for a moment, his eyes are not those of the man I fell in love with. They are wild, lost, and desperate —pools of anguish that scare the hell out of me.

"Please, Hannah. Don't do this," he pleads, reaching out a hand.

But the decision has already anchored itself deep within me. I need to protect what's most precious in my life: my daughter.

*Pack a bag for Lennie*, I command myself internally, the thought cutting through the fog. I refuse to let her witness any more of this pain and chaos. "Get help, Nathan," I say out loud as I back away from him. "For yourself. For us."

While Nathan remains downstairs, I quickly go upstairs, call Elena, and pack a suitcase.

Suddenly, I feel his presence behind me.

"Please, Hannah, let's talk about this. We can work it out."

I don't turn to face him; I can't. The image of the vase shattering against the wall is burned into my mind.

I'm finally beginning to believe that all this time my little girl wasn't confused. If he's capable of lashing out like that, who knows what she has witnessed in her father's presence, without me there?

I thought she was just imagining, misinterpreting things. I even wondered if at some point Lennie could have overheard me telling Nathan about my own violent dad, and she got it confused in her head.

I should never have doubted her.

"Work it out?" I say slowly. "Maybe, but let's do that once you get help, Nathan. You need help. Professional help. You need to grieve properly, not let the pain turn you into someone unrecognizable. The wedding is off until you find a way to heal."

Making my way to Lennie's room, my mind is racing, plotting, planning. We'll go to Elena and Darius. Lennie will be happy there.

I scoop her up, her silky hair spilling over my arm, her small body warm against mine. In her sleep, she mumbles something incoherent.

"Mommy?" Her sleepy voice tugs at me when I strap her into the car seat. "Where are we going?"

"To Aunty Elena's," I say. And with one last look at my home—a place once filled with love and now tainted by rage—I start the car.

Staying with Elena has another purpose too. I will be able to keep an eye on her, maybe plant a seed of doubt about anything that comes up in her hypnotherapy. Perhaps I can steer her away from the truth.

As soon as we arrive on Elena's doorstep and she opens the door for us, tears start to well up in my eyes. She wraps her arms around Lennie and me, holding us tightly.

"Come inside, my loves," she whispers after letting go, and ushers us into her home.

The familiar scent of warm cinnamon fills the air, instantly calming my racing thoughts. She guides us to the living room, where a crackling fire dances in the hearth. I know Elena wouldn't usually light it in the middle of spring, but she wants me to feel cozy and comforted. I feel so touched. This is just like Elena, always thinking of others, always there for her friends.

"I've already prepared the guest room for the two of you.

Hannah, how about you rest here and I take Lennie to bed? She's barely awake."

"Thank you." I pull my legs up on the couch, and watch as she carries Lennie up the stairs. When she comes back down, she heads to the kitchen and brings us both a cup of tea.

"Where's Darius?" I ask, taking the mug from her.

Elena sits down next to me. "Fast asleep. He went to bed early because he has a full day of clients tomorrow." She takes a sip, her eyes glancing toward the flickering flames. "What happened, Hannah?"

Lowering the mug to the coffee table, I take a deep breath before speaking. "I think I need something stronger than tea, Elena, honestly."

She responds to my wry smile with a chuckle and then goes to fetch us both a glass of wine, while I gather my thoughts.

I take a big gulp before I finally tell her. "Nathan happened."

"What do you mean?"

"I saw a side to him that I've never seen before. He became violent, unpredictable. It was as if a switch flipped inside him." I swallow hard before continuing. "Elena, I actually think he might have done it. I think he did hit Lennie. Or he lost his temper in a way that really, really scared her. I don't know what I'm going to do now, but I have to keep her safe."

# TWENTY-FOUR

When I wake up the next morning, Elena, Darius, and Lennie are out, and there's a note in Elena's elegant writing on the kitchen table alongside a large cafetière she's left out, all ready for me to fill with water.

I'm not sure coffee will be great for my headache, but I definitely need the boost of energy right now. Elena and I drank a lot of wine last night, or at least I did.

I pick up the note.

*I've taken Lennie to school. Wanted to let you sleep in. Why not take the day off? I'll call Josie and Lila to let them know they should hold the fort for you. Make yourself feel at home. I'll see you in the evening.*

I'm grateful for Elena's thoughtfulness, but I can't do what she suggests. I can't just sit around and do nothing. I have too much work to do at the shop to simply take the day off. And now I guess I'm going to need to do all the admin related to cancelling the wedding too. But I'm not sure I'm emotionally ready to tackle that right away. I drink an excessive amount of coffee and force myself to eat some of the homemade granola Elena left out for me, then I take a shower and get dressed.

As I walk out of the house, the bright sunshine feels overwhelming and brash, and I wish I had a pair of sunglasses with me.

Before I head to Bliss & Twine, hoping that immersing myself in work will provide some form of distraction, I drop by Honeywood to say hello to Gloria and I end up spilling my heart out as always, updating her on everything that happened last night.

At first, she says nothing, but then she reaches out and draws me into a hug. "I know this might be hard for you to hear," she whispers before letting go, "but I think this is for the best. I'm glad you and Lennie are safe."

She's right, it is hard to hear that. It was my decision to leave Nathan, but it hurts like hell.

"Do you want another chai? It might help soothe your nerves," Gloria offers kindly.

I shake my head and smile gratefully. "Thanks, but not today. I really need to get to the shop. I have a few things I need to take care of." I give her a quick hug before heading out the door.

The walk to Bliss & Twine is a short one, but every step feels heavier than the last. As I push open the door to the shop, the familiar smells of fresh flowers and scented candles envelop me, offering a temporary sense of comfort.

The morning light filters through the large display window, casting a warm glow over the colorful array of blooming plants, and I take a deep breath, trying to push away the lingering unease from the events of last night.

"Hi Hannah." Josie appears from the back room, carrying a bouquet of vibrant peonies. Her face lights up when she sees me, but the smile quickly fades as she narrows her eyes. "Everything okay?"

I force a smile, not wanting to burden her with my troubles. "Just a rough night, that's all." I head over to the counter, where a pile of orders awaits my attention.

Josie follows me, frowning. She sets the peonies down and reaches out to squeeze my hand. "You know you can talk to me, right? Whatever it is, I'm here for you."

"*We* are here for you." Lila joins us from the office. "Come on, tell us what's going on. You haven't been yourself lately."

I take a deep breath, feeling their support surrounding me like a soft blanket, and I decide to share a brief version of what has been going on. Not everything, of course, since as lovely as they both are, they're still my employees and I don't want to bring my personal drama to the workplace.

"Nathan has been struggling since his father died, and I don't know how to help him. It's been hard."

Lila places a hand on my shoulder, her eyes filled with empathy. "I'm so sorry, Hannah. That must be incredibly tough for both of you, and Lennie, I'm sure."

"Is there anything we can do to help?" asks Josie. "Maybe we could take on some extra work so you can take some time off?"

"You're sweet, but I need the distraction of work right now. I appreciate the offer though."

"I have an idea," she continues. "I remember you said your mom died a while ago, and it seemed like you were holding a lot of pain about it. Why don't you visit her grave, take along some flowers? At times like this, we need our mothers. And I wonder if processing those feelings and connecting your memories of her might help you navigate Nathan's grief?"

Lila nods. "That's not a bad idea. Sometimes talking to people we've loved and lost is a really good way to find clarity. That's been my experience, anyway."

"You can do it today; we can hold the fort here," Josie

continues. "And if you don't want to do it alone, I'd be more than happy to come with you."

"I don't know," I say, raking a hand through my hair.

I haven't been to my mother's grave since her funeral, and a part of me is scared about the memories that might resurface. But I do kind of want to connect with her, find comfort in her memory.

"Okay, let's do it," I say. "You're right, I think it's time."

The cemetery is only a short drive away, but every minute feels like an hour as Josie and I make our way there in silence. When we arrive and step out of the car, the air is heavy with the scent of freshly cut grass and the sun hangs low in the sky, casting a web of shadows over the rows of headstones.

"You can do this," Josie encourages me softly, her hand resting on my shoulder. I nod, taking a deep breath to steady myself before we start walking toward the gate.

Then I turn to her. "Would you mind if I go in alone?" I ask, my voice trembling a little.

"Of course not. Take all the time you need. I'll be right here waiting for you when you're done," she says, giving my hand a reassuring squeeze.

I nod and push open the gate slowly. The last time I was here, I was a mess. I was so broken and barely able to say goodbye to my mother.

Finally, I come to a stop in front of her headstone, and I trace the letters etched into the stone, sinking to my knees.

Amelia Livingstone.

Then suddenly, it's as if I lose control of my body.

My hand shoots out and grabs the slab of stone, gripping it tight until I snap a nail.

I came here looking for some sort of emotional release. I thought maybe it would be good for me. But as I clutch the cold stone, the pain I have bottled up inside for so long spills over, raw and unfiltered, poisonous.

"Why did you do it?" I whisper first through gritted teeth. Then I start to shout, and my palm slams against the gravestone. "Why didn't you stop him? Why didn't you believe me?"

Anger spreads through my veins like fire. I feel like I'm that little girl again, carrying the very same pain.

I remember my father locking me up in the dark attic to punish me. I remember the way his hard mechanic hand felt against my back. I remember its heaviness on my shoulder. I remember the boiling anger in his eyes.

I drop to my knees right into the dirt and cry my heart out. Eventually, I stand up and walk back to Josie, who looks deeply concerned as she scans my face.

"Are you okay, Hannah?" she asks.

"I don't know." I wipe the tears from my eyes and take a deep breath.

Josie wraps her arms around me in a tight hug, offering silent support as I let the emotions wash over me. "Let me drive, okay?" Her voice is soft and comforting, and I nod silently, grateful for her presence. Grateful to not be alone.

She helps me toward the car, guiding me with a gentle hand on my back.

Back in the town center, as we pull up outside the shop, Josie turns to me. "I'm so sorry I suggested this. Maybe it wasn't the right time; you have so much going on already. I just thought it might help. If you like I could pick Lennie up from school today."

"That's really kind of you, but you don't have to. You've done enough for me already."

If Josie picks Lennie up from school, Lennie might mention that we slept at Elena's, and then Josie would know that I walked out on Nathan last night. I'd like to keep that between me, Elena, and Gloria for now. I don't want the whole of Stoneview knowing my family is falling apart.

"Come on, let's go in," I say. "I'm honestly fine, Josie. I just want to get back to work now."

I go to my office, but I can't focus at all. At one point, I'm in the middle of creating boutonnieres that should be delivered tomorrow, and I'm just not paying attention; I prick my finger repeatedly on a piece of sharp wire.

Finally, I give up and tell Josie and Lila that I'm going to Elena's shop. I step back out into the sunshine, and I take the opportunity to walk there and get some fresh air to help clear my mind.

As soon as Elena sees me, she pulls me inside and puts up her "closed" sign.

"Hannah, what are you doing here? You look terrible. I told you to take the day off and have some time for yourself."

"I'm fine, don't worry. Thanks for taking Lennie to school. You didn't have to do that."

"That's what friends do. I can even pick her up later if you want."

"No, it's all right. Today is the last day of school before summer break and I want to be there."

The way my friends and employees are offering to help me out with Lennie is truly heartwarming, and they do say it takes a village. But I need my daughter to know she can rely on me, now more than ever.

Elena frowns. "But didn't you mention signing her up for the school's summer art program? The one that starts this coming Monday?"

Lennie is so passionate about art that when the school announced a daily summer art program, which ends on the day of our wedding rehearsal, she practically begged us to sign her up.

"Yeah, I did sign her up, but I still want to help her mark the end of the semester today. I might take her somewhere to celebrate."

"That sounds like a wonderful idea, Hannah. I'm sure Lennie would love that. Come on, sit down," she says and goes to get me a hot mug of tea, which I wrap my hands around, enjoying the steam as it rises to my face.

"Now tell me, how are you feeling?"

"Honestly, I'm a mess. Everything is falling apart."

I lower the mug onto the coffee table as Elena sits down next to me.

"Last night you were thinking Nathan got angry with Lennie, scaring her, even hurting her at some point? Hannah, you've known him almost all your life. Do you really believe he's capable of something like that?"

"All I know is that I was abused as a child, and from the outside everybody thought my father was the perfect man. The loving father. Which he was, when there were other people around. Only I got to see his other side, the one not even my mother saw. Plus, I know Nathan didn't have the best model in his own father. He always said he'd never be like him; he was so determined to be a different kind of dad to Lennie: hands-on, gentle, kind. But we don't always measure up to own standards or expectations of ourselves, and his father's death was such a trigger for him. What I saw last night..."

I pause and take some more calming sips of my tea, chamomile with a hint of honey.

"What if Lennie really is telling the truth, Elena?" I continue, pressing my palms and fingertips into the burn of the hot mug. "I can't deny Nathan has a temper. You should have seen him last night."

Elena shifts closer and puts her arm around my shoulders. "Like you said, Nathan is just going through a lot right now."

"My mother never believed me, you know? I told her so many times what was happening and she kept telling me that I was making it up. What kind of mother would I be if I don't learn from my past, if I do that to my daughter?"

We keep talking for a little while, before Elena gets a call and goes to her office to take it. When she comes back and sits down with me again, she hesitates.

"Hannah," she says finally. "I know you don't want to hear this, but I really think you need to see Darius for another session. So many memories are coming up from your childhood and you need help processing them. Maybe you can even have him try hypnotherapy on you?"

I nod. "I was at my mother's grave today."

"Oh, really?" she says, her eyebrows raised.

"Yeah. Josie and Lila suggested I go, that it might help me process some things."

"And did it help?"

"I'm not sure." I rub a palm down my face. "I broke down. It was bad."

"I'm so sorry, Hannah. I'm really, really sorry about what you went through as a child, but this is different. Nathan is different. And Lennie is not you." Elena pauses. "Plus, Lennie needs you to think clearly and look after your mental health. That's why I think it's so important you see Darius again. I'm worried about you. You've been talking about your dad a lot recently; are you sure you're not the one who put this whole thing in her mind, somehow? And maybe all these things are simply coming up because you're getting married and it's a big change, you know—"

"Look, Elena, I feel guilty enough already, please don't put even more blame on me for this," I snap.

Elena blows out a slow breath. "I'm sorry if I hurt your feelings, but I'm your best friend, I can't just stand by and watch.

I'm afraid you're going to destroy your relationship with Nathan and maybe even do harm, however unintentionally, to Lennie."

"I know you think the solution is to go to therapy again. But will I be seeing a therapist for the rest of my life? I'm tired of running to one every time something difficult comes up in my life."

"Therapy isn't a sign of weakness. It's just a tool to help you heal. You've been through so much, and it's natural for past traumas to resurface during times of stress and change. Seeing a therapist doesn't mean you'll have to do it for the rest of your life, but it can provide you with the support you need right now. And you should talk Nathan into seeing someone as well."

"I did ask him to, after what happened last night, but I'm not sure he will."

"And what if he doesn't, Hannah?" Elena asks. "Then what will you do?"

I just don't know. I can't bear the thought of losing him, but I also can't risk returning Lennie to a home where she isn't safe.

A little while later, Elena opens up her store again and I'm finishing my second cup of tea while she chats with a customer. She left her phone on the coffee table between us, and I spot a WhatsApp message coming in.

It's from Josie, and to my surprise, I can see my name is mentioned. I lean forward to read it, hoping Elena won't see me. Josie's asking Elena if I'm okay, and if she thinks Josie should go and get Lennie from school today.

My heart sinks at the thought of my friends and colleagues all talking about me behind my back. Discussing my capabilities as a mother. And why would Josie bring up the topic of picking up Lennie, when I already told her there is no need, that I will? Why would she go over my head and ask Elena?

I know they all mean well, that they care about me, but it still hurts.

And if they knew the whole story about what Nathan and I did to create our perfect family, I don't think they would ever understand, and I certainly don't think they would care about my welfare anymore.

Would they want to take Lennie away from me?

# TWENTY-FIVE

## LENNIE

As we drive back home, I press my nose to the window, making the glass foggy with my breath.

We have been staying with Aunty Elena and Uncle Darius since Mommy got mad at Daddy. I don't mind because their house smells like lavender and old books, and it makes me think of fairy tales. It also means not being around Daddy.

But I miss my tree house, the salty air, and the way the ocean sings me to sleep. So, Mommy and I come back home sometimes after school when Daddy is at work.

"Are you excited to see your tree house, Lennie?" Mommy asks.

I nod. I hope Whisper will be there, waiting for me. I hug my sketchpad to my chest and listen to the crayons rattling inside their box. Maybe me and Whisper can draw together.

"Can I take a nap in my room before we go back to Aunty Elena's?" I ask, unbuckling my seatbelt when the car stops moving. I miss my own bed; it's comfy at Aunty Elena's, but it isn't the same.

"Not today, sweetie. Remember, we're only here so I can

check on the garden and you can play in your tree house. Then we have to leave. Go on then. Have fun."

"Okay." I get out of the car and skip ahead, my sandals slapping against the cool concrete as I head to the side of the house.

As soon as I reach the tree house, I climb up fast, and once I'm inside, I call for Whisper, but she's not here today.

Feeling disappointed, I climb down again and go to the beach to find some new shells for my collection. The sand is cool between my toes as I walk along, searching for pretty shells. I find two of the nicest ones, one that shimmers like a rainbow and another that's striped like a candy cane.

I put them both in my pocket and run back to check up on Mommy in the garden. She has her green gardening gloves on and the big floppy hat she wears when the sun is bright.

Whisper is my special angel who looks after me, but Mommy doesn't have one like me. That's why it's my job to protect her.

The garden is where Mommy feels happiest, but today she's even more sad. She is bending over the roses with her watering can, but her body looks like it's swaying a little from side to side. Suddenly, she stops and sits on the bench. Her hand presses her forehead, and she stays really still. Then she gets up again slowly and starts weeding again. But every few minutes, she has to sit down.

"Mommy, are you okay?" I go to her. "Do you want me to help you?"

"No, sweetheart," she says, her voice soft and distant. "I'm fine. Go and continue playing."

"I found some shells on the beach; do you want to see?"

Shells make people happy. Maybe when Mommy sees them, she'll feel better. I take the rainbow-colored shell and hold it up to her face, and her eyes light up for a moment as she watches it shimmer in the sunlight.

"Oh, sweetheart, that is absolutely stunning. You have such

a wonderful eye for finding treasures. Thank you for showing it to me."

I take out the candy cane-striped shell from my pocket and offer it to her too. "And look, Mommy, this one is even prettier. You can keep it."

She reaches out and takes the shell from my hand, gently running her fingers over its stripes and smiling. "Thank you, my sweet angel," she whispers and I can see tears in her eyes.

"Why are you crying, Mommy?"

"Because I'm so happy to have you as my daughter," she says, her voice quivering. "You bring so much joy and love into my life, and I'm just so thankful." She reaches out and hugs me.

"Can I go and play now?" I say, squirming out of her arms again. She feels better, so I'll go and check if Whisper is in the tree house now.

I skip away from Mommy, feeling as light as a bubble because she's happy again. As I get nearer to the tree house, I can hear the soft rustling of leaves and the creaking of the wooden floor.

"Whisper, are you there?" I say quietly when I'm at the top, pushing open the trapdoor.

"Of course, my lovely Lennie." She's sitting on the bean bag, holding one of my books. "I just arrived."

"I was here before. Where were you?"

"Everywhere, with you on the beach, and even in the garden with you and your mommy. Don't forget that I'm with you even when you can't see me."

"Even at Aunty Elena's?"

"Even there." Whisper nods, her eyes shining like jewels. "And when I can't be close, I have an assistant who keeps an eye on things for me."

"An assistant? Another angel?"

"Yes. So, don't worry, you're always safe, with us looking out for you."

I sit down on the floor next to Whisper and she strokes my hair. "I'm sad today," I say.

"Why, little one?"

"I heard Mommy tell Aunty Elena that there won't be a wedding anymore."

Whisper sighs. "Sometimes, Lennie, things changing can be for the best. Your daddy gets angry, and he's upset your mommy a lot."

I nod, but my eyes burn, and I look away from Whisper. "I know. I don't think I want Mommy to marry Daddy anymore, but I really wanted to wear my pretty bridesmaid dress."

Whisper puts a hand on my head and says softly, "You know, Lennie, even if there isn't a wedding, I'm sure you'll still get to keep your pretty dress."

"Really?" I clasp my hands together. "It won't go away?"

"Of course not," she reassures me with a smile. "You can wear it to other special events. Maybe even your own parties in this very tree house."

"Yay!" I jump into Whisper's arms, squeezing her tight as I bury my face in her shoulder. "Thank you, Whisper."

When I let her go, I tell her that Mommy is still not feeling well.

"That's okay. I made more magic medicine while you were gone." She pulls a small bag from behind her and hands it to me. "Remember not to be seen when you give it to her."

I take it from her and look at it for a moment. "But the other ones didn't work."

Whisper sighs again. "It can take a few tries to find the right potion. Magic is a funny thing, you know? But I have a feeling that this one might just do the trick."

That night, Mommy and I go to a restaurant together and when she's talking to the waitress by the jukebox, I put the potion in her food. After dinner, when we're walking to the car I ask her if she's feeling better.

"What do you mean, sweetheart?"

"Is your head not hurting anymore?"

"You have to stop being worried about me, baby. Mommy is fine. I'm all better, I promise."

I really hope she's right and the potion is finally working.

Now if only there was a magic potion to get my daddy back too.

Maybe I'll ask Whisper for one.

# TWENTY-SIX

## HANNAH

The garden shears clink as I snip away at the hedges. It's early June and the sun's rays bathe the garden in warmth. I step back to admire my handiwork. The hedges stand tall and proud, with a satisfying neatness. Then a car engine hums into the driveway.

I straighten up, wiping sweat from my brow with a dirt-streaked forearm, and turn toward the sound. It's Nathan's sedan.

My heart pounds. He's not supposed to be here—not yet. I'd hoped for us to be gone before he returned from work, like yesterday when we were here. The man who emerges from the car is a stranger in Nathan's skin, a disheveled echo of the man who once seemed indestructible. He's dressed professionally in a suit with sharp lines and a perfect fit, but his hair and beard have grown wild and unruly. His eyes, which used to be bright and full of life, now seem haunted.

I am frozen as he approaches me, and the closer he gets, the harder my heart hammers against my ribcage. I take a deep breath, focusing on the scent of the sea, grass, and freshly turned soil.

"Hey," he says, his voice rough as his hands hang awkwardly by his sides.

"Hello," I say slowly.

When he says nothing more, the air grows thick and charged between us. Then he closes the gap, leans down, and places a kiss on my lips, and I let him.

"Where's Lennie?" he asks, straightening up, eyes searching past me toward the house.

"She's in the tree house. She loves it up there."

Nathan nods. He knows, just as I do, that for Lennie, it's more than a play area—it's her safe haven. A place where she can escape to a world of her own making.

"Can I—can I call her, say hi to her?" he asks hopefully.

"Let her play," I say softly. "She needs her space."

Silence stretches between us again.

"Hannah, I just want to see my daughter."

"Maybe she'll come down in a bit. She's so happy talking to her imaginary friend. I don't want her to be disturbed."

Nathan shifts from one foot to the other and runs a hand through his hair. "Fine. Can we talk, then?" It's more of a plea than a question.

My nod is robotic. "Yeah, sure."

The truth is, I really don't want to talk. I'm afraid we'll end up arguing again. But he looks so sad that I can't find it in me to turn him away.

I drop my shears, remove the gloves, and we make our way inside to the living room, where we used to spend countless hours, our limbs tangled, hands stroking skin and hair, watching movies or just relaxing and savoring the ease of each other's company.

"I'm so sorry," he begins finally, his voice low, almost inaudible against the whispering curtains. "For the vase... I shouldn't have thrown it." His gaze drops to his hands, and I can see a faint tremor. "I was having such a bad day, and that news about Elena and the hypnotherapy really shocked me."

I fix my eyes on him. "We all have bad days, Nathan." My voice is steady, but inside, I am a tangle of nerves. "But—"

"I know, bad days don't justify what I did." He lifts his head to meet my gaze again. His sharp blue eyes, usually so full of conviction, are deep pools of regret. "It won't happen again, Hannah, I promise."

I think he is sincere, I really do. But I need to be certain, for Lennie's sake, that we are safe with him. "Nathan, will you agree to see a therapist?"

He bristles, a stubborn tilt to his jaw. "I don't need therapy, Hannah. I can handle my own problems. I've dealt with worse on my own before. I can handle this."

"But you 'handling it' isn't enough anymore, not for us," I counter as I stand up, moving toward the door. "Lennie and I have to go."

"Wait." His hand reaches out, stopping me just as my fingers graze the doorknob. His touch is light, hesitant. "Fine. I'll talk to Darius, okay?"

I nod, tears in my throat.

Nathan is better than me at weighing every word he says, a skill honed in the courtroom. I don't think we need to worry about him letting something slip that he shouldn't. And I'm pretty sure that most of the conversations will revolve around his childhood anyway.

"Thank you, Nathan," I whisper, my voice cracking with relief. Maybe this is going to be the turning point we desperately need.

"You're welcome. But I need you to promise me something in return."

My heart thuds. "What is it?"

"Move back home, please. Let's carry on with our plans to get married."

His words echo through me and they seem so genuine, so earnest, that I can't help but waver. The memories of love and happiness we once shared, they tug at my heartstrings, reminding me of what we used to be.

Shouldn't I take this chance to mend what has been broken? To get my family back? Nathan is going to get therapy, and he is clearly so genuinely sorry for letting his temper get the better of him.

Maybe everything will be okay.

I let out a breath I didn't realize I was holding and slowly sink back onto the couch, its fabric cool against my skin. I rub my head, wishing I could think clearly, but everything is confused and blurred.

"Okay," I say at last. "We'll come home, at least for now."

Nathan's face softens as he hears my acceptance, relief flooding his features. Then he pulls me to him, his lips finding mine in a tender kiss. And in that moment, I allow myself to believe that we can rebuild what we've lost. We talk for a while, his hand caressing my arm, and we agree the wedding should go ahead. He's right, we've been through so much already. How could anything tear us apart now?

"Well then, I guess we should start planning the rehearsal dinner," I say after a while, noticing a strange thickness in my words, a struggle to pronounce them. I need to rest.

"Of course, I'll help with whatever you need." He pauses to scratch his beard. "Thank you, Hannah."

I place a hand on his cheek and gaze deep into his eyes. "I need a promise from you as well."

"Anything, baby. You name it." His eyebrows knit together.

"Promise me that I'll never again see what I saw that night. Your anger scared me and I don't want Lennie to see it."

Nathan's eyes brim with tears. He wraps his arms around me. "I promise, Hannah. I promise that I will work on my anger, on myself. I never want you or Lennie to be afraid of me. I love you both too much to let my anger destroy us. I will do whatever it takes to be the husband you deserve and the father Lennie needs."

Pulling away finally, I smile up at him. "Okay. We need to tell her we're moving back in together. But let me go talk to her first."

Nathan nods, his eyes still damp as he rests his head in his hands.

"Lennie," I call as I make my way to the tree house, trying to ignore the unsteadiness in my feet. "There's something I need to talk to you about. Can I come up?"

"No, Mommy," she calls back, her voice firm. "I will come down to you."

Respecting her wish, I watch as she descends the ladder carefully. She lands softly on her feet and rushes into my open arms, clinging to me.

"Lennie, sweetie, I have good news. We're coming back home. Mommy and Daddy will be getting married, after all. Daddy is going to get some help and we're all going to be okay."

I knew she would push back, but I couldn't have prepared myself for the torrent of emotions that floods her little face. She pulls away from me abruptly.

"But I don't want you to marry him," she whispers, her voice trembling.

I talk to her gently for a while and finally convince her to come back into the house with me, and before we go into the living room to join Nathan, she helps me to make us all some iced tea. She seems to perk up a bit as she does so, telling me she's adding her "magic ingredients."

I really want Lennie to see that everything's okay, that we're a family unit again and that both Nathan and I are focused on her.

So it frustrates me enormously when we go into the living

room and Nathan is pacing up and down the porch, on his phone, clearly having a heated discussion.

When he comes back inside, he quickly tries to smooth the anger away from his face and says it was a work call.

But I heard him mention Lennie.

Why would he be talking to anyone from work about his personal life, about our daughter?

And if it wasn't work, why is he lying to me?

# TWENTY-SEVEN

The scream is so loud and piercing that it startles me awake, my heart racing and adrenaline coursing through my veins.

I haven't heard my daughter scream like this since she was a little baby, and I know she must be dreaming, but it kills me to hear her in such distress.

Nathan is blissfully unaware next to me. Somehow he continues to sleep, snoring softly with one of his arms covering his head.

I run down the hallway, and Lennie's cries get louder the closer I get to her room. As soon as I open the door, I see her tossing and turning in her bed, and the covers are rumpled on the floor. I rush over and pull her into my arms, getting into bed with her.

"It's all right, sweetheart." I brush the damp hair from her face and kiss her. "Everything is okay, Mommy's here. You're safe."

"Mommy," she whispers and curls herself into my body.

"I'm here, my love. I'm here." I hold her closer. "It was just a bad dream."

As though my words have triggered something within her,

she starts crying, heart-wrenching sobs that rake through her small body, making her tremble in my arms.

"Do you want to tell me about the dream?" I ask when she calms down a little, but she simply shakes her head and continues to sob. It's only after I urge her for a few more minutes to talk to me that she finally opens up.

"It was Daddy," she hiccups and says nothing more as she buries her head into my chest.

"Daddy? You dreamt about Daddy?"

"He threw things and shouted, and he hit me." Her voice is so small, so broken, and my heart shatters.

We came back home yesterday, but I'm already thinking it was a bad idea, it was too soon. I was confused and feeling ill, and definitely not in the right frame of mind to make choices like that. But I don't know what to do, I can't keep messing Lennie around. She has barely spoken to Nathan. Last night he did everything to try and get her to let him in again, but the walls she has built up are impenetrable. She kept her distance, her eyes filled with fear whenever he tried to approach her.

I know something is going on with Nathan, and his temper has concerned me deeply. But he's the man I love, and I can see the genuine remorse and love in his eyes, and the pain he so clearly feels at his daughter's reaction to him. I might not have all the answers and I don't fully understand what is happening with him, but am afraid, too, of throwing everything away. Everything I fought so hard for. And I know Lennie is such an impressionable little girl, her imagination so vivid. I keep swinging back and forward, unsure what to do, how to be the mother she needs me to be.

"It was just a dream," I repeat to Lennie, stroking her hair, but she only begins to calm down when I bring all her favorite teddies into the bed with her.

As I pass her the new panda teddy, I gently reminder her

that her daddy bought it for her because he loves her. But then she tells me he didn't give it to her at all; it was Whisper.

Then she gasps and covers her mouth, as if she wasn't supposed to say that.

It strikes me as a bit odd, but Lennie is clearly so distressed and confused that I change the subject, instead telling her a story about a mermaid who swims far out to sea and finds a magical kingdom.

After she falls asleep again, I cover her up and head downstairs to the kitchen. When I picked up Lennie from art club earlier, Mrs. Perkins pulled me aside and told me that Lennie's art pieces have been rather dark lately. One of their projects was all about summer, and while the other kids painted happy scenes with picnics and sunshine, Lennie painted a sun that looked more like a fireball, with angry reds and smoky blacks swirling around it. She also drew a sad-looking little girl sitting alone in a corner, surrounded by broken toys. Mrs. Perkins was concerned, and she asked me if everything was all right at home. I assured her that everything was fine, but I hoped she didn't see the worry on my face.

In the kitchen, the blinds are up, and I can see the star-studded sky above the garden, the night breathtakingly clear. It's a beautiful sight, but suddenly my mind jerks me away from it.

I'm back in a memory from my childhood.

It was an evening after dinner, and I was playing with my doll, Pepper, brushing her long black hair when my father walked into the room. I could see immediately that he was having a bad day. Just from looking into his eyes, I knew I was about to be his punching bag, his stress ball. I could already feel the pain even before his hand struck the back of my neck.

He had been on the phone earlier, discussing something about debts. Mom had gone out to meet a friend, so it was just me and him alone at home.

I was ten at the time and I knew that when my father was in a terrible mood, he took it out on me. I never understood why. I was only a child, and it broke my heart to see him transform from a loving father to a monster. I never knew what each day would bring.

It wasn't always like that. There were times when we were such a wonderful family, and he was loving and attentive. On those days, he bought me gifts and made me feel like the most special girl in the world. But then there were days when he turned into something else, something dark, and unrecognizable.

My mother never believed me when I told her he hit me. He made sure to always do it when she was out of the house. Despite the bruises, Mom buried her head in the sand, and I had to go through it all alone. Maybe she just didn't want to confront it and accept the kind of man she married.

I can't imagine Nathan ever being like my father. But am I doing the same thing my mother did to me? Should I believe my daughter, no matter how impossible it might seem?

I close my eyes, wishing I could open them again and find everything different. I desperately want to go back to seeing Nathan and Lennie attached at the hip, running around on the beach, collecting shells and playing hide and seek.

"Are you okay, Hannah?" I hear Nathan say behind me.

I don't turn around immediately but continue to stare out of the window, the pain in my chest deepening. Behind me is the man I'm about to marry, but things are so messed up right now. Was it a mistake to come back home, to give us another chance?

"Hannah," Nathan repeats, "are you okay?"

No, I tell myself firmly. I know this man. I have known him since we were children. There's no way he would not care about his daughter's pain. There's no way he would hurt her.

I wipe away my tears, turn around slowly and nod, then shake my head. "Honestly, I don't know. Lennie had a bad dream. She was screaming. She said the dream was about you, about a time when you hit her."

Nathan pinches the bridge of his nose. "Hannah, please tell me you don't believe this."

"I'm just telling you—"

The speed at which Nathan slams his fist into the table makes me jump out of my skin.

"Dammit, Hannah, you do believe her, don't you? You really think I'm capable of that?"

"I don't know what to believe, Nathan. I don't," I say, stumbling backward.

"You seriously think I'm a monster? After everything we've been through, I can't believe you trust me so little."

When I say nothing, he pushes back his chair, knocking it to the floor, and without picking it up, he walks out of the kitchen. A few minutes later, the front door bangs shut.

I feel like the worst person in the world, and I know I'm going to need to make a decision now. What is the right thing to do, for my daughter?

# TWENTY-EIGHT

## LENNIE

In the morning after breakfast, Daddy tries to talk to me, but I don't say anything back. I'm still mad that we came back home, and I don't want him and Mommy to get married anymore.

When I see his face start to get angry, I quickly finish my cereal and run upstairs. Running up the stairs is not allowed, but I want to get away fast. I don't like Daddy's angry face. Whisper came to see me in my room again before I went to sleep last night and she told me to stay as far away from Daddy as I can. She says I should stop thinking about him as my daddy, because he isn't really. She said that I'm like a princess in a story, taken away from her real parents; a king and queen in a castle far away. And one day I'll get to go back to them and live in their magical land.

I can hear Daddy walking around at the bottom of the stairs, calling for me to come and talk to him, but I ignore him. Inside my room, I close the door. Then I sit on the floor, leaning my back against it. If Daddy tries to open it, he still won't be able to come in because I'm strong. I'll push very hard with my back. I wait and listen, but he doesn't come.

I can hear every sound in the house from here. Mommy and

Daddy are still downstairs and they're arguing again. I'm scared for Mommy. Maybe Daddy will hurt her too, like Whisper said. I stand up from the floor and slowly walk out of my room.

They are in the living room, so I sit on the stairs where they can't see me. Daddy's voice is getting louder and I'm starting to get scared, so I run outside to my tree house.

I'm so happy to find Whisper up there waiting for me.

"Are you okay?" She hugs me tight.

I like it when she hugs me. I also used to like Daddy's hugs, but I don't anymore.

"I'm scared of Daddy," I say to Whisper.

"I know, pumpkin. But I'm here now. You know I'll never let him hurt you."

"Thank you, Whisper."

"And you know what?" She cups my face. "I have a surprise for you that will make you feel so much better."

"A surprise?" I feel myself grin. I haven't been smiling much lately. But I love Whisper's surprises.

She reaches under the bed and pulls out a box wrapped in shiny gold paper. "Here it is."

"Can I open it?" I ask, bouncing up and down.

"Yes, of course you can."

I take the present and sit down on the floor with it, and while Whisper watches me I pull away the wrapping paper and open the box.

Inside, there is a small case, like the ones Daddy carries when he goes to court.

"What is this?" I ask, feeling excited.

"Have a look inside." Whisper smiles and lifts the case from the box. "Go on, press that button under the handle."

When I do, the case pops open, and inside are many coloring pencils, crayons, paints, and also a notebook with lots of empty pages.

"Lennie, I know you love to draw. But do you know that I'm

very good at drawing too? I want to teach you. I can show you all my tricks."

"I know how to draw really well already. I go to my school summer art class every day."

"I know you do, but I want to show you how to draw even better. You're going to become a real artist."

"I like that idea! What are we drawing first?"

"We're drawing your feelings. How about we draw how you feel about your daddy?"

"I feel angry." I pick up a green coloring pencil and hold it up.

"Why are you so angry with him, Lennie?"

"Because he keeps making Mommy sad and shouting, and he doesn't spend time with me anymore. And you said he doesn't love me, and that means he broke his promise. Because he said he'd love me forever."

"Good." She pats me on the head. "Now why don't you draw how angry you are? You will draw as many emotions as you can. Let me show you."

Whisper pulls out a big, black pencil from her bag and opens a special book. She sits me on her lap and takes my hand in hers, helping me move the pencil across the page.

The pencil moves fast and makes squiggly lines that show how mad I am. Then like magic, there is a man on the paper, a man with a big frown on his face and angry eyes. His hand is raised in the air like he wants to hit something.

"Who is that?" I ask Whisper.

"That's your daddy, Lennie. But we're not done. Now we'll draw you."

Softly, Whisper holds my hand, and we keep drawing. My pencil dances across the paper, making me look real. I see myself next to the scary man, and my hands are covering my head.

"What's that?" I point to a blob on the floor next to me.

"Those are your tears," Whisper explains gently. "Your daddy is hurting you and you are crying, but it's okay to cry, Lennie. It's okay to let your emotions out on the paper."

"Daddy looks scary. I don't like it."

"But you feel better now, don't you?"

I nod my head and smile because I want Whisper to be happy, but I'm not sure I feel better. I look down at the drawing I made. I don't remember Daddy hurting me like that, but Whisper said it was true, and she never lies. "Can we color it in?"

"Of course, Lennie! You can color it however you want. Pick any colors you like to show your feelings." I walk over to the table where the box of crayons sits, my eyes lighting up at all the bright shades. Coloring is my favorite part of drawing.

Then I hear Mommy's voice calling for me in the house.

"You need to go, Lennie, before your mommy comes looking for you. You can come and color in later. I'll hide everything under the bed."

I stand up and give Whisper a big hug before I climb down the ladder and run to the house, hoping Mommy and Daddy have stopped fighting now.

I find Mommy standing on the porch, wearing her yoga clothes, and she smiles and takes my hand.

"Want to join me for some yoga?"

"Yes. Can I wear my yoga clothes too?"

"Of course you can. I already put them out on your bed. Go ahead and get dressed, then we'll meet in the living room."

Upstairs, I put on my soft, stretchy yoga clothes. They make me feel cozy, like a warm hug. I hear the soft music Mommy is playing downstairs, and it makes me feel happy and calm.

When I get to the living room, Mommy is there with her mat and mine is there too, all rolled out next to hers. The room smells like the sage incense Mommy likes to light sometimes when she does yoga.

I sit down on my mat with my legs crossed, and Mommy smiles at me. The music is so peaceful, like when you close your eyes and pretend you're in a magical land.

We start by taking big breaths, in and out. Mommy says that when we blow out, the difficult feelings go away too. I breathe away the sadness I felt when I saw the drawing Whisper did for me, and it feels nice.

Then Mommy and I stretch our arms up high, like reaching for the stars. I try to touch the ceiling with my fingers, but I'm too small.

We do more stretches, like being a big tree with branches that sway in the wind. Then we lay down on our mats, and Mommy says it's time to relax. I close my eyes and imagine myself floating away on fluffy clouds to the happy kingdom where my magical mommy and daddy live.

I can't wait to go there one day, away from Daddy. Maybe my mommy from this world can come too. But would she want to stay with Daddy instead?

# TWENTY-NINE

## HANNAH

The moment I step out of Honeywood, the hot, sticky air envelops me. I pause to take a swig of water and a pill for my headache, and then take deep breaths, trying to calm the anxiety that has been plaguing me since Lennie and I returned home last week.

Then my phone vibrates and when I look at the screen, I see an unfamiliar number. "Hello?" I sound a little frail and distant, strange even to my own ears.

"Hannah, it's June Crane. Are you on your way?" The woman's voice is sharp, edged with panic and something else... disappointment? "My baby shower is starting in ten minutes and the flowers aren't here. You said you would be here two hours ago."

June Crane. The name doesn't ring a bell, and I feel a lurch in my stomach. "I—I'm so sorry, June."

A baby shower? Why wouldn't I remember all the planning, the emails back and forward that confirmed the booking? Why is my mind going completely blank here?

"We've been trying to reach you for over an hour now. The

event starts in literally ten minutes, and we even stopped by your shop. No one's there."

I pause on the sidewalk, the world tilting slightly under my feet. How could I forget this?

"June, I can't apologize enough. I... This has never happened before. I'm afraid the truth is that I forgot. I'm so sorry." What can I say?

Lately my mind has been scattered, like puzzle pieces waiting to be put together. And nothing seems to be helping, not the pills Nathan has been giving me to help the headaches, and not the glasses of wine late at night that I drown myself in, hoping they will quiet my thoughts.

We've been home for a week now, and Lennie has barely spoken to Nathan, even though he's been trying everything to get her to let him in again. It feels like the walls she has built up are impenetrable. It breaks my heart to see the desperation in Nathan's eyes as he reaches out to our daughter every day, pleading for her to trust him again. And it's not even just Nathan she's pushing away anymore. I've been trying to connect with her, to get her to laugh and play with me, read her favorite books, but all she wants to do is go and talk to her imaginary friend Whisper.

I've decided she really needs to get therapy, it's the only way forward. I'm going to talk to Darius about it soon, but I've been dragging my feet, because I remember how painful therapy was for me. It was necessary, and I know it's important for Lennie too. But she's already so fragile, she's been through so much emotionally, and I'm afraid of putting one foot wrong, making a mistake that would shatter her already fragile psyche. I'm doubting every thought I have and every decision I make, terrified of doing anything that would hurt her.

Nathan was so upset that night when Lennie had the nightmare, and he accused me of believing the worst of him. He hasn't had another anger outburst since then, but I can no longer relax. I'm walking on eggshells, watching and waiting in fear, wondering if it's only a matter of time before the next explosion. I nearly left him again that night, I'd started packing up my suitcase when he got home, but he begged me to stay. And I did, only because he is keeping his promise; he has had two sessions with Darius already, and he agreed Lennie should get therapy soon too. I'm hoping this will help Nathan address his anger issues, and mend the shattered bond between him and our daughter. Isn't it worth trying? Isn't our once happy family worth fighting for?

I really need it to work, I need everything to be okay again. Honestly, I'm falling apart. It's hard to think clearly when your brain is filled up with fog and you keep forgetting what you did even hours earlier. The stress has just become too heavy, and I don't think I can handle much more.

If I'm honest, it's not just that I'm hoping therapy will fix things for Nathan and Lennie. I'm also scared that if I leave Nathan, I won't be able to look after Lennie on my own. What if I mess it up? What if I put her at risk? What if I go back to those dark days, the ones I thought I'd left behind?

What if she's taken away from me?

I'm really struggling to trust myself now, far more than I'm struggling to trust him.

"Please tell me you're joking. You forgot?!" June is saying, her voice rising in anger.

Heat wafts in waves from the pavement, wrapping around me as I tighten my fingers around my phone. I swallow hard.

"I'm so sorry. I—I'll make this right. I can be there in half an hour with the flowers, June," I say, my voice barely more than a whisper over the line.

But I know some mistakes can't be undone; there are consequences.

There's a pause, and then June exhales sharply, her disappointment and annoyance palpable. "Hannah, by the time you get here, it'll be too late. The guests are arriving—" Her voice breaks, and I hear the clink of silverware in the background, the murmur of voices. "We'll... we'll make other arrangements."

I squeeze my eyes, trying to stave off the hot tears threatening to spill out. This woman trusted me on one of the most important days of her life and I've let her down.

"June, I'm so sorry," I choke. "You will have a full refund. I'll process it immediately. Please believe me, I never meant for this to happen."

"Sorry just doesn't feel good enough, Hannah." Her tone is resigned now, not angry, and that somehow makes it worse. "I'll be expecting that refund today."

"Of course, of course," I stutter. "I—"

The line goes dead, and I'm left staring at the screen. I glance around me at the crowded street, but dots appear before my eyes, blurring the faces of passersby. Everything feels so distant and the world itself seems to spin around me. I take a heavy step, then another, pushing ahead slowly toward Bliss & Twine.

Finally I slam the door behind me, the familiar tinkle of the bell mocking me as I step into the space that used to be my sanctuary. The scent of lilies and roses does little to calm me down today. Being a florist has always brought me so much comfort. Flowers used to be my refuge when the world turned ugly. When I struggled to forgive the ugliness within myself. But now I can't find any peace here either.

Lila should be arriving in half an hour when I leave to get Lennie from school, but for now I'm alone. At my office desk, my fingers fly across the keyboard, pulling up orders, searching for an explanation for how on earth I could have forgotten a baby shower. Anything that would excuse such a big mistake.

There's nothing. There's no record of the baby shower order, nothing at all.

I punch in the client's name, and finally there it is—an email stamped Thursday, twenty-eighth of May. That's two weeks ago. It contains all the details of sunflowers and yellow daisies for June's baby shower. It's in the Archive folder, not the Spam folder, and it clearly says that the order was confirmed over the phone.

I scroll through the rest of my inbox, wondering if I will find a follow-up message from June, confirming any changes or updates. But there's nothing.

"Damn it, Hannah," I curse myself, furious and frustrated to the max. How could I have been so careless?

It's like enormous chunks are flaking away from my recent memory. I asked Nathan the other day about the panda he gave to Lennie, the one she said was from Whisper. And he knew nothing about it at all; he just looked at me like I was crazy. He'd tried to speak to Lennie and engage her in make-believe about her toys, and she'd told him the panda was from me. Had I really just completely forgotten about it?

What other things have I forgotten about? With trembling hands, I push back from the desk and head to the small fridge tucked under a counter laden with ribbon spools and floral wire. My reflection in the stainless-steel surface doesn't look like me anymore. It's haggard, eyes rimmed with red, a stranger wearing my skin.

The pop of the champagne cork is as loud as a gunshot in the silence. As I pour the liquid into the glass, bubbles rise to the surface. I keep champagne in the fridge for when we have a particularly large order to celebrate, but today I need it myself. The liquid shimmers in the glass as I lift it to my lips, then I stop.

"You can't do this," I whisper, setting the glass down. My mind races to Lennie, her smile, her laughter, the way she looks at me with so much innocent love and trust in her eyes. She's waiting for me to pick her up from school. I cannot fail—not when it comes to her.

If I start drinking from this bottle, I know I won't be able to stop until I've drowned myself in regret and despair.

Like I've been doing a lot lately, after Nathan and Lennie are fast asleep.

"Pull yourself together," I order the pale woman reflected in the fridge, and I take a deep shaky breath.

Lila will be here soon. I will be ready and composed, the perfect picture of a woman who can handle anything—even when I feel like I'm splintering apart.

So, instead of the champagne, I open the fridge again and pull out a bottle of Elena's lemonade. Then from a drawer, I fetch the bottle of the pills Darius prescribed me—my lifeline. I shake out two capsules.

"Take as needed for anxiety." I tip back my head and swallow them down with a gulp of lemonade.

The bitter taste lingers on my tongue and I grimace, but the lemonade helps to wash it down and, slowly, I feel the knot in my chest loosen. It's a temporary relief, I know, but one that I desperately need in this moment.

It feels like I'm losing my mind, but I can't reveal the extent of it to anyone. With my family's history of mental illness and my own, I know I could potentially even lose my daughter. I need to be very careful, to hold it together, or at least to keep up the facade of stability, even when I feel like I'm unraveling.

As I finish the glass of lemonade, a knock on the door startles me. Lila's here. I take a deep breath, forcing a smile to my lips, and go to open the door. "Hey, Lila," I greet her, trying my best to sound upbeat.

"Hi, Hannah," Lila replies, her voice laced with concern as she fixes the scarf she has twisted around her long black hair. "Are you okay? You look a little off."

"I'm fine, just a little tired," I say, brushing off her worry as I run her through what needs to be taken care of in my absence.

But before I can step out, Lila extends her hand, holding out a brightly colored children's book. "Oh, before I forget," she says, her eyes sparkling with excitement, "I got this for Lennie. It's *Rapunzel*, you know, the story of the princess who discovers her mother is not really her mother and has been keeping her captive."

"Yeah, I know the story." I glance at the book then back at her. "That's so kind of you, Lila, but Lennie actually already has a copy of *Rapunzel*."

Lila doesn't seem deterred, her determination evident in the set of her jaw. "I know, but I thought she might appreciate having another copy, especially from me. I know she loves the story. This is also a different edition and these illustrations are different, more vibrant. It's actually my favorite book from when I was a child."

I hesitate for a moment, my stomach tightening with a twist of paranoia. Why does Lila want to give Lennie something so personal and meaningful? It's kind of her, but wouldn't she want to keep the book for her own child, one day? I think back to that strange text on Nathan's phone, the one I think I must have imagined.

I'm clearly too tired to think straight, my anxiety causing me to second-guess everything. So, despite my reservations, I accept the book with a grateful smile. "Thank you, Lila. I'm sure Lennie will love it."

With that, I tuck the book under my arm, then I'm out the door and walking slowly to my car, feeling like I'm suffocating in the heat with each step.

"Pull it together, Hannah," I whisper to myself. "For Lennie."

# THIRTY

"Looks like you have a visitor," Josie says as she walks past me on her way to the till, where two customers are waiting. "Mr. Handsome Fiancé is about to walk through that door."

"Nathan?" I look up from cleaning the water fountain and peer through the window in time to see my fiancé get out of the car on the curb by Bliss & Twine. For a moment, he just stands there, his hands in his pockets.

He looks like himself again, clean-shaven, and his hair combed and neat.

There he is: the distinguished, calm, and confident man I fell in love with, the man who has the power to own a court-room and then come home and play make-believe with his daughter. The man I would do anything for.

On the days he goes to the office, he usually gets so absorbed in work that he rarely has the time to step away. So I did not expect him to come to see me at the shop today, and certainly not after what happened last night.

After we put Lennie to bed, I mentioned again that she should see a therapist herself soon. I'm getting increasingly concerned, not only about what Lennie keeps saying about

Nathan, but also about this imaginary friend of hers. Before the end of the semester, her schoolteacher told me Lennie keeps to herself in the class, that she doesn't have many friends, and when I ask Lennie who her best friend is she just says it's Whisper.

I don't know how to help her out of her bubble and into the real world, and I'm worried that the longer this imaginary friend phase lasts, the harder it will be for her to tell truth from fiction. But Nathan had changed his mind, and we had a big fight over it. The bottom line is, he is worried that the therapist will take Lennie's side and believe whatever she tells her about him.

Our argument was so intense that this morning, we barely said a word to each other. But here he is now, and arguing is the last thing on my mind. I frankly don't have the strength for it, especially with this lingering headache that just won't shift.

I desperately want everything to go back to normal between us. And of course I'm still upset, but right now, I appreciate that he's trying. I watch as he makes his way to the door and I feel a sudden urge to run to him, to throw my arms around his neck and pretend there's not this dark cloud hanging over us.

The bell chimes as he enters and looks around, his gaze sweeping over the flowers. It's been a while since he came here. Our eyes meet and I smile back. God, I miss him. I really do. It's still there, after everything that has happened. The deep soul yearning I've felt for him for so long, that magnetic pull, that overwhelming feeling that without him I'm lost and untethered, like an astronaut floating away into the darkness.

"Hey, sweetheart," he says, walking over to me. "Busy day?"

I shrug as I cross the distance between us. "My days are always busy. Making the world a beautiful place is hard work, you know?"

"I can understand that," he says with a grin. But now that we're standing in front of each other, I see it again, the emptiness in his eyes, the heaviness.

He's here and he's smiling, but he's still a shell of himself. Maybe it will just take some time before he comes back to us fully.

"Come here." He opens his arms and I walk into them without hesitation, and while Josie and Lila make themselves busy around the spacious shop to give us some privacy, we hold on a little longer to each other.

"I didn't know you were stopping by today," I say when we finally pull apart.

"Spur of the moment. I was meeting up with a client and decided to drop by afterwards and take you out to lunch."

Tears fill my eyes instantly. What he's doing is such a small gesture, I know, but it honestly feels like he's giving me a lifeline.

"Hey, you're crying?" He brushes my cheek with his thumb.

"I'm sorry. I'm just a little emotional, I guess." I pull my gaze from him to see some customers enter. Now's not the time or the place for this. "I'm just tired."

"Then allow me to take you out of here for a while. Do I have permission to take my fiancée out to lunch?"

"Yes, you are allowed," I chuckle.


Ten minutes later, after I finish up a few tasks, we head out of Bliss & Twine and he drives me to the Stonehill Tavern, a quaint little diner by the river on the other side of town from the beach. It's a place where we have made some lovely memories over the years.

The atmosphere is serene, with soft jazz music playing in the background and the gentle murmur of conversation filling the air. The decor is rustic, with dark wooden furniture and dim lighting. We settle into a booth by the window, where warm sunlight pours in and we have a beautiful view of the water. It almost feels like a first date.

"I think we should talk about yesterday," he says after we order our food; shrimp and rice for me and steak for him. "I said some hurtful things and I regret every word."

He certainly did say some hurtful things that caused the argument to escalate. Words can be weapons and nobody can take back the damage they do, any more than they could erase a wound they physically inflicted. Or a life they took.

"I know. I did too." I squeeze his hand. "Can we please just move on from this? You're going through a painful time, and it will take a while before you heal. But we need to be careful about not hurting each other in the process or, more importantly, hurting our daughter."

Dipping my head to the side, I gaze into his ocean eyes and take a deep breath. "Nathan, are you sure you want to get married soon? I just wonder if we all need a bit more time."

"No, please, no." He suddenly gets to his feet and comes to kiss me hard on the lips before returning to his seat after a moment. "I want you, me, and Lennie to get back to normal, to be a happy family. I want you to be my wife. We've waited too long."

I smile at him with warmth spreading through my chest, as the waiter brings us our food.

As we eat, we avoid talking about difficult subjects and focus on happier things such as our wedding, and the rehearsal that will happen the night before.

"Have you finalized all the bookings for our honeymoon, by the way?" I ask.

"Of course. Rhodes is waiting for us. I hope you're ready for the adventure."

"I am. I'm so happy you are taking time off so we can go immediately."

"I wouldn't have it any other way."

Elena and Darius have offered to have Lennie stay with them while we are on honeymoon, and I'm looking forward to some quality time with Nathan, even though we'll both miss Lennie a lot.

"I have an idea," he says, pouring peppercorn sauce onto his steak. "How about we pick Lennie up from school together today and take her for ice-cream? We could spend some time together as a family?"

I hesitate, wondering how Lennie will react to this idea. But we do need to start rebuilding our family, and I know she needs to see that her father is trying.

So, I smile at Nathan and nod in agreement. "That's a fantastic idea. But I took her out for ice-cream yesterday. We could do something else. Or what the hell! It's Friday, so let's just do ice-cream again at a different place for a change." I push back my chair. "I'll be right back."

I walk into the ladies' room and clench the edge of the sink tight, closing my eyes and pulling in deep breaths. I suddenly feel dizzy again.

Then I notice it, a scent I recognize, a dance of lavender and vanilla.

Panic sweeping through me, I rush out of the bathroom, telling myself it's all in my head. But the scent is following me still, lingering in the air, wrapping itself around my neck like a noose that tightens with every passing second.

As I return to the table, Nathan shoots me a concerned look. "Are you feeling okay? You seem a bit flushed. Is something bothering you? Do you think it's something you ate?"

"It's nothing." I quickly swallow the water he passes me and try to push my thoughts back into the past, where they belong, where they will stay.

Later, as we make our way to the car, I can't shake the feeling that everyone is staring at me. And when I sit in the driver's seat, my eyes are drawn to Lennie's stuffed panda bear lying between the front seats. Its button eyes seem to follow me accusingly too, a silent judge.

# THIRTY-ONE

We're at Lennie's school, parked outside with Nathan sitting in the passenger's seat, clasping and unclasping his hands.

"Nathan, we don't have to do this, you know?" I say. "We can try another day, if you're feeling too stressed."

"No," he says, his voice steely and determined. "I want to do it today."

"Okay." I unclip my seatbelt. "I'll go get her. I do think this will be good for us all."

As I head to the school entrance, I watch as children who are attending the various summer activities at the school pass me by, skipping and laughing at each other's jokes. They all look so happy and carefree. But when I see Lennie, she doesn't even have a smile on her face. Instead of coming to meet me in the schoolyard, I find her sitting on one of the benches in the hallway, hugging her bag tight against her body. And instead of jumping up and running toward me like she used to, she approaches me slowly, as if she doesn't really want to.

"Hey, little one. I missed you today."

"Okay," she says simply and takes my hand.

I crouch down to her level, holding her shoulders with both my hands. "I have a little surprise for you."

"I don't want to go to Bliss & Twine," she says, and my heart deflates. She's usually so excited to go there; the fact that she doesn't want to anymore says so much.

"That's fine." I plaster on a smile. "What do you want to do, then? I know I took you out for ice-cream yesterday, so how about we go to Spinning Wheels? Daddy is waiting for us in the car. He can't wait to hang out."

Spinning Wheels is a new amusement park in town, and it's been on Lennie's wish list for ages. She used to chatter away about the colorful Ferris wheel and the teacup ride her friends at school had told her about. But now, she simply shrugs her shoulders, her eyes avoiding mine.

"Whatever," she mutters, her voice barely audible.

I swallow my disappointment. "Oh, honey, why are you so sad?"

"I just am. And I don't want to go there with Daddy." She's pouting now, like she did as a little baby. "Can I just go with you alone?"

"I'll be there right with you darling, we'll all be together. You don't need to worry, okay?"

Lennie sighs. "Fine."

"And sweetie, I want you to know Daddy is really excited to spend time with you. It was his idea, he misses you."

She shrugs. "He doesn't love me anymore."

"Oh Lennie, please don't believe that, it's not true. You are Daddy's favorite girl and he loves you more than anything. As do I."

"But Whisper told me that Daddy doesn't love me. It's true."

I used to be fine with Lennie having an imaginary friend. Many children do. But the thought of Whisper turning Lennie against her father, maybe against me? That can't be normal, and I don't know what to do about it.

"Darling"—I pull her to me and hold her tight—"Whisper is wrong. I promise you that Daddy loves you."

"Whisper is my guardian angel." Lennie detaches herself from me. "Guardian angels always tell the truth."

"Well, this time she's lying," I say a little too firmly. "Now let's go to the car."

"Hello, angel," Nathan says when we get in.

"Hi." Lennie stares out the window, arms folded across her chest.

"Did Mommy tell you that we're taking you out for ice-cream?" he asks.

"Change of plans. We're going to Spinning Wheels," I interject. "I think it would be more fun."

Nathan nods. "Ah, yeah! Sounds great, I can't wait."

I glance at Lennie in the rearview mirror and see no reaction whatsoever.

During the drive, Nathan tries to no avail to encourage her to speak. But to my surprise, the moment we drive into the parking lot of Spinning Wheels, her eyes light up. It's as if a switch has been flipped, and suddenly, she's giggling and bouncing in her seat.

"Mommy, look! They have all the cool rides!" Lennie exclaims gleefully.

We spend the next few hours at Spinning Wheels, going on every ride Lennie wants to try, so long as they're appropriate for her age. I accompany her on some of them and enjoy seeing her smile brighten up her face.

It feels like ages since she's been so carefree. As for me, I'm normally an adrenaline junkie, I love rollercoasters, but today my headache is growing and I feel lightheaded even from the gentle twirl of the kiddie rides.

Thankfully, Lennie is completely oblivious to my discomfort, her laughter echoing through the air. She still doesn't give Nathan much attention and only allows him to hold her hand for brief periods of time, but it doesn't dampen the magic.

Nathan doesn't give up, either. He continues to work hard to make Lennie laugh and smile. "Does someone want some cotton candy?" he asks as we walk past a colorful cotton candy stand.

Lennie's eyes widen and she nods, her pigtails bobbing up and down.

We get a giant stick of fluffy pink cotton candy and after a little while we head back to the car. On our way home we stop by our favorite pizza place, Drew's Pizza Shack, and Lennie's eyes light up again; she loves pizza from Drew's.

As we settle at our red and white checkered table, Nathan leans back with a contented sigh. "I can't remember the last time I had this much fun," he says, a genuine smile spreading across his face. "Thank you so much for this, my love."

I grin back. "You don't have to thank me. I'm just glad we could have this time together."

Lennie squirms in her seat, her eyes darting between us. "I want a pizza with lots and lots of cheese!" she declares mischievously.

Nathan chuckles. "Well, then, my little cheese monster, you shall have the cheesiest pizza in town."

When our server, Lana, comes over to take our order, she flashes us a warm smile. "It's been a while! The usual?"

Nathan nods and replies, "You know it, Lana. Hot pepperoni for me, mushroom and rocket for Hannah, and the cheesiest pizza you've got for the little one."

Lana scribbles down our order. "Coming right up. Anything else for Miss Lennie?"

"How about some garlic knots?" I suggest, knowing how much she loves them.

Lennie claps her hands together. "Yes, garlic knots! Lots and lots of them."

Everything continues to go well right up until we pay and are getting ready to leave.

"I just need the bathroom quickly. You two can go ahead and wait for me in the car," I say.

That's when everything comes crashing down.

When Nathan gets up from his seat first and reaches for Lennie's hand, she lets out a scream so loud that it reverberates through the entire restaurant. People turn their heads, their conversations abruptly halted. Panic floods my veins, and I scramble out of the booth.

"Lennie, what's wrong?"

"I don't want to go with that man. Don't leave me alone with him, Mommy."

Nathan freezes, his hand still extended toward her. His face is contorted with confusion and pain.

"What are you talking about, Lennie? Why are you talking about me like I'm a stranger? I'm your daddy." He tries to touch her again, but Lennie recoils.

"No, you're not. You're not my daddy. Leave me alone."

# THIRTY-TWO

"What the hell was that all about?" Nathan asks as soon as we get home and Lennie runs upstairs to her room.

Trembling, I pull up a stool at the kitchen island and cover my face with my hands.

"I don't know," I say finally. "I don't know why she's saying this. I'm honestly at a loss."

"Hannah, what... what's going on here?" His face is still a bit pale with shock. "I just can't understand why she's afraid of me. Why she'd say I'm not her father." Nathan's voice is almost a whisper.

"I know. And I think you might be right. I'm scared if she talks about it to someone else, they'll think you hit her. I know you'd never do that, but she keeps saying you did."

"But that's ridiculous." He shakes his head, looking close to tears.

"Look, I know. I don't know why she's got such an idea in her head. She keeps saying Whisper told her. I don't believe it, okay?" I get to my feet and try to touch him, but he shrinks away from me.

I watch as he sinks onto a stool. "My own daughter is afraid of me. This can't be happening."

At the pizza shack, it was clear that Lennie was genuinely terrified of being left alone with him. It reminded me so strongly of me when I was her age, afraid to be left alone with my own father.

"It'll be okay, Nathan. You've been kind of hard to reach lately and she's lashing out, that's all."

"My daughter thinks I'm a bloody monster, not just hard to reach," he snaps.

"Don't you dare shout at me," I say, beginning to lose my cool. "This isn't my fault."

He drops his head into his hands and grunts out loud. "I know. I'm sorry. So, you think this is all because I've not been spending enough time with her and I've been so down lately?"

"Maybe, I don't know. But I told her that you love her, and you just need time to heal after losing someone very important to you—"

"My father was not important to me." The ice in his tone sends a chill down my spine and I shift in my seat.

"But she doesn't know that, Nathan. She doesn't know anything about him. She doesn't even know that's who died."

"Yeah, you're right." He buries both hands into his hair. "What can I do to make her feel better? We should never have entertained the idea of her having that imaginary friend."

"I think your main focus right now should be rebuilding your relationship with Lennie," I say gently, reaching out to place a hand on his arm. "She needs to feel heard and understood."

"Should I... Do you think I should go up there right now and talk to her?"

"I'm not sure that's a good idea. Maybe you should just get some rest and talk to her tomorrow."

Nathan agrees and stands up, walking through the door, and he spends the rest of the evening in his office while I take care of some household chores. But after I help Lennie with her bath and tuck her in, I decide to bring up the topic.

"Lennie, why did you scream at Daddy like that at the restaurant?" I ask gently.

She fidgets under the duvet, her small fingers playing with the edge.

"I didn't want you to leave me with him."

"But sweetie, I was going to the bathroom, and Daddy was just going to take you to the car."

Her lower lip quivers, tears pooling in her eyes. "I didn't want him to get mad at me again and hurt me."

Just then, I see Nathan appear in the doorway, his eyes filled with pain. He rushes to Lennie's side, kneeling down beside her bed.

"What did you just say, sweetheart?" Nathan's voice cracks with emotion.

Lennie clings tightly to a stuffed animal, sniffling as tears stream down her cheeks. "Daddy... you... why don't you love me anymore? Why did you get mad and hurt me?"

"Baby, you know I would never hurt you." Nathan reaches out to touch Lennie's arm, but she flinches away.

"Lennie, why are you saying all these things?" I say. "Please, sweetheart, you can't believe that Daddy would hurt you." I hear my voice wavering.

"I want to sleep, Mommy," she says and turns in her bed to face the other way.

"No, Lennie," Nathan says firmly. "We need to talk about this. You know—"

"Nathan," I begin, "I think it's best if Lennie gets some rest now. We can talk about this another time."

His shoulders slump. "All right. But we can't just ignore this, Hannah."

I nod. How did we end up here? Just a few months ago, our little family felt so complete, so full of love and happiness. I wonder if we'll ever recover.

# THIRTY-THREE

I wake up from a horrible nightmare, my pajamas drenched with sweat. I could try to get back to sleep, but it's already morning and my alarm will ring any minute.

I'm exhausted and my head is pounding, but at least I don't need to work much this Saturday. I do have to stop by Bliss & Twine at some point and make a few deliveries, but that shouldn't take too long. I slide out of bed and go to the closet to change into some yoga pants and a tank top, but I have to move slowly because I feel so weak.

I head downstairs, closing the door quietly so that I don't wake Nathan. In the living room, I open the French doors that lead out onto the porch to let in the sea air, before I unroll my yoga mat, facing the ocean. The morning sunlight streams through, and I settle into a seated position where I take a deep breath and close my eyes, letting the stillness envelop me. The rhythmic sound of the waves crashing against the shore helps me to drown out my thoughts. I begin to stretch, feeling the tension in my muscles gradually dissipate, and as I flow through the poses, the outside world fades away.

Inhale, exhale. Inhale, exhale. *Grounded.*

It is in this state of tranquility that I hear Lennie crying upstairs, the sound pulling me out of myself. My stomach tightens as I rush up the stairs, and I find Lennie sitting up in bed, arms around her legs.

I rush to her side, sitting on the edge of her bed. "Lennie, sweetheart, what happened? Did you have another bad dream?"

"Yes, a really, really bad one about Daddy getting angry," she says, burying her face into my stomach.

I stroke her hair, feeling the rapid rise and fall of her small shoulders as she sobs.

She keeps saying things like that and it breaks my heart. Her relationship with Nathan is really shattered at this point and I have no idea how to get them back to where they used to be.

No matter what Nathan says, it's time for me to get her started with therapy. It might be painful for her, it might even make her more vulnerable for a while. But I can't just do nothing, and I'm clearly unable to help her on my own.

Nothing matters more to me than being a good mother to my daughter, and I've never felt like more of a failure than I do now.


Nathan joins us at breakfast with his cup of coffee and he tries again to get Lennie to talk to him. When she refuses, the frustration on his face is unmistakable.

I never thought it would come to this. It's like I'm at a crossroads where I have to choose between believing that my daughter can have the close father–daughter relationship that I always wanted for her, the one I desperately longed for myself, and my willingness to admit that we have both failed her.

My thoughts drift to my wedding, imagining myself walking down the aisle toward Nathan, but instead of excitement, now I'm overcome with dread.

Then I think of my increasing symptoms, the awful headaches, the dizziness, the spells of forgetfulness. And the document I filled in the other night while drinking my way through a bottle of wine.

This isn't how a bride-to-be is supposed to feel, to act. Am I making a terrible mistake?

After breakfast, Lennie can't get out of the kitchen fast enough, and when Nathan touches my shoulder as I'm washing up, I jump. "Oh, hi," I manage, trying to regain my composure. "Sorry, I'm just lost in thought."

He raises an eyebrow. "So, you're afraid of me too now?"

I swallow hard. "No, Nathan, of course I'm not."

But the truth is I *am* increasingly feeling uncomfortable around him, and I don't know how to stop it. It's as if Lennie's fears are now being transferred to me.

He puts both hands on my shoulders and draws me close to him. I want to pull away, but instead I find myself leaning in. His touch sends conflicting signals to my mind and heart. Without warning, tears start to well up in my eyes, and I turn away, hoping he doesn't notice.

"Hey, come on now." He pulls me closer, holding me tight. "I need you to trust me. You know me, Hannah. You know I love my daughter. I would never hurt her. Or you."

But I know he broke that exact same vow before, to another woman.

## THIRTY-FOUR

### LENNIE

My room is dark, but a little moonlight is peeking in through my princess curtains. I was sleeping, but now I'm awake because Mommy and Daddy are shouting again in their room. It's making my stomach feel achy and it's hurting my ears.

I pick up Mr. Buttons and hug him tight, whispering into his soft fur. "I'm scared, Mr. Buttons."

I don't want to stay here and listen to all the yelling.

"Mr. Buttons, should we get out of here?"

Mr. Buttons nods, so I get out of bed and tiptoe to the door.

We have to be very quiet so Mommy and Daddy don't hear us. I'm not allowed to go downstairs alone in the night.

I know the staircase really well, so I don't need to switch on the light. I can feel every step that will take me down, avoiding the places where it creaks. I hold tight to the railing with one hand while my other hand holds Mr. Buttons.

My heart is beating fast, and when I get to the bottom of the stairs, I get scared again. I understand why Mommy and Daddy don't like me to come downstairs by myself when it's dark. It feels strange down here and there could be monsters hiding in the shadows.

Maybe I should go back to my room and cover my head with the duvet, then I won't hear Mommy and Daddy shouting so much. I look back up the stairs, but then I hear someone whispering my name.

"Lennie."

I can't see her, but I know it's Whisper. She always comes when I'm sad.

Then she steps out of the shadows, and she looks bright and safe in her white clothes.

"Hello, dear Lennie," she murmurs as she pulls me into a hug. "Where are you going? Are you sad?"

I nod. "Mommy and Daddy are shouting and I wanted to get away."

"I understand that," Whisper says, stroking my hair. "So, how about we go on a little adventure? That way you won't hear them anymore."

"Okay, I love adventures. Where will we go?"

"I'll show you." She takes my hand and leads me to the front door.

I'm not allowed to be downstairs alone and I'm not supposed to leave the house at night. But Whisper is here, my guardian angel and my best friend. So nothing bad can happen to me.

Whisper holds my hand as we walk out through the door, and we go around the house to the back where I can see the sea.

"You like the beach, don't you, Lennie?"

"It's my favorite place in the world."

"Well then, let's go for a walk on the beach."

I've never been on the beach in the dark except when we had bonfire nights. That was when Daddy was nice, when he still loved me.

We start walking down the path to the beach, the moon showing us where to go. The sand feels soft, a little cool under my bare feet. I like how it squeezes through my toes.

The waves are loud, but it's a nice noise that makes me feel happy.

"Whisper," I ask, "does Mommy not love Daddy anymore?"

Whisper sighs. "Let's just say she loves you more than she loves him."

"Do you think she's going to send him away, then? I want him to go away."

"We'll just have to wait and see."

Once we're far away from the house, we stop and watch the waves. Mr. Buttons is happy that I also brought him with us because he doesn't get out of the house much. I hold him against my body but make sure his face is looking at the ocean.

"I know things are hard right now, Lennie," Whisper says. "But I hope you know that I'll always be here to take care of you, and my helper is watching over you too." Her voice is so calm, like the breeze.

"How do you always know when I'm sad?" I ask.

"A good guardian angel always knows when her favorite person is sad or in danger."

"Like magic?"

"Exactly. How about we sit down here for a while?"

I nod and sink down onto the sand.

"Do you think Daddy will love me again soon?"

Whisper touches my cheek. "Sweetheart, I wish I could tell you that everything is going to be okay, that he will love you again, but sometimes people change, and they don't change back. So, I've been thinking, would you like to go away with me? To get as far away from him as possible, to a place where he won't be able to hurt you anymore? We could go to the magical kingdom we talked about, where your other mommy and daddy live.

"I want to go away from Daddy, but I love my mommy. I don't want to leave her."

"But sweetheart, your mommy is not good at protecting you."

"But she loves me. You said that she loves me more than she loves Daddy."

"Yes, she does, but she doesn't know how to protect you. I do. I'm your guardian angel. That's my job."

"When do you want us to go?"

"Maybe we can even leave right now. It would be a great adventure."

I'm thinking about it, but then I hear a sound coming from far away. It's my mommy's voice.

I jump to my feet, picking up Mr. Buttons. "I need to go back home before Mommy knows I ran away."

"Okay." Whisper stands up as well. "Run along home, and we can plan our great adventure next time we meet. Remember to keep it secret."

"I promise."


When I get closer to home, I see that Mommy is not alone. She's standing with Daddy in front of the house.

"I'm here, Mommy," I shout back.

When Mommy sees me, she starts running toward me and when she reaches me, she wraps her arms around me, crying.

"Oh, Lennie, why did you leave the house all on your own, at night? You know you're not allowed to do that."

"It was too loud. I wanted to get away from the yelling."

Mommy holds me tighter but when Daddy comes and tries to hug me, she pulls me away and takes me to the house.

"I'm so sorry you heard us arguing, darling. It must have been really upsetting to hear that, but I promise you it's all okay. We're all right, and we love you so much. But please, please never do that again," she says softly when we get inside my room, and she sits me down on my bed. "It can be dangerous out there."

"I have Whisper to protect me," I say.

"No, Lennie." Mommy puts both her hands on my shoulders. "You can never leave the house on your own again, ever. And I don't want you to talk to Whisper anymore."

"But I wasn't alone, Mommy. I was with Whisper, and she's my guardian angel," I say.

Mommy continues to tell me to never leave the house at night and to stop talking to Whisper, until finally I nod and give her my promise.

When Daddy comes into my bedroom, I can see that his eyes look wet. I think he's crying like Mommy, but I don't understand why. He doesn't love me anymore, so why does he care?

"You really scared us tonight, Lennie," he says. "We were about to call the police, so they could look for you."

When they finally leave the room, I pick up my panda, Snowy, from where she fell onto the floor, and I put her carefully on the chair near my bed so she can see me. Whisper told me Snowy is one of her helpers and that she can magically see me through Snowy's eyes. It makes me feel safer to think that Whisper is watching over me in the night.

As I start to feel sleepy, after Mommy has tucked me in, I think about my big adventure with Whisper. I will wait until Mommy and Daddy are sleeping. Maybe I'll leave a drawing behind for Mommy, of the kingdom I'm going to, so she knows where to come and find me.

# THIRTY-FIVE

## HANNAH

After we've tucked Lennie in, we head back to the kitchen and I put on some coffee. There's no way I can sleep tonight, after my daughter ran out into the dark all on her own, because of us. Because of the fighting between her parents, the two people who are supposed to keep her safe.

The atmosphere between me and Nathan is thick with tension. Tonight feels like the point of no return. We don't have anything more to say to each other, and we're both clearly in shock. I can't believe we upset Lennie so much she left the home at night. She's always been scared of the dark, but clearly we scared her even more.

What would have happened if I didn't decide to go to her room to check up on her? If we hadn't been out calling for her so soon after she left, would she have kept running away down the beach? So close to the water? She's not yet a strong enough swimmer to be safe in the ocean on her own, but no child has a bigger imagination than Lennie, and she loves to pretend she's a mermaid or a pirate. Would she dive into the waves, never to be seen again?

Or would she come across another danger, out there alone

at night? A stranger, someone who might snatch her away from me?

I feel sick with anxiety at all the things that could have happened to her, could still happen, if ever she runs away again. "Nathan, we can't keep doing this. Last night you—"

"Yes," Nathan hisses, "it's always my fault, isn't it? I feel like I'm losing my daughter, and you're not helping."

The next few minutes are full of hushed, painful words until I finally leave the room, go upstairs and sink onto our bed, my heart heavy and my entire body feeling completely drained.

I never thought our daughter would feel the need to escape her own home.

To my surprise, when Nathan comes in he walks straight into the closet, coming out a few minutes later with the suitcase he uses when traveling.

"What are you doing?"

"To be honest with you, I don't know. I don't know a damn thing these days."

"You're moving out?"

He clenches his jaw. "If Lennie is scared enough to run away from me, maybe I should give her some space."

"Maybe you're right," I sigh. "We're so broken apart right now, I don't know how to fix us. We can't possibly get married like this."

"No, I really do want to get married. We've been through so much Hannah, we can't just throw everything away because we're going through a difficult time. All couples have their problems, all families do. We'll make this work, we just need to take some time apart to process and let things settle. It doesn't mean we don't love each other anymore. Let's not do anything hasty, okay? I will see you at the rehearsal." He meets my gaze. "I just need to be alone right now, and I want to give Lennie some time away from me, you as well. I'll check into a hotel. And after the wedding, you're right, we should get Lennie started on therapy. I'll talk to Darius about it this week. We'll all be okay."

I watch silently, tears falling down my cheeks as he packs his suitcase, and when he's done, he comes over to me, holding my hands tight. "I don't know what's happening to us, baby, but I really hope we can fix it. There's nothing I want more than that, to have my family back. I miss you. And I miss my daughter."

"I miss you too," I say, pressing my lips to his.

After Nathan leaves, everything shatters inside me. I wrap my arms around my knees, trying to stop myself from feeling like a complete failure.

After a while, I go to the closet and reach up onto one of the shelves, pulling out a box filled with photos of me and my parents.

I drop them all on the bed. My parents are smiling into the camera. In some of the photos, my father has an arm around my shoulders. Other times, I'm sitting on his lap, or I'm wedged between the both of them. A perfect, happy family.

As anger bubbles up inside me, I pick up the photos that have my father in them. Then I head to my desk and yank open the drawer, grabbing a pair of scissors. Gritting my teeth, I start snipping away, shredding every one of those photos to pieces.

I'm lying on the bed surrounded by fragments of my childhood when my phone rings; it's Elena. I press the phone to my ear, but I'm too racked by sobs to say anything.

"Hannah, what's happened? Are you okay?" Her soothing voice makes me cry even harder.

"Yes... No, I don't know."

"Do you want me to come over?"

"No." I blow my nose. "I'm going to be fine. It's just too much right now. Something happened."

"Yeah, I got a call from Nathan, and he told me you might need someone to talk to. He said you two had a fight?"

"It was terrible. Lennie ran out of the house onto the beach; if I hadn't noticed she was missing, God knows what would have happened to her."

Elena clears her throat. "Sweetie, with everything going on right now, are you sure you still want to get married in a few days?"

"I don't know." I swallow hard.

"I understand," she says softly. "This is a lot to process, and it's completely normal to feel unsure about everything right now."

"Is Gloria with you?" I ask when a familiar voice on the other end of the line interrupts my thoughts.

Elena hesitates for a second, then coughs. "Yeah. We... we went to the movies and we ended up going out for a drink afterwards."

There's a pregnant pause.

"Hannah, I hope you're not upset that we didn't ask you to come with us," Elena says uncertainly. "It's just that we thought you wouldn't want to go out, with everything going on."

"Sure, I get it. Thanks for the call. I should go. Get back to your drinks."

I wouldn't normally mind them meeting up without me, I'm not that needy. But a burning sense of insecurity is spreading through me; I feel like they might be shutting me out because I'm not easy company anymore. Am I really such a mess that even my own friends are avoiding me? I wonder if they've all been talking about me again, like Elena was with Josie.

I feel like I'm on the verge of losing everything, and I have never felt more lonely.

After a few hours of scrolling mindlessly through my phone because I can't sleep, I hear the sound of the bedroom door opening. Through blurry eyes, I see a shadowy, familiar figure standing in the doorway.

"Nathan?" I whisper, my voice hoarse from crying as I switch on the night light. "Is that you?"

He steps into the room, his face etched with worry. "I'm back," he says softly, then drops his suitcase. "I'm so sorry about everything, Hannah. I shouldn't have let it get to this point."

"What made you come back?"

"I just... We can't keep running from our problems. We need to face them together. And honestly, I know I've not been the best lately, but I'm worried about you too. I can see you're struggling, and I don't want to leave you to manage Lennie alone especially when you're feeling like this."

I wipe the tears from my eyes. "I'm just so scared. We're swinging back and forward, together and then apart, again and again, and I feel so lost. I don't know what to do anymore," I admit, my voice trembling.

He sits down beside me, taking my hand in his. "We'll figure it out. We'll fix everything. We always do, remember? It's you and me against the world. Always."

# THIRTY-SIX

I wake up in the morning to find Nathan's side of the bed empty. For a moment, fear grips me—what if he changed his mind and left again? I peel back the covers and head out of the bedroom, my heart pounding. The hallway is silent except for the soft hum of the central air system.

I pause at Lennie's door, pushing it open with the gentlest touch. She's still fast asleep, hugging Mr. Buttons to her chest. She breathes evenly, lost in dreams that I hope are peaceful and untroubled. I linger, watching her, drinking in her sweet expression, before I pull the door closed and go downstairs.

As I reach the bottom step, I can smell something rich and savory, the aroma of something being cooked. Nathan hasn't touched a pot or pan since his father died, hasn't once offered to help with meals. He let all those duties fall on me as he retreated further into his grief.

I go into the kitchen, and there he is, my Nathan, standing at the stove with his back to me. He's humming a tune I can't quite place, flipping pancakes.

"Good morning, my love," he says, glancing briefly over his

shoulder. "Have a seat, I'll have breakfast ready soon. Did you sleep well?"

I hesitate, my mind still grappling with the abrupt change in his behavior. "Yes, fine," I say, watching as he plates our breakfast: herby pancakes with scrambled eggs and crisp rashers of bacon.

"Where did all this come from?" I ask.

There's a smile playing at the corners of his mouth. "Well, I thought it was time for me to join you. To have breakfast together as a family. I know it means a lot to you, to start the day right."

I just nod, lost for words. It feels a bit like a dream. One minute Nathan was gone, and now he's back, acting like the perfect husband and father again.

"Here, my love." He pours me some coffee. "I'll go and wake Lennie in a bit."

"Thank you," I say. It's disarming watching him play the doting partner, after he nearly left last night. But my mind is swirling in fog these days, everything confused and abstract. Maybe I wouldn't feel so lost in our relationship, if I could just think straight for a few minutes.

"Anything else you need?"

I shake my head, tucking a loose strand of hair behind my ear. "No, this is great, it all looks lovely."

He nods and sits down with me.

We did make up last night. He did come back home. And yet, part of me feels as if the time we have together is borrowed, that any moment, another argument will explode between us and shatter the illusion of domestic bliss. I try to push those thoughts aside and focus on the present.

"Mommy?"

I turn to see Lennie rubbing sleep from her eyes as she pads softly into the kitchen. Her hair is tousled, and her brown eyes are blinking with sleepiness.

"Good morning, sweetie. We were just about to come get you." I open my arms for her to enter into for a hug.

"Morning, Lennie," Nathan says gently. "I made breakfast. Why don't you sit down with us and have some?"

Lennie's gaze lingers on him. Then, with silent steps, she approaches the table and takes a seat.

"Did you make pancakes?" she asks as the knot in my stomach loosens a little.

"Sure did," Nathan replies, his smile warm and reassuring. "And I made some just for you, with chocolate chips, the way you like them."

He places a stack of pancakes in front of her, dusted with powdered sugar, and I see my little girl's face light up.

"What do you say, Lennie?" I prompt.

"Thank you," she replies, beaming at us both.

My fingers curl around my mug and I exhale slowly, not realizing I had been holding my breath. I watch her pick up her fork and tuck in happily.

"Pass the salt?" Nathan asks, and I slide the shaker across the table.

"Thanks." He sprinkles it over his eggs, then continues to dig in, as if this shared meal is something ordinary that we do every day. Then slowly he begins to talk to Lennie, ever so gently drawing her out of herself, asking her about her dreams and her artwork, telling her a story he'd heard about a little boy who found a dinosaur footprint on a beach somewhere. He doesn't push her to open up about all the difficult feelings she's had lately, but I can see he's working toward it. He just wants to rebuild a foundation between them first.

I'm silent, unable to join in as they talk to each other. I can't shake the feeling that we're actors in a play where I can't remember my lines. As much as I want to believe that things are changing, that we might find our way back to the way things used to be, I'm still haunted by doubt. And there's a sharp pain deep inside my head that I just can't shift.

"Guess what, Lennie?" Nathan says when he finishes. "I've got a surprise for you."

Her fork halts mid-air and she looks up at him with wide eyes.

"You'll love it, I promise." Nathan hurries out of the room and returns moments later, a gift-wrapped box in his hands.

"Here you go, sweetie." He places the package in front of her, and then takes a deep breath. "I want you to know I love you, Lennie. I know things have been hard recently, and I haven't been the best of dads to you, and I'm really sorry." He chokes a little then, and clears his throat. "I've been talking to Uncle Darius, to help me understand my emotions and learn to handle them better. Helping people is his job and he's really good at it. And Mommy and I think you should talk to Uncle Darius too, soon. It's okay to need help sometimes, and it's good to talk to people when things get tough. It's okay if you don't want to spend much time with me right now, but I want you to remember that even if I make mistakes sometimes, I'll always love you, and I'd never hurt you. I've bought you something as a little reminder whenever you play with it, that your daddy loves you more than anything, and that will never change."

Lennie hesitates, then reaches out with small fingers to pull at the ribbon. The paper falls away to reveal a ginger toy cat. When Nathan flips a switch on its belly, it meows, takes a few mechanical steps on the table, and then rolls onto its back.

"Wow," Lennie breathes as she pats the synthetic fur.

"See? I told you you'd like it," Nathan says, the pride in his voice unmistakable.

I watch Lennie cuddling her new toy, and it's as if my heart is stitching itself back together, piece by fragile piece.

"Thank you, Daddy! Her name is Lily." She wraps her arms

around Nathan's waist. "Can I play with her in the tree house after art school?"

"Of course, sweetie," I say with a warm smile. "Take her to your room for now. I'll come up in a bit to help you get ready."

Lennie nods and darts out of the room. Just then, I catch a glimpse of movement outside in the garden from the corner of my eye. I go to the window, but there's no one there. Could it have been the branches swaying in the wind? My heartbeat races as I turn to Nathan. "Did you see that?"

He frowns. "See what?"

I shake my head, trying to push away the uneasiness creeping over me. "It was probably nothing. Just my imagination." I reach for a napkin to wipe the sweat from my forehead, pull in a breath and force a smile. "That was such a good idea, Lennie's gift. Where did you find it?"

He sighs. "Actually it was from someone I know. She said Lennie would love it. Look, Hannah, I know I haven't been the best father or husband lately. I've not been myself, but I promise you that I'm trying to change." He pulls me to my feet and into his arms. "I can't wait to get married to you. It will be perfect, and so will our life together. Our new beginning." He pauses. "But there's something you need to know first. Something I've been keeping from you. I should have told you before now, but there never seemed to be the right time."

I freeze, wondering what bombshell he's about to throw at me now. What more can this family take?

Slowly, Nathan sits down at the kitchen table, and stares at his hands.

"When I heard the news about my father's death, I discovered something else about my family."

"Go on," I urge him after a pause.

"Someone got in touch with me, someone we know, saying she's actually my sister. Apparently, when my mother left us, she was pregnant and she escaped, wanting to protect her baby from my father. Clearly, she didn't care enough about me to take me with her, or maybe she knew my father would never let her get away with taking away his son."

I sit down unsteadily, my mind racing with a million questions, but I wait for him to continue.

"This woman has been around us for ages, knowing that I'm her brother, that Lennie is her niece, but she never told us who she really is. She said she was too nervous that I'd reject her. She'd written a letter to me years ago and I never replied, so she thought I wanted nothing to do with her. Thing is, I don't remember receiving a letter at all, and it's obviously not something I'd forget. It must have been lost in the post. Then when she heard the news about our father's death, she reached out to me again thinking I might want some support. I was so angry, Hannah, that she'd been lying to us, not revealing her true identity. It reminded me so much of my ex, and all her lies."

"What did you do?"

Nathan shakes his head. "I yelled at her, I was furious, and the way she reacted to that... She told me I was like our father. I've been trying to ignore her since then. I just can't deal with this right now. And I know I should have told you before now, but I have been so confused about the whole thing. I didn't want you to pressurize me into building a relationship with her and letting her hang out with Lennie. The more time has gone by, the harder it's been to bring up. So, here it is, the whole truth. Lennie has an aunt, I have a sister. That's who the toy cat is from."

I interrupt him then, no longer able to hold back. "Nathan, who are you talking about exactly? Who is your sister?"

"Lila," he says in a low voice, finally meeting my eyes. "Your assistant, Lila."

. . .

I'm still reeling from Nathan's news when he receives an urgent call and has to leave for the office.

I make my way to the garden and take a seat by the fountain to gather my thoughts, and as soon as I sit down on the bench, I notice something at my feet—a cluster of small white flowers.

Picking up the delicate blooms, I study them closely, admiring their intricate petals before realizing with horror what they are.

This is poison hemlock. It's unmistakable. A deadly plant with small white flowers hiding dangerous toxins.

A plant I would never grow in my garden, especially with a young child who plays out here all the time.

I shoot up to my feet, dropping the cluster of blooms back on the ground as if it burned my skin.

My heart races as I glance around the garden.

How did poison make its way into my home?

I search the garden thoroughly for more poison hemlock, and don't find any sign of it, so I can only assume it was carried in on the ocean breeze somehow.

As the days go by, I focus on Lennie and Nathan, and try to keep up my strength.

Something is really wrong with me and I even briefly wonder if I might be experiencing early pregnancy symptoms, but the tests come back negative. I take some time off work and tell myself that as our family begins to heal, so will I, and I just need to coax my mind back into a place of clarity through yoga and gardening.

# THIRTY-SEVEN

On the day of our rehearsal, I open my eyes to a bright room, promising what should be a beautiful morning. But my heart feels impossibly heavy. Last night, I was tidying Lennie's room when I saw it: a piece of paper folded into a small square, and it changed everything.

I unfolded it to see a drawing that is now imprinted on my mind forever. It showed a small girl with pigtails crouched on the ground, shielding her head with her palms, and a puddle of tears next to her. A man loomed over her, his arm raised. The arrow pointing to the man read *Daddy* and the arrow pointing to the girl read *Lennie*.

I now reach under my pillow to retrieve it, and I trace my fingers over the figures.

Then my phone beeps on the bed beside me. A message from Nathan—who has already left for the office—appears on the screen, urging me to check my emails.

I open the email app and see a new message from him with the subject line: *A Letter to My Future Wife*.

I tap on the email.

My love,

We have been through so much together and waited for this moment for what feels like forever. I have never felt closer to anyone than how I feel with you. You are my true love, my heart, my everything.

You have to believe that I would never hurt Lennie or do anything to harm our family.

I apologize for not being the best at expressing myself lately, and I'm really sorry for not telling you about my sister for so long. I promise there are no more secrets between us, and all I can say is that I need you in my life and I can't wait for you to be my wife tomorrow. See you at the rehearsal tonight.

My vision blurs with tears. Just as I'm about to put the phone aside, it rings, and it's Elena.

Her voice comes through loud and clear. "Hey there, beautiful bride-to-be. Are you looking forward to the rehearsal later?"

How can I tell her the truth, that everything has already fallen apart? How can I tell her what I'm planning to do?

"Ugh, I feel like I haven't slept all night."

"Don't worry, we can cover up any signs of a sleepless night. That's the magic of makeup."

"Well, looks like I'll be relying heavily on that magic today," I reply. "I'll see you later."

After hanging up, I pull myself out of bed, feeling as stiff and weak as an elderly woman. I shuffle down the hallway to Lennie's room. The courage to talk to her, knowing what I need to do later, doesn't come to me immediately, so I just chat with her casually as I get her washed and ready for school.

"You'll look so beautiful in your bridesmaid dress tonight,

Lennie," I say. "When you come home from school, it will be right here waiting for you."

She looks up at me with her big, innocent eyes, and a small smile tugs at the corners of her lips. "I can't wait to be a princess."

"You are my princess, even without the dress." Sitting next to her on the bed, I take her hand in mine and pull out the drawing from my pajama pocket.

"Sweetheart, I need to talk to you about something. Did you draw this?" I ask.

Shrugging, she doesn't answer.

"Is this you and Daddy?"

After a few moments of silence, she finally speaks up. "I was drawing my feelings," she says softly.

"I see." I take her hand in mine. "Can you explain the drawing to me?"

"This is Daddy." She points to the figure looming over the small girl. "And this is me."

"Can you tell me what Daddy is doing here? And why is his hand like that?"

"He hit me," Lennie says, pointing to the raised hand in the drawing. "That's why I'm crying." She gestures toward the tears on the floor.

I squeeze my eyes tightly, trying to hold back the tears. "Honey, do you really remember Daddy doing this to you?"

She shrugs and says she's not sure, as she reaches for Lily the cat, pressing her to her body.

"Lennie, do you know what the rehearsal dinner means?"

"It means we get to practice for the big wedding tomorrow," she replies, her voice filled with excitement. "There will be lots of people and pretty decorations, and I'll be wearing my dress."

"Do you want to go, baby?"

"Yes, Mommy. I want to go," she says softly, her voice barely audible. "I want to wear my dress."

"And does that mean you changed your mind? Do you want Mommy to marry Daddy?"

"No," she whispers.


Closing myself in the bathroom, I sink against the door and dial Gloria's number.

"Gloria," I whisper when she picks up. "I need a friend right now."

There's a long pause when I finally finish spilling my heart out, and just as I'm about to ask if she's still there, she speaks.

"Hannah, nobody knows what this feels like better than I do, and I can promise you that if you don't do the right thing by Lennie and act now, you will regret it for the rest of your life. Like I did. Please make the right choice. You need to put a stop to this, right now. You know what you have to do."

I hang up the phone and look over at the bathroom cabinet where the door is slightly ajar, revealing neat rows of pill bottles.

Gloria is right: I do need to act. I've failed as a mother, and I'm going to make up for that now.

# THIRTY-EIGHT

## LENNIE

In my art club room, the clock is louder than Mrs. Perkins as she teaches us how to draw water that looks like it's real.

My legs swing back and forth under my desk because they don't know how to stay still today, not when I have so many important things waiting for me.

I don't want Mommy to marry Daddy. But I really want to wear my dress at the rehearsal, and I know they're going to get married anyway. So I'll not think about what Whisper said, just for a bit.

"Please, Lennie," Mrs. Perkins says, "try to focus on your work. A few more minutes, then we're done."

I nod and look down at my paper. Then I draw a big sun on the page, with arms reaching out like it wants to hug everyone. Mrs. Perkins said no more drawing angry suns like I did last time, so this one is a happy, yellow one.

I'm proud of my drawing, but I can't stop thinking about the rehearsal dinner tonight.

Finally, the bell rings so loud it makes me jump. I shove my crayons into their box and slide off my chair.

"Have fun tonight, Lennie." Mrs. Perkins smiles at me. "And have a great summer break."

"Thank you, Mrs. Perkins." I skip to the door, my heart racing.

But when I look outside, I don't see Mommy. Other kids are hugging their parents, but I'm alone.

Mommy promised that when I finish, she would be outside waiting for me.

"Don't worry, Lennie." Mrs. Perkins comes to stand next to me, putting a hand on my shoulder. "I'm sure your mommy will be here soon."

I try to smile, but I'm scared. What if Mommy forgot about me? Is she going to have the rehearsal dinner without me?

I sit down on the front steps of the school, feeling sad as everyone leaves with their parents until there are no more kids left.

Tears well up in my eyes as Mrs. Perkins finally leads me back inside. "It's okay, sweetheart. I'll give your mom a call and see what's going on."

I nod and sniffle, trying to stop my tears. Mrs. Perkins takes me to the office and dials my mom's number on the big phone. It rings and rings, but no one picks up. Mrs. Perkins frowns at me.

"Is my mommy not coming?" I ask in a small voice.

Mrs. Perkins lets out a big sigh. "Don't worry, we'll figure it out." She picks up the phone again and dials another number. "Let's call your dad," she says softly. And this time, someone finally answers.

# THIRTY-NINE

## HANNAH

The chill of the tiled floor seeps into my cheek, and my eyelids are heavy, as if they've been stitched shut. Through the fog of my semi-consciousness, I sense that something terrible has happened to me.

The living room door swings open with a creak and a thud, footsteps punctuating the silence, until a shadow looms in my line of sight.

"Hannah!" Nathan says, his voice low and hard.

I try to respond, to form words, but my mouth is dry, my lips refusing to cooperate. When I finally sit up, I spot a packet of pills lying beside me, an empty bottle of wine next to it.

Nathan looks down at the pills as well, then back at me. "Jesus Christ, Hannah. How could you?" His tone cuts deeper than any knife.

"Mommy, are you playing?" Lennie's small, worried face hovers at the edge of my vision, but Nathan immediately steps in, blocking her view.

"Go to your room, Lennie," he commands, his voice steady but edged with sharpness.

"Is Mommy okay?" Lennie asks.

"Yes, she just needs some rest," he replies without looking away from me. "Off you go, Lennie."

There's a blur of golden curls as Lennie retreats from the room.

"Look at you," he hisses, crouching down, his eyes ice-cold. "You promised. You promised Lennie you'd pick her up, and you just left her there waiting for you while you washed your pills down with wine. On the day of our rehearsal."

I want to cry, to scream, to beg for forgiveness, but I can't bring myself to speak. I blink away the fog, trying to focus on his face.

Then he suddenly makes a strange noise, and pulls me close to him, wrapping his arms around me tightly. It's a hug unlike any other he's given me before, as if he's terrified of letting me go. I can feel the desperation in his grip.

The pills. The alcohol. My blood goes cold. I know what it looks like.

When he lets go, there are tears in his eyes, but I can see anger is still there, simmering just beneath the surface.

"Rehearsal dinner," I murmur as he helps me up and steers me upstairs, my voice thick and hoarse.

Nathan says nothing until we're upstairs.

In our room, he sits me down on the bed. "Hannah, what were you thinking, mixing pills with alcohol?"

A shiver traces my spine as memories claw their way through the haze—my mother, lifeless on her bed with pills strewn next to her. She left me without a word, without a goodbye.

"It's not what it looks like," I say as firmly as I can. "I need to... I need to talk to Lennie."

Slowly, I get up and stumble toward the door and head to Lennie's room. She's sitting cross-legged on her bed, hugging her toy cat, Lily, to her chest.

"Lennie, baby, I'm so sorry." My throat is thick with tears as I kneel beside her.

"Mommy, why didn't you come?" Her bottom lip trembles.

"Something happened, sweetheart. I made a mistake. But it won't ever happen again." I reach for her hand, desperate for her forgiveness.

"Are we still going to the rehearsal?" she asks.

I nod. "Yes, angel. We're still going, and you'll be the most beautiful bridesmaid."

"Okay, Mommy." Lennie's face brightens and she wraps her arms around me as I breathe in the comforting smell of her vanilla shampoo.

"I'll be right back with your dress." I get to my feet.

Back in our bedroom, Nathan is slipping into his neatly pressed shirt.

"Nathan..." My voice is a broken thing, scared and small.

He doesn't turn, his back a silent rebuke.

"Please, I need you to forgive me. I don't know what happened, I swear."

"Forgive you?" He turns to face me, his eyes like chips of ice. "All this time you've been doubting me as a father, but all along it's you, Hannah. You're the one endangering our daughter. You are the bad parent."

"Baby, nothing like this will happen again. I promise."

His back to me again, he adjusts his tie.

"Nathan, please talk to me."

He whirls around again then, his eyes blazing with a sudden intensity that pins me to the spot.

"If you ever pull something like this again," he warns, his voice low and threatening, "I swear to God, Hannah, I will take Lennie away from you. And if you think I'm going to let you care for her alone again, you've really lost your mind this time."

That shatters the last of my defenses. I want to scream, to

explain that I don't remember doing it, that this isn't me, it can't be. But my words dissolve before they leave my lips.

I understand the terror that must have gripped Nathan when he found me, the confusion and anger he's feeling now. Nobody understands more than me.

"Please," I choke out. "Don't say that. Lennie is my whole world."

He doesn't respond, simply turns back to the mirror, adjusting the cufflinks I gave him for a recent birthday.

"Get dressed, Hannah," he says without looking at me. "We have a rehearsal to go to, my colleagues are going to be there, they'll already be on their way. We're not canceling it now, it's too late. I'll call the wedding off during the rehearsal and apologize to everyone in person, and we'll have to figure out a new arrangement between us. You can see Lennie sometimes, with supervision. *If* you get help. Now, I need to drive by the office. Elena will be here in a few minutes to look after Lennie. I didn't tell her what happened, just that you need a hand. I'll send a car to pick you up."

He exits the room without another word.

# FORTY

After Nathan leaves, I hurriedly message Elena and tell her not to come, saying that I've already left with Lennie and I'm taking her for ice-cream. Then I set about making myself coffee before getting dressed. I have two large, strong mugs because one simply won't do. A hangover is overtaking my senses, my vision blurred by wine I don't even recall drinking. This wasn't the plan.

"Get a grip, Hannah," I murmur to myself, cradling my second mug with both hands, its warmth seeping into my trembling fingers. My reflection in the window over the sink startles me—pale, with dark circles under my eyes that would take quite a bit of makeup to cover up.

I take a sip, grimacing as the coffee scalds my tongue.

Back in the bedroom, I head into the closet and climb slowly into some comfortable clothes, instead of my rehearsal dress. Trying to feel more human, I apply makeup mechanically. Mascara, eyeliner, lipstick—it feels like I'm fitting on armor, preparing for a battle.

"Mommy?" A small voice calls out from the doorway, and I turn to see my little girl standing there.

"Hey, sweetheart." My voice is steadier than I feel. "You ready to get dressed?" I plaster on a smile, pushing down the nausea.

She nods.

"Let's make you look like a princess." I reach for the dress she's been so excited to wear and hold it out in front of me.

A few minutes later, I guide the zipper up Lennie's back. "There we go." I step back to admire her, the ache in my head momentarily forgotten.

The dress clings to her small frame, the soft fabric flowing down in delicate layers of tulle.

"Mommy, am I pretty?" She spins around, her eyes shining with excitement, sending warmth spreading through me.

"More than pretty. You're breathtaking."

The sound of a car horn interrupts us and I look out the window, drawing in a deep breath.

"It's the cab Daddy sent for us. Come on, princess." I reach out to take Lennie's hand. Her small fingers slip into mine and we descend the stairs together.

I help her into the back seat before sliding in beside her.

"Mommy, where's my flower crown?" she asks as soon as the car starts pulling out of the driveway.

"Ah, I nearly forgot. We have to pick it up from the shop."

"Yes, I can't be a princess without my crown."

Lennie's chatter feels like distant white noise as the taxi winds its way through the streets.

"Are you okay, Mommy? You look funny."

"I'm fine, baby."

I glance out the window, watching the familiar sights pass by in a blur. There's Honeywood, the park where Lennie loves to play, my favorite bakery. The landmarks of our life, a life I am going to leave.

"Mommy, why are you breathing like that?" Lennie's voice reaches my ears again.

"Like what, sweetheart?"

"Like when you run and breathe very hard."

"I'm just excited for later, Lennie. Everything's okay," I lie.

"Okay," she replies.

"I can't wait to see you wearing your crown," I say.

"Are we almost there, Mommy?"

I force a smile. "Soon, darling."

I try to steady my heart. I know what I have to do, and it's time to tell my little girl.

"Actually, sweetie," I say, my voice trembling. "After we pick up your crown, we're going to have a little adventure."

"An adventure?" Her eyes light up.

"Yes," I exhale. "Just you and me."

As we get closer to the shop, my resolve hardens. My plan is unpolished and desperate, but it's all I have for now. Gloria was right; I have to act. After we pick up Lennie's crown to keep her happy, we'll leave town. We'll go to stay with a distant cousin of mine. Someone Nathan doesn't know.

"Is it a secret adventure?" Lennie asks.

"Very secret. But very fun."

"Like when we play hide and seek and you can't find me because I'm so good at hiding?" She giggles.

"Exactly like that," I reply, my throat tight.

"Okay, Mommy!" Lennie claps her hands, delight dancing in her eyes.

I look back through the window of the cab. The world outside is a smear of colors, and I clutch at the seat, fingers digging into the faux leather.

When we stop at Bliss & Twine, I will grab some cash from the till and avoid using our joint bank account card with Nathan, and then I'll get a different cab. I don't want to leave behind a trail that could reveal our whereabouts.

Before I change my mind, I pull out my phone while Lennie hums next to me and I dial the number.

"Hello, Hannah?" The voice on the other end sounds excited and a little breathless.

My throat constricts, and I force the words out before I lose my nerve. "I won't be at the rehearsal. I'm leaving town with Lennie. I don't know when I'll be back."

"Wait, Hannah, what—"

"I need to do this."

I press "end call" and the screen goes dark. It's done.

I lower the phone from my ear with sweat dripping down my temples.

My heart is racing a hundred miles an hour and I'm so glad I'm not driving. I feel like I'm on the verge of a panic attack. I'm terrified of the consequences of my actions and the uncertainty of what lies ahead.

But there's no room for hesitation now. There's no going back.

It's my responsibility to protect Lennie from pain, something I wish my own mother had done for me. She never left my father, but I have control over what happens to my child. And I won't let anyone take her away from me.

I dreamed of being Nathan's wife for such a long time. And since Lennie was born, my only wish has been for us to be a happy family and put the past behind us.

But the drawing I found yesterday sent shockwaves into me, and Nathan's words today, saying he'd take her away from me? I can't bear it.

I unlock my phone again and make another call.

# FORTY-ONE

The bell above the shop door chimes as I push it open, and Lennie's hand feels small and fragile in mine as we hurry inside.

"Mommy, why are we running?" Lennie is confused, but I don't have time to explain.

We need to act fast.

"It's all part of the adventure, baby," I say to her. "We need to hurry because we have a train to catch."

As I head over to the till, I spot the delicate circlet of flowers on the counter, so I grab it quickly and hand the flower crown to Lennie. There's a note next to it left from Lila, saying she can't wait to see Lennie in her bridesmaid dress.

Lila. After Nathan's revelation, the two of us decided to wait a little while before talking to her, and I'd taken some time off work anyway, so it was easy to avoid the subject. It wasn't okay that she lied to us about her identity for so long, but at the same time I can understand why she wanted to meet her brother and connect with her niece, and why she'd struggle to know how to do so when he'd ignored her previous attempt to reach out.

He thinks her letter was lost in the mail, but the truth is that all those years ago I opened a letter from someone claiming to be his sister.

Nathan was away from home going through a stressful trial and asked me to check his mail for a piece of evidence he was expecting. I decided not to tell him what I read, because he was already under so much strain, and after the trauma we'd recently been through with his ex, I just didn't think he'd be able to handle anything more. I wasn't in the best place myself then mentally, either, and in the end I never told him about it at all. Honestly, with everything else that was going on, it totally slipped my mind. A bit like things have been falling away from my memory recently too.

It never occurred to me that the woman who came in a few months ago looking for a job at my shop was that same sister. The letter she had sent did not include a picture, and she signed off with just an initial. There was no way I could have known it was her, trying to get close to the family she thought had rejected her.

I realize now that it was Lila at the funeral: I can't believe I didn't see it before, with her big sunglasses, and the hat covering her long black hair, but she was so far off and I'd never have expected to see her there.

It's also no surprise that she kept a distance from the other mourners. After all, Nathan said that when she revealed her true identity and tried to talk to him again, he reacted so badly to her and told her to stay away from his family.

Anyway, Nathan and I came to the decision that Lila means well, she's just gone about things the wrong way, and both of us should be understanding of that since we all make mistakes. Some worse than others. We wanted to get past the wedding day and give Lennie some more time to get back to normal before telling Lila that we want to build a relationship with her as a member of our family: Lennie's real aunty.

I guess that will never happen now.

Beaming, Lennie perches the flower crown on top of her head. "Can we go now, Mommy, to Miami?" She must have overheard me on the phone.

"Very soon, angel." I force strength into my voice. "But there's something I need to do first."

As she chatters about the princesses and enchanted forests she thinks we'll find in Miami, I open the till. My fingers are swift, snatching bills and stuffing them into my handbag.

"Are we going now?" Lennie's impatience bubbles up.

"I just need another minute, baby."

Then I hurry to the office and open the safe. My heart pounding, I gather the stacks of money and stuff them into my bag.

Back at Lennie's side, I bend down in front of her and place both my hands on her shoulders.

"Listen to me carefully, Lennie," I say. "Whatever happens, I want you to know that Mommy loves you more than anything in the world, okay?"

"Okay." Lennie smiles.

Then the bell above the door chimes, and I whirl around, my heart lodging in my throat.


"Going somewhere?" Elena's voice is hard and cold, her eyes sharp as she scans the scene before her—the open till, my fearful expression.

"Seriously, Hannah, you were just going to run off with Lennie?"

I immediately regret calling her earlier. I should have just left with Lennie quietly and called when we were a good distance away.

"Elena, please, just let us go."

"Mommy, is Aunty Elena coming with us on the adventure?" Lennie asks, her hand reaching up to touch the delicate crown on her head.

"No, sweetheart," I say, but my eyes are fixed on Elena. "Only you and me."

"An adventure, huh?" Elena echoes. "Is that what you're calling it?"

"We need to go, Elena, please don't try to stop us." I take Lennie's hand and try to maneuver around Elena, but she steps in front of us, blocking the path to our only exit.

"You can't run away from your problems. This isn't going to work."

"Come on, Elena. Let us leave. Do it for Lennie."

Elena turns to Lennie with a forced smile. "Lennie, sweetie, why don't you sit over there for a moment? Me and Mommy need to talk in the office."

She reaches into her bag for her phone and switches it on. For a second, I'm afraid she's calling Nathan, but instead, she hands it to Lennie.

"That's a new drawing app I downloaded for you. Why don't you give it a try while Mommy and I have a chat?"

Lennie's eyes light up as she takes the phone. "Thank you, Aunty Elena!"

I steel myself and follow Elena into the office.

She rounds on me, her eyes blazing. "Nathan just told me, Hannah. He told me everything." Her voice slices through the air. "You didn't pick Lennie up from school because you were passed out on the floor? With pills, Hannah, pills... and alcohol?" She paces in front of me.

"Look, it's not what you think," I stammer, but the words are hollow and I know she won't buy them. "I don't even remember drinking the wine or—"

"Stop lying to me. I don't even know who you are right now." She jabs a finger at me; I've never seen her this angry before. "You're unfit to be a mother, Hannah. You've been saying all this awful stuff about Nathan, but all the time, were you just trying to cover up for your own failings?"

I open my mouth to defend myself again, but nothing comes out.

She's about to say something more when she suddenly stops, her breaths coming in short gasps as if she's been sprinting. I watch, unable to move, as a horrible realization dawns on her face.

"No, it can't be," she whispers, more to herself than to me, and her head tilts to the side, as if listening to a distant echo only she can hear.

Then she collapses into a chair. And without her uttering another word, I know.

I know she's unraveled the thread of my darkest secret. I can see it in her eyes, in the way they reflect a mixture of horror and disbelief.

I stand frozen, unable to tear my eyes away from her as I watch the past claw its way back into the present, and I'm helpless to stop it.

With an effort that seems monumental, Elena rises again, her movements sluggish, as if she's wading through water.

"I know what you did," she whispers, her voice carrying the weight of betrayal and shock. "You poisoned her, Nathan's ex. You did it together, on their wedding day. You tried to kill her. And you confessed that night, didn't you? Then you tried to make sure I'd never remember and never tell anyone, with that car accident."

The edges of my vision blur, and a cold sweat breaks across my forehead.

"No, that's not how it happened, Elena," I gasp out, shaking my head so fiercely it feels like it might snap off. "That's not the whole story. You've got it wrong. I never meant it to go as far as it did, I never really wanted to kill her and Nathan didn't either, but he'd found out things about her that you'd never believe. I just wanted to protect him from her and stop the wedding, she was dangerous. She'd lied about who she was. And the car accident wasn't our fault."

"Look at you." Elena stands up and walks toward me, fury etched across her face. "You're totally deranged."

I grab the edge of my desk for support, the wood pressing into my palms. "Elena, please," I beg, but my voice doesn't sound like my own. It's the whimper of a cornered animal.

"You don't deserve Lennie," she spits out. "You're unstable, a danger to your own child." She's close now, close enough that I can see every line etched into her face.

"Stop," I whisper. "I love her. I would never—"

"Love? You don't know what that means. You don't deserve to have a daughter. I need to call—"

"No!" I shout. I can't let her do anything that would make me lose my daughter.

With a desperation that surprises even me, I lunge forward, my hands finding Elena's shoulders, pushing with all the force I can muster.

She stumbles backward but recovers quickly, charging toward me with a force that takes me completely by surprise. The collision sends me reeling.

As I let out a scream, my foot catches on the edge of the rug in front of my desk, sending me sprawling to the ground. The back of my head connects with the floor, and a vase from the nearby shelf is knocked over, falling on top of my head.

Pain explodes in a burst of white light behind my eyes. Through the haze, I see Elena, her face a mask of anger, panic, and fear.

Then I turn my head slightly to see Lennie as well. My little girl, peeking through the door she's nudged open, her eyes wide with terror.

I want to reach out to her, to reassure her that everything will be all right, but my limbs feel heavy and unresponsive.

"Lennie," I whisper, but my voice is trailing off into silence as darkness creeps up on the edges of my vision.

I watch helplessly as Elena rushes to Lennie, gripping her by the arm. "We have to go, sweetheart," she says, pulling her away from the scene with urgency. Lennie screams, kicking hard at Elena; her flower crown falls off and tumbles to the floor.

As consciousness slips from my grasp, the last thing I register is the fear in my daughter's eyes.

# FORTY-TWO

## LENNIE

We're in Aunty Elena's car and she's driving too fast.

"Aunty Elena?" My voice is small, squeaky, like a mouse. "Is Mommy okay? She fell down."

Aunty Elena looks back at me only for a short time and continues to drive. In the mirror in front of her, I see that her eyes are big and scared.

"Everything's going to be all right, sweetheart," she says, but her voice is shaking. "I'm going to take very good care of you."

"Can we go back now? Mommy needs us and I forgot my crown, and my shoes. I took them off because they were pinching me." I turn in my seat to look through the window, squinting to see if Mommy is running after us.

"No, Lennie, we can't go back. I just need to call someone real quick."

"Who are you calling?" When she doesn't answer, I press my face against the cool glass window. My tummy feels funny. "I want my mommy."

"Please," Aunty Elena's voice shakes as she speaks on the phone, which she has put on speaker on the seat next to her, "Gloria, you have to help me."

"Elena, what's happened? Are you and Hannah on the way to the rehearsal? I'm already here," says a woman on the other end of the phone. I think I recognize her voice, but I'm not sure who it is.

"I... She's hurt. It was an accident, but—"

"Who? Elena, who is hurt?"

"Hannah. She fell hard. I pushed her, Gloria. I didn't mean to do it, but I had to stop her."

"Stop her from what?" The woman's voice is getting louder.

"From taking Lennie away," Aunty Elena sniffs loudly. "Lennie is not safe with her or Nathan, she's in better hands with me."

"I don't understand. What are you doing? Where are you going?"

"I can't tell you. I just—I love this little girl so much. I need to protect her."

"Where are we going?" I ask quietly from the back seat.

"Somewhere safe," Aunty Elena says briefly, before continuing her conversation with the woman on the phone.

"But Mommy—"

"Shh, Lennie." She takes a deep breath. "Gloria, Hannah is in the back of Bliss & Twine. In the cool area where they keep the flowers. I don't know what to do. I think she might be dead."

I cry out loud. I don't want my mommy to be dead. I know what that means. It means she's gone to be with the angels in heaven and I won't see her anymore.

"Dead?" The woman gasps. "What? What the hell did you do?"

"I—I was trying to protect Lennie. But I didn't mean to hurt her."

"Okay, listen to me. Whatever happened was an accident, right?"

"Yes, an accident," Aunty Elena repeats. "I'm Lennie's godmother, she means the world to me. I have to keep her safe."

"Exactly," the woman says. "Just stay calm. I don't understand what happened, but I'm sure you did what you had to do and that it's not as bad as you think it is. We'll sort this out."

I hug my knees to my chest, trying to make myself smaller, invisible. I wish Whisper could come now and make me feel better. She's my guardian angel, so she must know where I am. But today, I can't even hear her voice in my head.

Aunty Elena wipes her eyes. "Gloria, please, just go check on Hannah, okay?"

"Of course, I'm heading over there now. She's probably just unconscious. I'll get her to the hospital and I'll call you as soon as I know more."

When she stops talking on the phone, Aunty Elena says, "Don't cry, Lennie. Everything's going to be okay, all right?"

I hug my knees tighter, squeezing hard. I know I'm wrinkling my bridesmaid dress, but I don't care.

"Where are you taking me?" I can taste the salty taste of tears on my tongue.

"I'm taking you to my sister's in New York. She has two children your age, and you will really enjoy getting to know them. It will be one big, fun adventure."

"New York?" I know that place. I've never been there, but Daddy used to go there for his work. He used to say he would take me there one day.

"Yes, sweetie. You'll be safe there. I promise."

"But what about Mommy?"

"We'll talk about that later. Right now, we need to keep moving."

"But I don't want to. I want my mommy," I scream then, and try to open the door, but it's locked.

Aunty Elena hands me a piece of gum from her bag and tells me to stay calm, that I can pick the music we listen to if I'm good. It tastes like toothpaste, but I like it. I just have to be careful not to swallow it because I don't want my insides to stick together.

We drive for a long time and Aunty Elena and I sing along with the songs. And then, after driving for a while, we stop at a big grocery store. She buys me a new pair of shoes, and all my favorite snacks like chocolate chip cookies and fruit punch juice boxes. She even surprises me with a bag of gummy bears.

"Thank you, Aunty Elena," I say.

"No problem, Lennie. I just want to make our adventure super special."

When she's paying for the snacks, I see some pink sunglasses with sparkly crystals. I pick them up and try them on.

"You like them?" she asks me, and I nod.

"Then let's buy them for you. They go perfectly with your dress."

As soon as we get in the car she puts on the music again, but I'm tired now. I want silence. I can't stop thinking about Mommy. She always told me that when we're not together and I think of her, she will know and think of me too. So, I close my eyes and imagine seeing her in my head.

I think about her soft laugh, her warm hugs, and the way she stroked my hair when I couldn't fall asleep. I hear her telling me that everything will be okay.

When I open my eyes again, I know Aunty Elena was lying. Mommy is not dead; otherwise I would not hear her voice in my head.

"Oh, Lennie," Aunty Elena says. "We have a long journey ahead of us, filled with so many exciting places to explore and discover."

I nod. "But we can't go too far, okay? Because Mommy will never find us then."

Aunty Elena goes quiet for a while before she speaks again. "Lennie, it's time to stop thinking about your mommy and daddy now. That's why we're on this adventure together, to get away from them and keep you safe."

"I'll never see my mommy again?" I ask, my voice shaking.

Aunty Elena reaches behind to pat my hand. "I'll be your new mommy, sweetheart."

# FORTY-THREE

## HANNAH

I don't know how I got here, but I'm lying on the concrete floor of the back room, where I keep fresh blooms that have just arrived from the flower market. Their heady scents fill the air, mingling with the musty smell of damp rotting leaves. An icy coldness is seeping into my bones, as if I'll never be warm again, and my head is throbbing painfully.

My hand trembling, I reach up to touch my head and pull my fingers away. They're wet with blood. A memory flashes: Elena. Falling and hitting my head. A vase crashing on top of me, Lennie's scared little face. Then the darkness.

"Lennie," I whisper, my voice cracking in the silence. How long have I been out? Minutes? Hours? Panic starts to simmer, but I push it down.

With an extreme amount of effort, I drag myself into a sitting position, leaning against the cool metal shelving. My hands fumble in the dark, searching for something—anything— that could help me.

"Think, Hannah, think," I mutter, trying to piece together the scattered shards of my mind.

"Help," I call out, my voice refusing to rise above a whisper. But who would hear me anyway?

A metallic taste fills my mouth, and I realize it's blood, dripping down from my head into my mouth.

I have to get out of here.

"Help," I try again, louder this time, but the darkness swallows the sound. I'm alone, alone with the flowers and the shadows, and this terrible coldness saturating my body.

"Come on, Hannah. Move," I command myself, and inch by inch, I crawl toward the door, even as the immense pain in my head urges me to give up, to surrender to the darkness again.

"Lennie?" The word scrapes against my dry throat, emerging as a hoarse whisper.

It would be so easy to close my eyes and sink back into unconsciousness. But I can't. I need to get to Lennie.

Another memory flashes in my mind. Elena, her face contorted with rage as she screamed at me.

"You don't deserve Lennie!" she had hissed, eyes wild.

"Where did you take her, Elena?" I gasp out loud even though there's no one to answer. How could Elena, my oldest friend, take my daughter away from me?

Images flash before me—Lennie's tiny hands patting the sand into castles, her smile as she found another seashell treasure for her collection.

"God," I choke out and swallow hard, "I know I haven't been good. I've done terrible things, and I've hurt people. But please forgive me," I beg through sobs. "For the sins I committed. Don't take my daughter away, don't punish her because of me. She needs her mother."

More memories come to me then—the sharp tang of eucalyptus as I arranged bouquets, the softness of Lennie's cheek as she clung to me.

"God, if I die, please protect her," I plead. "Don't let her pay for my mistakes. She's innocent. Please, just keep Lennie safe. Don't let my darkness touch her. Not ever."

I pour out every regret, every unspoken apology.

When I'm done praying, I only feel more determined. I know I can't give up. I need to fight. Lennie needs me.

Gritting my teeth against the throbbing in my skull, I push myself to my feet and stagger slowly, impossibly, toward the door. Next to it, I find the light switch and flick on the light.

Then I reach for the doorknob, but it doesn't budge.

"Help!" I shout, banging on the door with all the force I can muster.

Desperate, I send myself crashing into the door again with a thud, but it doesn't move. Pain shoots through my shoulder and I stagger back, cradling my injured arm.

I slump against the door, and I'm about to surrender to despair and fall to the ground when, faintly, the distant chime of the bell above the shop door pierces the silence.

My heart thudding, I press my ear against the door, straining to hear the sound of voices or footsteps.

"Please, help me," I call, but no one answers.

Minutes pass, and just as I begin to doubt my own ears, there's a click, then the door opens and someone is filling the doorway as I stumble away from it.

My heart stutters, and my mouth falls open in a silent gasp of recognition.

It can't be. But it is.

She's back: Nathan's ex-wife... my former friend.

The woman we thought we'd got rid of, forever. She's changed, but her face is unmistakable.

"Brynn," I breathe out. "What are you doing here?"

# FORTY-FOUR

"Hello, Hannah," says Nathan's ex, her voice smooth and calm as she steps into the room, and the door swings shut behind her with a soft click.

Her looks have changed since I last saw her, with her hair now a dark shade that's almost black instead of the usual auburn, and her eyes green instead of brown. She must be wearing contact lenses, but I wonder about the hair. Did she dye it to this new color or was this her natural hair color all along? She still wears the same perfume, that soft sweet scent of lavender and vanilla, so at odds with the violent, dangerous woman I now know her to be.

With her presence dominating the space, the room feels even smaller than it did before, and the air crackles with electricity.

"Wh-what are you doing here, Brynn?" I ask again, stammering.

She tilts her head and smiles. "I think you know."

Her sudden appearance leaves me speechless, but I can't say I'm entirely surprised. Deep down, I always feared she would come back one day, seeking revenge for the hurt I caused her. It's a fear that I pushed away and tried to forget.

Yet here she stands, a painful reminder of my past actions. I was the one who came between her and the future she dreamed of with Nathan, I was the one who tore her world apart. But she didn't deserve to be happy after all the terrible things she did and planned to do. She claimed she really did love Nathan, that she'd changed her mind and wasn't planning on murdering him on their honeymoon. But even if that was true, leopards don't change their spots, and I'm confident she would have gone back to her old ways before long. What Nathan and I did was self-defense. We didn't kill her, of course we didn't. But I thought we'd done enough to get her out of our lives forever.

Casually, she eases herself onto a crate near the door. "You might want to call me Whisper," she continues. "That's what Lennie knows me by."

I blink, trying to push through the fog. "Whisper?"

"You know, her imaginary friend. Her *guardian angel*," Brynn continues, a smug smile playing on her lips. "Lennie and I, we've known each other for a while now. She trusts me."

"What are you talking about?"

"Funny, isn't it? While you thought you were living your perfect little life, the two of us became really close, playing inside her tree house. It started small, a nudge here, a lie there, until I convinced her to trust me completely. It was all me, Hannah. I made sure she was terrified of Nathan. I made her believe he was dangerous, that he hurt her."

Shock courses through me like a live wire. How could I have let this woman get close enough to my daughter to manipulate her?

"How could you? How—?"

"It's simple really. I wanted your life and Nathan's life to crumble like mine did when you stole everything away from me." She presses a hand to her belly. "It's your fault I lost my baby before I even got a chance to hold it in my arms. You and Nathan don't deserve Lennie."

I sink to the ground, words dissolving before they can leave my tongue.

She's right. If it wasn't for us, there would have been no need to rush off to the hospital with Brynn, and the car accident that caused her miscarriage and Elena's injury would never have happened. But Nathan and I didn't know she was pregnant, or we'd never have done something so drastic.

Brynn watches as I suffocate under the weight of guilt, her eyes showing a mix of satisfaction and malice.

As much as my heart goes out to her for the pain she endured after losing her child, her manipulation of my daughter is unforgivable. She doesn't have the right to use my own child as a pawn in her revenge scheme.

"I have another little secret." She leans forward, her eyes gleaming. "You know those chais you love so much at Honeywood?" She pauses for effect, the corners of her mouth twitching upward. "Well, they've had a special ingredient just for you."

"Wh... What are you talking about?"

"Your friend, Gloria. She and I have been working together. Ever heard of poison hemlock?" She doesn't wait for me to respond before continuing, "I only had Gloria give you small doses, but I thought they'd take effect more quickly than they did. Of course, I also added another special something that triggered those hallucinations you were experiencing. I must say, you were quite entertaining to watch as you descended into insanity." Her lips twist into a sickening grin. "Then the day you neglected to pick Lennie up from her club, I tried to finish you off with the wine and pills, when you were so out of it you didn't even register what was happening. But you survived that, somehow. Frankly, it's a miracle that you're standing here right now."

My blood turns to ice as I recall the cluster of poison hemlock I found in the garden. It's exactly the kind of twisted thing Brynn would do. She left the flowers for me to find, to frighten me; she was so confident and so brazen. She knew she was winning, she knew she had already won. She's a killer, and she enjoys it.

Unlike Nathan and me. What we did was wrong, I know that. But we are both glad our actions didn't end her life; we only wanted to punish her and stop her from continuing her murderous plans. We were desperate, spiraling out of control. Our hearts had been broken by Brynn and her cruelty.

So yes, I expect this of Brynn.

But Gloria? How can she be a part of this? Sweet, kind Gloria, who has been such a good friend to me.

"Gloria wouldn't do that," I say unsteadily. "You're lying. She's my friend."

"If anyone knows that our real enemies can sometimes turn out to be our dearest friends, it's you, Hannah. The truth is, Gloria was being a good friend to me, not you."

The headaches, the disorientation, the forgetfulness. The sense of slipping away from myself. It wasn't stress. It was all orchestrated by Brynn, and by Gloria—my own friend.

"But how?" I gasp, finally. "How did you know I was here, now?"

"Ah, dear Gloria called to tell me." Brynn smiles. "So, I couldn't resist coming to sort things out once and for all. It's over, Hannah."

"Please," I whisper, my voice barely audible now. "Lennie needs me."

Brynn's laughter echoes through the room. "Don't worry, Elena will take great care of her. It's all in your will, isn't it? The one Gloria advised you to write a few weeks ago? That was my idea, of course. I got Gloria all anxious that Nathan might kill you. She kept going on about it, and worrying about Lennie.

Elena was the obvious choice to take Lennie, and honestly, she should have her, after what you and Nathan put her through. It's your fault Elena lost her ability to have children. Did she tell you that? The doctors think the trauma of the car crash on our way to hospital all those years ago, with all of us inside, led to early menopause. None of that would have happened if it weren't for you. Just how many women's lives have you destroyed, Hannah? You know you deserve everything that's happening to you now. And with you gone, Nathan won't stand a chance at getting Lennie either. I have more than enough proof that he's not a safe father."

"But you manufactured all of that, and the car crash was not our fault. We were trying to save your life, get you to hospital. It's all lies, just like it's all lies about Nathan."

"Does it matter?" she replies coolly. "It's not lies to Lennie anymore, she believes it. It might as well be true."

I want to scream, to fight, but my limbs are stuck; it's as if the air is mud around me.

"Time for your final act," Brynn announces as she pulls a small bottle from her pocket and uncaps it.

Then she walks toward me and, with her free hand, she grips my chin, forcing my mouth open. I try to fight her off, but my body refuses to cooperate. The liquid drips onto my tongue, and slides down my throat. I feel abject terror rising within me now.

I'm going to die.

I'll never see my daughter again.

Finally she releases me and I slump to the floor, the room spinning.

I watch as she pulls out a pen and a piece of paper. "Let's write that suicide note, shall we?" She pauses. "Any suggestions?"

I try to speak, but I can barely hear my own voice over the roaring blood in my ears.

"How about something simple?" Brynn starts writing. "I'm sorry for everything. I can't do it anymore. I can't bear the weight of my mistakes any longer. I did many terrible things that are impossible to forgive. I hope you can find it in your hearts to forgive me. Goodbye." She looks up at me, smiling broadly. "Perfect, wouldn't you say?"

No, I want to shout, but the darkness is creeping in, stealing my voice, my strength. The image of my daughter flickers in my fading thoughts, a moonbeam in the night.

"Goodbye, Hannah," Brynn whispers as she comes to kneel down next to me. "It's almost over. You're about to be free of it all—the pain, the fear, the burden of motherhood you so clearly can't handle."

I want to throw myself at her, but the darkness is starting to overcome me. Instead, I focus on Lennie's little white shoes by the door. *Lennie.* My darling little girl.

# FORTY-FIVE

## LENNIE

We're still in the car, and Aunty Elena is on the phone again. This time she's talking to Daddy. Whisper said Daddy doesn't love me, but right now, I just wish he would come and get me, and take me home.

I want to speak, so he knows I'm here, but Aunty Elena warned me that when she's on the phone, I shouldn't make a sound.

"Where are you? Everyone's here at the rehearsal waiting. What's going on? I can't seem to get through to Hannah either. Where's Lennie?" Daddy's voice crackles through the speaker and I curl my fingers around the puffy skirt of my bridesmaid dress.

Aunty Elena turns around and puts her finger over her mouth. So, I bite my lip really hard to keep from yelling out for Daddy.

Then Aunty Elena turns back to face the road again. "Everything's fine. I spoke to Hannah, she was doing much better. She had to stop by the shop for Lennie's flower crown and then Lennie was a bit nervous, so she took her for ice-cream. But she and Lennie should be with you any minute now.

I'm not far away, either. I got caught up in something, but it's nothing to worry about."

Why is Aunty Elena lying?

"Okay, well please hurry," Daddy begs. "Almost everyone is here. I'll try Hannah again. I don't get why her phone keeps ringing but she won't answer."

"It's probably on silent," Aunty Elena says. "Look, Nathan, I've got to go. See you soon."

The car is quiet again and Daddy's voice goes away. I start to cry and Aunty Elena reaches behind and touches my leg.

"Don't be sad, Lennie. We are going to have so much fun together, you'll see. You're my favorite person in the world."

I don't say anything, I just stare out the window at the sky, which is now turning all dark. I wipe away my tears and try to believe Aunty Elena's words, but all I can think about is Mommy lying on the floor in the shop.

"I'm hungry," I say when we drive past some restaurants.

Aunty Elena sighs , then she smiles in the mirror. "All right, Lennie. We still have a long way to go, but maybe we can stop for a quick bite to eat. How about a burger? Would you like that?"

"Okay," I say.

She drives us to a tiny restaurant with a bright-red sign that blinks and says "open."

There are not many cars in the parking lot, but I can see some people sitting inside by the big window, their faces lit up by the lights. They look happy, like I used to be with Mommy and Daddy when we went out to eat.

The restaurant is kind of old, but it feels really nice inside. Aunty Elena takes me to a table near the window where we can see cars driving by.

We sit down at our table and a lady with messy hair comes over to take our order. She has a name tag that says "Maggie."

"Can we have two burgers please?" Aunty Elena says. "One with lots of cheese and one without. And two sides of fries."

Maggie writes it down on her notepad and asks, "Anything to drink?"

"Just water for me." Aunty Elena looks at me. "What about you, Lennie? Do you want a milkshake?"

I nod. "Can I have chocolate?" I ask quietly.

"Of course, honey. A chocolate milkshake it is."

Maggie writes down my order. "Okay then, two burgers, one with lots of cheese, two sides of fries, a water, and a chocolate milkshake. Coming right up!" She walks away.

As we wait for our food, I look up at all the old pictures on the walls. They're dusty and faded, but everyone in them is smiling. There's a big machine in the corner that plays music when you put money in it. When I hear music, I like to tap my foot, but not today. Today, I feel really sad. So, I rest my head on the table and watch as Aunty Elena takes out her phone and calls someone. But they don't answer, and she puts her phone away again.

Then she tries to talk to me, to cheer me up, but I don't feel like talking. I stare at the pictures on the walls, especially a black and white photo of a man and a woman dancing together like Mommy and Daddy used to do sometimes in our living room.

Soon, our food arrives, and Maggie places the plates carefully on the table. The smell of juicy burgers and crispy fries makes me forget my sadness a little.

Aunty Elena thanks Maggie with a tired smile, and as soon as the waitress is gone, she takes my hand. "Lennie, I know you're feeling sad right now, but I just want you to be safe, okay? I'm here to protect you."

"But you're not my guardian angel. Whisper is."

"Well, godmothers can be guardian angels too, you know?" She picks up her burger.

I shrug and take a bite of mine, but it doesn't taste so good. I look back at Aunty Elena. "I'm not hungry anymore. My stomach feels weird." I push my plate away.

"That's okay, sweetheart. We'll just pack it up and take it with us."


"Can we go back to Mommy, please?" I ask when we sit back in the car and Aunty Elena drives away.

When she doesn't answer me, I ask again. "I want to go and see if Mommy is okay."

"Lennie, not now, okay? I need to think."

"Please," I beg.

Instead of answering me, her shoulders start to shake, and she starts making loud crying noises.

"Aunty Elena, are you sad about Mommy too? Maybe Mommy misses us."

After a while, she stops the car at the side of the road and gets out.

I watch her walking around outside. She's still crying and hitting her forehead over and over again with her palm.

Then I reach for the door, and this time, it opens.

# FORTY-SIX

## HANNAH

My eyelids flutter and I gasp for air. I remember everything immediately: Brynn's face, twisted into a mask of rage as she forced the poison down my throat, telling me my life was over. My stomach clenches. Is she still here? If she is, I need to remain still.

A sharp cramp shoots through my abdomen, and I bite down hard on my lower lip to stifle a cry. The pain is excruciating, as if my insides are being twisted by a powerful pair of hands. Sweat beads on my forehead as I try to regulate my breathing, willing the pain to subside.

When the agony lessens, I manage to pull myself to a sitting position, using the shelf behind me for support. I swallow hard, forcing the bile back down, and I strain my ears to listen again.

There's another sound, footsteps, I think.

She's out there and if I don't do something, she will come back in to finish what she started. I can't die, not when I know my daughter is in danger. Brynn was working with Gloria all this time. What if Elena is too?

I know Brynn too well. She is dangerous, unhinged. I'd known she was wrong for Nathan for a long time, and when he realized the truth about her, the darkness inside her, he saw it too. I will do whatever it takes to protect my daughter from her.

Ignoring the pain in my stomach and head, I push myself up to my feet. Every movement sends jolts of agony through my body, but I grit my teeth and keep going.

I teeter on unsteady legs, the room tilting.

When I hear the sound of the door being unlocked again, my fingers fumble, grasping blindly for something—anything—to use as a weapon. Finally, I find the smooth handle of a broom and I hold on to it as tightly as I can.

Each breath is a battle, but I refuse to collapse, refuse to give in to the darkness.

"Come on, Hannah," I urge myself, "you've been through hell and back. You can take whatever comes next."

As the door slowly creaks open, I grip the broom tighter, every aching muscle in my body ready.

But it's not Brynn who appears. It's Elena, her frame outlined by the doorway. Confusion and fear scramble for space, but before I can say anything, Lennie squirms past her.

"Mommy!" Her voice is like a burst of sunshine.

"Lennie!" I drop the broom, my arms opening on instinct despite the protest of my poisoned muscles. The room spins as she crashes into me, but nothing else matters.

I've been given back my world.

I steady myself against the dizziness and hold her tight, feeling the beat of her little heart.

Then reality sinks in.

"Are you here to finish what Brynn started?" My voice is hoarse as I eye Elena above Lennie's head.

"Brynn... what?" Elena shakes her head. "What are you talking about? Hannah... I just wanted to see if you're okay," she says, her voice breaking.

"Okay? You took my daughter away and left me for dead. How do you expect me to be okay?"

"I just wanted to do the right thing." Elena's tears stream down her face, her voice trembling with regret. "I thought I was protecting her."

"Protecting her from her own mother?" I choke, as pain and anger burn through me like wildfire.

"Can you blame me, Hannah? I remember what you did now, to Brynn. The crash. You—" She glances at Lennie and looks back up at me. "God, you don't look well. Let me take you to the hospital, okay? We can talk there." Her voice trembles as she attempts to touch my arm, but I jerk away, holding Lennie even tighter against me.

"No!" I snap. "I don't need your help. I don't need anything from you."

"Mommy, Aunty Elena said you are dead, but you're not, right?"

"No, my love," I assure Lennie, my voice softening as I meet her innocent gaze. "I'm very much alive, and I will always be here for you."

Elena takes a step back, her face contorted with guilt. "I'm so sorry, Hannah," she whispers, wiping her cheeks. "Let's go and get you looked at, please."

I want to refuse again, but my legs wobble beneath me, threatening to give way at any moment.

The only thing holding me together right now is Lennie, and as soon as she lets go, I'm pretty sure I'll crumble to the ground.

Elena rushes to my side, linking her arm with mine, and together we slowly make our way out of the room with Lennie holding my other hand.

A few steps from the car, a fresh wave of dizziness washes over me, and I stumble, almost losing my balance, but Elena quickly wraps her arm around my waist, providing much-needed support. Dread rises within me. Am I dying? Is it already too late?

Elena must sense my fear because she tightens her grip around me, holding me up. "Hannah, stay with me," she pleads, her voice desperate.

Inside the car she tries to keep me awake, distracting me by handing me her phone to call Nathan.

My fingers tremble as I hold the phone while Lennie gently rests her head on my shoulder.

I dial Nathan's number, closing my eyes briefly. So much has happened that I don't even know where to start.

"Hello?" His voice slices through the silence. "Elena, where the hell are you? Hannah and Lennie are still not—"

"Nathan, it's me, Hannah."

"Hannah?" He sounds confused. "Where are you?"

"Something happened," I murmur. "I need you to meet me at the hospital."

There's a sharp intake of breath, the rustle of fabric. "Why? What's happened? What did you do? Is Lennie okay?"

"Something terrible happened, but it wasn't me," I say, but my voice is losing steam and I don't think I can talk anymore. "I can't tell you now, I'm sorry. I'll explain when you get there."

"Oh God, okay, I'm on my way."

"Thank you," I murmur, and the line goes dead. Silence settles once more, and Elena drives fast, her eyes fixed ahead.

My eyes are starting to drift shut again, but Elena notices in the rearview mirror and keeps urging me to stay awake. She tells Lennie to do the same, and Lennie keeps shaking me, telling me to keep my eyes open. I fight as hard as I can, but I don't know how much longer I can hold on.

Where is Brynn now? What if Nathan is in danger too?

What if Elena called the cops? Will they be waiting for me at the hospital?

Could Nathan and I be about to walk into a trap, arrested in front of our daughter?

## FORTY-SEVEN

The sterile scent of disinfectant hangs heavy in the air, and a doctor with a clipboard stands at my bedside. He's an older man, with a lined face and graying hair, and his eyes look tired. "Miss Livingstone. Good to see you awake. We've administered treatment for the poison." The doctor checks the IV line feeding into my arm. "You got here just in time. Now, the most important thing for you to do is rest."

But it's not rest I need; it's answers.

"We'll be keeping you here for observation, for a little while," he continues. "Maybe at some point you'll feel able to tell us what happened, who gave you the poison you told us about."

"Thank you," I manage.

Time loses meaning as I drift in and out of a fitful sleep until the door creaks open, and Elena steps into the room and comes to sit by my bed.

"Nathan will be here soon, and a nurse offered to take Lennie to the playroom down the hall. I thought it best to talk to you alone."

I nod and swallow hard. "Did you call the police on Nathan

and me?" My voice is hoarse, barely audible over the beeping of machines and the hushed footsteps outside my door.

She shakes her head, then her face crumples and a silent torrent of tears carves tracks down her cheeks. "No, Hannah," she breathes, and her hand finds mine, squeezing it. "I don't condone what you and Nathan did all those years ago, but God help me, I understand it now. Nathan and I talked. I know what you found out about Brynn, her true murderous nature, and what she was planning on doing to him after they got married. What she's capable of, how desperate you both must have been when you found out. You just wanted to stop her. And after what happened at your shop tonight, I can see how someone would do something drastic in the heat of the moment. I did it myself. I can't believe I almost kidnapped Lennie."

Relief washes over me.

"Thank you," I whisper.

Elena leans in toward me. "Hannah, I'm really sorry I hurt you. I'm the reason you're here."

"No." The words burn as they leave my lips. "It's not your fault. It was Brynn, she poisoned me. She came to Bliss & Twine after you left with Lennie."

Shock registers slowly on Elena's face. "She's back?"

"Yeah, and she's been here for a while."

Elena's mouth drops open.

"She's been poisoning me for weeks, with small doses hidden in my chai from Honeywood every day. That's why I had those headaches and spells of dizziness."

I watch as Elena's expression shifts from shock to horror. "In your chai? But how?"

"Gloria. She's been working with Brynn all along, spiking my drinks, smiling at me while she served me death in a cup."

"Gloria?" Elena sounds astonished. "No, I can't believe she would be involved in something like this. I don't understand. How does she even know Brynn? Why would she—?"

"No idea." My fingers stroke the cool sheets beneath me. "But I want to find out."

Elena stands up abruptly, pacing the small space between the bed and the wall. "And to think that we trusted her, we thought she was our friend."

We're silent for a while, then she turns back to me. "Where do you think they are now, Brynn and Gloria?" Her eyes search mine for answers I don't have.

I run through the possibilities. "Well, if Brynn believes I'm dead, she might have left town by now. She got her revenge; she thinks she won."

"And Gloria?" Elena interjects, her hands wringing together.

I glance toward the window as if she's hiding out there. "If she's smart, she's gone into hiding as well. But if she's panicking, and finds out I'm still alive..."

"Then she could be dangerous," Elena finishes the sentence for me, then her voice drops to a whisper. "A terrified person can do unimaginable things to cover up their tracks. God, Hannah. I feel terrible. I even called her, after you fell. I thought she'd go and help you, while I had Lennie. I guess that's when she called Brynn, instead."

"Yeah." My heart hammers against my chest. "And now, she could come back to..." I trail off.

Elena takes my trembling hand in hers. "We'll figure this out. You, me, and Nathan. Together. We'll find them before they can do more harm."

"Okay. Thank you." I cling to the lifeline she offers. The bond of friendship between us, strained and tested though it may be, still holds firm.

Then I tell her everything else that Brynn did, the lies she fed Lennie, how she must have come into my own home, my own garden. My mind had been so scattered I didn't think anything of it when Nathan's set of keys went missing, but now I know it was her.

When I'm done, as silence stretches between us once more, the door opens and my breath catches as Nathan walks in, Lennie cradled against his chest.

Her eyes are heavy with sleep as Nathan sets her down on the bed next to me.

She's so warm, solid, and real, and I hug her to me, feeling her heartbeat against my body, giving me back the strength I lost.

Nathan looks from Elena to me, his sharp blue eyes searching. I reach for him with an outstretched hand, but instead of taking it, he wraps his arms around me.

"I'm sorry, Nathan," I whisper into the crook of his neck, inhaling the familiar scent of him. "I don't know how to even—"

"Shh, sweetheart." His strong arms envelop both me and Lennie. "Just tell me what happened."

I send Lennie out with Elena, and then with trembling lips, I recount everything. Finally, I finish talking, and Nathan looks utterly horrified. "She was here? Going into our home, our garden, meeting our daughter, for weeks? She tried to turn my daughter against me? To kill you?" Now his voice is a low growl. "I'll find her, Hannah. I swear it. She's not getting away with this. Not this time."

Later, just as Elena heads to the door to leave, her phone beeps and instead of reaching for the door handle, she glances down at the message, her brow furrowing in confusion. "Oh, my God," she mutters. "It's from Gloria."

As she reads the message, her eyes widen in shock, and she comes to sit on the edge of the bed, sharing the contents of the message with us.

"I sent her a few messages and voicemails earlier,

demanding an explanation from her and telling her all about Brynn," Elena says, her voice trembling with a mix of anger and confusion. "And she just responded now. Listen to this: 'I never meant to hurt Hannah, I swear. I was tricked by Brynn. I thought I was doing the right thing. I was not aware of Brynn's past, not at all. Please, you have to believe me. I feel terrible for what happened. Please meet me at Honeywood. I'd like to explain and apologize in person.'"

# FORTY-EIGHT

A week later, Elena and I find ourselves sitting at a corner table in Honeywood. The air is heavy with tension and Elena's leg bounces nervously under the table, a physical representation of the anxiety that twists in my own chest.

I was only discharged from the hospital a few days ago and the memory of that night at Bliss & Twine still haunts me. My body feels fragile, and I know the recovery is going to be slow, both physically and emotionally. But I'm here. I'm alive, and most importantly, my daughter is safe. We told the police about Brynn, and I'm hoping they will catch her soon. There's a risk she'll reveal to them what we did to her all those years ago, and we're going to deny it, Elena too. If she's believed, we will face consequences. But it's a risk we have to take, to keep Lennie safe.

"Anything for you ladies?" Judy asks as she approaches our table with her notepad in hand.

"Not right now, Judy," Elena says. "Is Gloria going to be long, do you think?"

"Her call just ended, she should be here any minute," Judy replies before scurrying off to attend to another table.

Elena reaches for my hand, her grip firm and reassuring. "Are you sure you want to go through with this? We can walk away right now if you're not ready."

I shake my head. "I need to understand why she did this to me, Elena. I need closure."

Finally, Gloria emerges from the back, her eyes locking onto ours. She slowly makes her way over to our table.

"Hannah, Elena," she greets us with a tight smile as she sits with us. "Thank you for meeting me."

I don't say anything but my gaze remains fixed on her face, searching for answers in her eyes. The silence hangs between us like a heavy curtain, each of us waiting for someone else to break it. Finally, after what feels like an eternity, Elena speaks up.

"Gloria, what did you mean when you said you thought you were doing the right thing? How can you possibly have believed that?"

"Can I get you anything to drink first, on the house?"

"You're kidding, right?" I glare at Gloria, my frustration boiling over now. "After you've been poisoning me for weeks, do you seriously think I'd drink anything you offer me?"

Gloria's eyes drop to the table as she fidgets with her hands, and then she takes a deep breath before she speaks. "A while back, I was in an abusive relationship. I joined a Facebook group for abused women. That's where I met her, Brynn. She was so supportive and kind." She inhales sharply and continues, her voice barely above a whisper. "My relationship ended really badly, as you know, and Brynn helped me make it through. She helped me start over here in Stoneview. But in turn, she wanted me to pay it forward, to help someone else in the same situation."

"Someone else in an abusive relationship? So, she told you Nathan was abusive?" I rub my forehead with my fingertips.

"Yes. She said he was abusive to both you and Lennie, that we had to set you free."

"By poisoning her?" Elena cuts in incredulously.

"No. She told me it was an antidote, that Nathan was slowly poisoning you and it would counteract the drug, until we could figure out a way to get you out of the relationship for good." She grabs a napkin from the table, wiping tears from her eyes. "It sounds so stupid, but I really trusted Brynn. She was totally convincing and she had done so much for me. I didn't know the drug I put in your chais was actually harmful, I thought it was saving your life. I never wanted to hurt you, Hannah. I swear. Please, you have to believe me."

I take a deep breath, feeling a mix of emotions swirling inside me. Betrayal, confusion, anger, but also a deep sense of understanding and forgiveness.

"I thought of you as a friend, Gloria, and I trusted you. I wish you'd just talked to me, been honest about what was going on."

"I know, I should have. I followed Brynn blindly, and I was wrong. I really thought I was helping you." She reaches out and grabs both my hands. "I'm really sorry, Hannah. I never wanted any of this to happen. If I could go back and change things, I would in a heartbeat. Please say you'll forgive me."

"Where's Brynn now?" Elena interrupts. "Have you heard from her recently?"

"No, not since that night. I tried calling; I even went to where she was staying. But there was no sign of her. I promise you that if I ever do hear from her, I will let you know. I want to make things right. I want her to pay for what she did."

Part of me wants to hold on to the anger, but another part of me knows that Gloria was also a victim in all of this. She was manipulated, a pawn in Brynn's twisted game of revenge. Brynn had taken lives before, acting like she was some kind of avenging angel protecting women and children from abusive men. But she didn't always get her targets right, and now I think she'd developed a shark's taste for blood. Nathan and I thought we'd done enough to stop her from ever hurting anyone again, that she'd learned her lesson. We let her go, and in turn she promised to keep our secret, never to tell anyone that we had almost killed her. We thought we could leave the past behind, but we were wrong.

I squeeze Gloria's hands gently before pulling away. "I need time to process everything that has happened," I say softly. "But I appreciate your honesty, I really do." I pause and look from Gloria to Elena. "And if I do get past this and we all get back to being friends, please, no more secrets."

Elena nods and Gloria smiles hesitantly through her tears. "I promise." I can see the glimmer of hope between us that maybe, just maybe, things might one day go back to how they used to be.

Two days later, I'm tucking Lennie in when one of her stuffed animals—the panda—falls to the floor. I bend down to pick it up, but instead of placing it back on her bed next to the many other toys, I notice a flicker of something red in its eyes and I frown.

When Lennie stirs, I leave the room with the toy still cradled in my hand.

"Are you okay?" Nathan asks when I enter our bedroom.

"Yeah, but, you gave this to Lennie, right?"

"The panda?" He shakes his head. "No, I told you that I didn't. We discussed this, remember? Lennie said you gave it to her." He furrows his brow in confusion.

"Oh yes, I remember you said that. But I don't think I did give it to her, I don't remember that at all." I stop talking as I study the plush toy in my hands. There's that flicker of light again.

"What's going on, Hannah?"

"If neither of us gave it to her, who did?"

Suddenly, Nathan jumps from the bed and comes to take the toy from me. I watch as, before my eyes, he rips open a seam in its belly, revealing a tiny device hidden inside. My eyes widen in disbelief.

"A camera?" My heart slams into my chest.

"Brynn," Nathan says, his face darkening.

"Oh, my God!" My knees suddenly weak, I sink down onto the bed.

She has been observing us, listening to our conversations, infiltrating our lives in ways we never could have imagined.

She vanished after thinking she killed me at Bliss & Twine.

But she's still been here. Watching my daughter.

And the police still haven't tracked her down.

# FORTY-NINE

## LENNIE

Two Months Later

Me and Mommy are sitting in Uncle Darius's office again. We've been here lots of times because Mommy and Daddy said Whisper, my guardian angel, was a liar. She made me think things that weren't true about Daddy. That's why I have to talk to Uncle Darius, so he can help me tell the truth from the lies.

There's a special spot just for kids in the office with so many fun toys and books, but I already brought my two favorites, Lily and Mr. Buttons. I sit cross-legged, holding them tightly while Mommy is on the big couch for adults, smiling at me.

"Remember, Lennie," Uncle Darius says in his soft voice. "Whisper is just an imaginary friend. She lives inside your mind, and she cannot be seen. The woman you saw in real life was not her. Imaginary friends don't come out to play. That was a real person pretending to be Whisper, trying to confuse you."

"Is Whisper gone now? I don't hear her in my head anymore."

"Only if you want her to be," Uncle Darius replies, offering me a chocolate chip cookie, but I shake my head. "I'm sure she's just on a little vacation inside your mind, resting. But remember, you are the captain of your imagination, Lennie. You have the power to bring Whisper back whenever you want. But she's inside your head, she's not out here in the real world."

Mommy stands up from the couch and comes to hug me. Her blue silk top smells fresh and flowery.

"Where is the bad woman now, the woman who pretended to be Whisper?" I ask Uncle Darius while Mommy strokes my hair.

Uncle Darius clears his throat and looks at Mommy before looking back at me. "We don't know where she is, Lennie, but we are doing what we can to find her, and if you see her again, you need to tell us. We are the people you can trust, and we will keep you safe."

"Okay," I say and look up at Mommy. "Are we going home after this?"

"No, darling. We're all going to enjoy a nice picnic in the park, remember? Aunty Elena and Uncle Darius are also joining us."

"Will Daddy come?"

"Of course. He's with Aunty Lila and Aunty Elena already. They are preparing everything right now, so that when we get there, we can all have a delicious lunch together."

"That's so much fun. I can't wait."

"I'm also very excited." Uncle Darius looks up from writing in his notebook, with a smile and a twinkle in his eyes. "And Aunty Elena also made two extra-large bottles of fresh lemonade for the picnic." He pauses. "But Lennie, before we go, is there anything else you want to talk about? Anything on your mind? We have a few more minutes before we head out."

"Are guardian angels real?" I ask.

"Yes, Lennie," Darius replies with a smile. "Guardian angels are as real as you want them to be. They watch over us, protect us, and guide us through life. Some people believe in them strongly, while others may have different beliefs. But if having a guardian angel makes you feel safe and comforted, then they are very real for you." Then his face becomes a little serious and he leans forward. "Do you want to know something else?"

I nod.

"I'm pretty sure you still have a guardian angel watching over you. It just wasn't that bad woman who pretended to be Whisper. Your true guardian angel is out there, looking after you, even if you can't see them."

I smile a little. "Really?"

"Absolutely. You might even have more than one. So, even if you can't see your guardian angels right now, trust that they are watching over you and keeping you safe." Uncle Darius stands up. "I think we better get going now. We don't want to keep everyone waiting."

"Thank you so much, Darius." Mommy stands up as well. "We really appreciate your time."

"Of course, Hannah. Lennie is such a brave and special little girl. It's my pleasure to be here for both of you." Uncle Darius grabs his notebook and puts it back in his bag. "Now, let's go and enjoy the sunshine."

Feeling happy that I still have a guardian angel watching over me, I take Mommy's hand and we walk out the door while Uncle Darius leads the way. As we step outside, I can feel a warm breeze brushing against my face, and I close my eyes for a moment, imagining that my guardian angel is stroking my cheek.

When we arrive at the park, we don't have to search long before we see Aunty Elena, Aunty Lila, and Daddy waiting under a big tree next to a lake. They wave as we come near, and I know this is going to be the best day ever.

Before I sit down to eat, me and Lily run around the park, the green grass tickling my ankles. The park is so pretty and colorful, just like Mommy's flower shop. I laugh as I try to catch a butterfly with pretty blue and orange wings. It keeps flying away, but it's so much fun to chase it.

"Careful, Lennie!" shouts Daddy. I turn back, smiling at him, and nod. He always worries, but I'm fast. I can almost touch the butterfly.

"Look, Lily," I whisper, "it's dancing in the air just for us."

When the butterfly flies really high up, Aunty Lila comes over with a big smile on her face. She kneels down next to us.

"Are you having fun, you two?" She reaches out to redo my braid that has loosened from all the running around. She's so good at braiding hair, just like Mommy. I nod, my eyes still following the butterfly as it flies far away. Then I turn to look at my new aunty.

"Aunty Lila, can I come to your house again soon for a sleepover like last time?"

"Of course, my favorite niece in the whole wide world. Maybe we can convince your mommy and daddy to let you stay a little longer next time." She smiles warmly. "But for now, let's go get some yummy food!"

"Yeah!" I jump up, already feeling hungry from playing. Aunty Lila takes my hand as we walk back to the picnic area.

When Mommy sees me, she pats the spot next to her on the blanket. "The two of you are just inseparable, aren't you?"

Aunty Lila laughs as I plop down next to Mommy. "If you had the smartest, funniest, and most beautiful little niece like I do, you would understand." She pats Mommy's hand. "Don't be jealous, dear Hannah. You'll always be my favorite sister-in-law too."

"Any love left for me in this circle of family favorites, by any chance?" Daddy winks at Aunty Lila.

"We can always make room for you, Nathan," she says.

There are so many yummy foods on the blanket. Sandwiches with all my favorite stuff inside, colorful fruit salad, donuts with rainbow sprinkles, and even a big chocolate cake with fancy frosting!

While Aunty Elena prepares a plate for me, I pick up Mommy's hand. "Can I wear your ring, Mommy?"

I love Mommy's new wedding ring. It's pretty and shiny, and I like how she smiles every time she looks at it.

"Sure, darling. Just be careful not to lose it." She takes it off and puts it in my hand. I feel like a princess when I put it on my finger.

"I promise," I say, holding my hand up so the little diamonds sparkle in the sun and make rainbows.

"I can't believe we finally did it." Daddy wraps an arm around Mommy. "Even without the big party, it was perfect."

Mommy nods and leans into him. "The best decision we've ever made."

"And I still got to wear a bridesmaid dress," I add proudly.

Mommy laughs and ruffles my hair. "You were the prettiest and best bridesmaid ever!"

Aunty Elena joins in. "That's right, Lennie. You were the star of that beautiful wedding. Now it's time to eat."

I take a big bite of my sandwich and look around at all the other happy people having picnics in the park under the shining yellow sun.

When we finish eating, I go play for a little bit more and then it starts raining a little, but it's okay because we already had our picnic and ate most of the food.

While the grown-ups hurry to pack our things, I look up at the sky and spin around in the rain with my arms out wide. The drops tickle my face and forehead as I giggle and twirl faster and faster, my dress spinning with me.

"Come on, Lennie," Daddy calls out, holding an umbrella over his head. "Let's get going before it rains harder."

I run over to Daddy, still spinning in the rain, and he puts his arm around me, then we walk back to the car under the umbrella, but it's too small for Aunty Lila to fit under, so she runs faster to the car and gets in.

When it rains harder, we wave goodbye to Aunty Elena and Uncle Darius as they run to their car.

But before I get in the car, I see something.

Near the park gate, I see her.

The woman who said she was Whisper. The woman who lied to me about Daddy.

I start breathing hard and Mommy comes to me. "What happened, Lennie?" she asks.

I blink hard, and when my eyes open again, the woman is gone.

"Nothing," I say, but my voice shakes a little.

I'm scared to say what I saw in case the words become true. I hope I only imagined her. As I sit in the car and watch the raindrops chasing each other down the window, I fix my thoughts on one of them. A magic raindrop. And this time, I wish my guardian angel stays only inside my head, forever.

# A LETTER FROM L.G. DAVIS

Dear reader,

I just wanted to take a moment to say thank you for reading *The Missing Bridesmaid*. I hope you've enjoyed all the twists and turns in the story as much as I did writing them. It has been a privilege to guide you through the streets of Stoneview one last time.

One character that is near and dear to my heart is little Lennie. Breathing life into her and immersing myself in her world, particularly her enchanting tree house, was an absolute delight. I hope she added an extra touch of magic to the story and that you connected with her as well.

If this book left you wanting more, and you want to be the first to know about my future books, I invite you to join my email list. You'll be among the first to know about new releases, exclusive content, and other exciting updates.

*www.bookouture.com/l-g-davis*

I have a little favor to ask. If *The Missing Bridesmaid* resonated with you, please consider leaving a review to help other readers decide on whether to dive into the series. Your feedback is invaluable to me, and I appreciate you for taking the time to share your thoughts.

I love hearing from my readers, so don't hesitate to reach out anytime to share your thoughts, feelings, or just to say hello. Your messages truly brighten my day.

Thank you once again for coming along on this journey with me. There are more stories to be told, more mysteries to unravel, and I can't wait to share them with you.

Yours always,

Liz

www.lgdavis.com

 facebook.com/LGDavisBooks

 x.com/lgdavisauthor

 instagram.com/lgdavisauthor

# ACKNOWLEDGMENTS

Writing a book can be a rewarding experience, but sometimes it can also feel like an endless uphill battle. If I didn't have a team of dedicated people supporting me every step of the way, I never would have made it to this point.

I'm extremely grateful to Bookouture, my publisher, and all the amazing people who played a part in bringing *The Missing Bridesmaid* to life. It takes a team effort to turn words into a published book, and I want to thank the editorial team, cover designers, publicity and marketing teams, and all those behind the scenes who helped make my dream a reality. Your hard work and dedication have not gone unnoticed, and I am forever grateful for your contributions to this project.

It also helps that I have the best editor in the world—Rhianna Louise. Her insightful feedback challenged me to dig deeper into the characters' motivations, pushing the boundaries of what I thought was possible. Rhianna, thank you for believing in me and my stories, even when I doubted myself. Your guidance and expertise have been invaluable, and I appreciate your role in shaping this novel into what it has become. You're more than just an editor to me, you are a dear friend, and I couldn't have asked for a better partner in this writing journey.

A special thanks goes to my husband, Toye, and my two amazing children. They have always been there to lend an ear when I shared my thoughts and ideas, and they offered words of encouragement when doubt crept in. My dear husband, I apologize for occasionally waking you up in the middle of the night to read aloud a passage I was proud of, or to share an idea that struck me at odd hours. Your patience and understanding mean everything to me. I love you so much.

Last but not least, I want to convey my deepest and sincerest appreciation to all of my readers. Knowing that my stories have touched your hearts, and connected with you in some way, brings me so much joy and fulfillment. Each time I receive a heartfelt comment or review from one of you, it reminds me why I do what I do. Your support means everything to me, and I'm forever grateful for each and every one of you.

I love and appreciate you all. This journey wouldn't be as much fun without all of you by my side.

With warm regards,

Liz

# PUBLISHING TEAM

**Turning a manuscript into a book requires the efforts of many people. The publishing team at Bookouture would like to acknowledge everyone who contributed to this publication.**

## Audio
Alba Proko
Melissa Tran
Sinead O'Connor

## Commercial
Lauren Morrissette
Hannah Richmond
Imogen Allport

## Data and analysis
Mark Alder
Mohamed Bussuri

## Editorial
Rhianna Louise
Lizzie Brien

## Copyeditor
Donna Hillyer

Made in the USA
Monee, IL
27 June 2024